WINDSWEPT

MARA MAHAN

SKYSHIP FANTASY PRESS

For the Skyship Crew. Our ship might be stuck in a bottle,
but that's no reason to stop adventuring.
Thanks for sailing with me.

Also for my mom, because she said so :)

CHAPTER ONE
Gale

"Guinevere, will you marry me?" Gale sighed and smoothed back his straw-blond hair, re-straightening his threadbare canvas shirt for what felt like the hundredth time. "No, wait, that's not right…"

He fixed the angle of his cracked shaving mirror against the rocking of the ship, looked himself in the eye, and tried again. "Guinevere, I'd be honored if you'd see fit to marry—damn, that's wrong too…"

The ship groaned as though in agreement. Gale sighed again and tried another tone.

"Please, Guinevere—"

"Shift's up, Gale. Final turn's yours to… what're you doing?"

Gale dropped the mirror face down and leapt to his feet. "Blazes, Crawford—y'damn near scared me to death!"

Crawford raised his eyebrow and leaned forward, glancing skeptically from Gale's face to the upturned mirror. "Aye? An' what has you so jumpy?"

"Ain't no business o' yours." The two men stared

1

each other down for a long moment, then simultaneously burst out laughing.

"Ain't no business o' mine? Ain't no business o' mine? Blast and becalm me, Gale, I drop a pin an' you're jumpin' outta your skin—hell if that ain't my business, mate. All the years I've known you, I don't think I've ever seen you strung so taut."

Gale gave a rueful smile. "Aye, I s'pose you're right. It's Guinevere, Crawford. I'm... I'm gonna ask her to marry me."

Crawford froze. "Guinevere? As in Guinevere Syren—with the shop on Green Street? That Guinevere?"

"Aye," Gale said, nodding. "I'm gonna ask her as soon as we make port. Way I see it—if I don't hurry up and get my act together, I'll go ashore one day to find she's gotten sick of waitin' an' moved on with her life without me."

"Aye..." Crawford nodded slowly. "Well, one way or the other—right now you got a windshift to run. Better get on that, or the captain'll keelhaul us both."

Gale laughed. "Aye, but then he'd go an' lose the two best windworkers in all of Alinor!"

Crawford grinned. "Fine then. Worse than keelhaulin—Cap'n might dock our pay."

"Now there's a penalty to fear! Gods know my wallet ain't already loose enough. I'll catch you later, aye?"

"Aye, now get outta here 'fore I kick you up that ladder myself."

Gale laughed again, giving Crawford a cheerful salute as he swung himself up the ladder and onto the deck.

Out under the sun, the ship bustled. Sailors went about their work, shouting orders and singing shanties as they filled their nets with shining silver fish. A gull flew down and landed on the deck, where it turned into a man. He pointed out a new school of fish to another sailor, who promptly jumped overboard, shifted into a dolphin, and swam away to herd the school towards the ship. Likely they'd ask Gale to push the vessel that way in a few minutes so they could scoop up the school before any of the other ships could reach it.

Gale leapt into the rigging and climbed his way to the top of the mast, where he took his place beside the lookout in the crow's nest. Down below, the signalman made a broad gesture with his left hand, sweeping it outward and up. Gale nodded to himself and called the magic in his blood, summoning a stiff breeze from the sea to push the ship further out into the wide blue world—right up to the edge of Alinor's domain.

The ship pulled within a hundred yards of the edge before Gale stopped the wind, becalming the ship. The other sailors scurried about, readying the nets, and Gale leaned against the low handrail to await his next order. Occasionally he would divert a stray breeze conjured by some other ship's windworker or readjust his own power to account for a shift in the world's wind, but the tasks left his mind with plenty of time to wander.

Though he tried to be attentive and watch the signalman, Gale found his gaze wandering out over the open ocean, away from the distant shore and the innumerable masts and sails of the other assorted fishing boats. The light in the waves, the color in the water—it distracted him like little else could. The deep, beautiful murky green of Alinor's home water shimmered comfortably next to the brilliantly sparkling blue over the domain border—that unnaturally straight line in the sea that no ship dared to cross—and beyond that, the world was a patchwork of blues and greens and silver-greys, all the way out to the horizon.

The waves gleamed, swelling and ebbing with the breath of the world, and the waters shifted—sea blurring with sky and vanishing, giving way to foreign patches of water as the domains of the ocean disappeared and reappeared to the gods' chaotic design. Gale's eye drifted lazily over this tapestry of constant motion, eventually coming to rest on the single line of color that neither moved nor vanished. One narrow band of red-tinted water stretched out beyond the bounds of human sight, reaching all the way to the distant shores of Mikare.

"What d'you think it's like out there, Harisin?" Gale eventually murmured to the lookout. "Sailin' on the Rose Line, I mean."

"Eh? Hard and dangerous," the older man replied, running the back of his hand across his nose, "Line to Mikare—may as well call it a straight shot to Mother Ainsley's Keep. I swear near half the men who set out across those waters end up dinin' with the old girl in her cold halls. Sure, the other half that make it back get paid in gold—but I don't value any cash as worth more than my life. Now put the thought out of your head, lad. The signalman is wavin' us home."

Sure enough, Gale glanced down and saw a rather irate signalman flagging him down.

"What do you know," Gale said as he called up a landward breeze, "I thought we'd be out here for at least another hour or two."

The lookout snorted. "What, you lose track o' time with your head in the clouds, Gale? We ain't got long 'til sundown, now. I don't know about you, but I wanna be good an' drunk afore curfew falls."

"Aye," Gale laughed, filling the sails with wind, "that's a fair plan, and no mistake! Have a drink for me, will ya? I won't be able to make it, tonight."

"That girl o' yours again?" Harisin snickered. "Boy, she's really got you wrapped around her finger. You used to know how to have fun."

Gale shrugged, giving an easy smile. "I say it's worth staying sober if it means seein' her smile."

Harisin rolled his eyes and laughed. "Aye, you say that now—but if I know a thing about it, you'll be drinkin' to forget her scowl the day after you go and get yourselves hitched. Mark my words, Gale—it ain't worth the time or the effort."

Gale grinned and commandeered a tiny breeze to sweep his hair back out of his eyes. "If that's what you think, Harisin, I don't reckon you're doing it right."

* * *

Three quarters of an hour later, every able-bodied man was back in human form and working to bring the ship safe into port. As Gale pushed the vessel forward, the rest of the crew got to work hauling lines, securing cargo, and doing everything they could to see the ship docked safely. When that was done and the massive barrels of fish had been signed over to the dockworkers to unload, Gale received the three shiny silver coins that made his five days at sea worthwhile.

Swaying happily to the motion of a ship that no longer rocked beneath his feet, Gale pocketed his pay and strolled away, down towards the dockside market.

The setting sun lit the sky and the sea with a light like fire, lending a warm orange glow to the narrow market streets. The black-pebbled beaches, the low stone buildings—everything looked as though some whim of the gods had painted them gold. Even the people seemed brighter than usual; the normally sullen dockworkers bustled cheerfully among the ships, the returning sailors sang as they wandered from tavern to tavern, and even the cutpurses and pickpockets seemed to be going about their evening work with a particular odd glee.

Gale shouldered through the crowds, greeting everyone he met with a grin and a friendly "good evening," albeit with one hand guarding his wallet. He'd need every coin to pull off what he had planned.

The door to the Sunrise Blue Tavern swung open as Gale passed. Warm firelight spilled out onto the street, coupled with energetic music and raucous, happy laughter.

Gale hesitated—then shook his head and got back to walking. Guinevere would be waiting.

The thought brought a dreamy smile back to Gale's face. One glance from her was enough to make his heart pound. Her kiss was better than the finest wine. He found himself humming as he strolled past the taverns, past the fishmongers and fruit salesmen, down to the little shop in the back alley off Palm Street where the seaside district met the far edge of the nobles' quarter.

Gale pushed the door open, and a little bell chimed to welcome him. Behind the tall counter, a tiny old woman looked up from her book.

"You back again, Gale, y'scoundrel? I hope you have coin in your pocket, this time. I ain't gonna work for free."

"Aye, you old sea witch. I've got the coin, if your dry old bones still have a drop o' magic left in 'em. I ain't payin' 'less the job gets done."

"Rascal. I don't need to take that kind of talk from you. Come here." The old woman hopped off her stool and spread her wrinkled, tattooed arms, the silver beads in her hair clinking with every motion. Her wizened face split into a broad, weatherbeaten smile.

Gale grinned back and embraced her. "It's good to see you again, Missus Smith. Been too long since we last spoke."

Missus Smith cleared her throat, giving a few gruff coughs to hide her own affection. "Wouldn't have been so long if you'd have come back to visit sooner, boy."

"Aye, well—you made me swear not to return 'til either I had the coin for the job or the sense to give up on it, and I've yet to grow any more sense. I do got the brain to know you didn't raise me to go around breakin' my word, though."

The old woman clicked her tongue and chuckled. "Boy, I reckon by this point I didn't raise you so much as I ruined you. I figure it a wonder you grew up at all."

Gale laughed. "Ruined me? Gave me life, more like. What manner of man would I have been if you'd never brought me to the sea? A kitchen boy? A lawman? A clerk?"

Missus Smith reached up and lightly cuffed the side of Gale's head. "A whole lot politer, that's what." She paused, staring up at Gale's face for a long moment, examining the cast of his features and the light in his eye. "A kid with magic like yours... I couldn't stand the thought, knowing your talent was stuck rotting away in some children's home. The Brother Gods hate waste, an' I ain't about to offend them. But that don't mean I did it for you—I'm a selfish woman and I wanted your power on my ship, and you'd best not forget that. But... I s'pose you could've turned out worse."

Gale nodded amicably. She gave this speech nearly every time he stopped by to visit. Sometimes when he wasn't paying attention, he found himself mouthing along. Now, though, he called a grin. "I turned out fine. I'm doin' fine. What I've got suits me fine, an' I'm gonna thank you whether you like it or not, Missus Smith."

"Aye, everything you are is thanks to me," Missus Smith agreed, nodding as she hobbled back around the counter to her stool, "I done you too many free favors, boy. More than my share, Brothers help me." Though she frowned, the stern look did not reach her smiling eyes.

"Well, don't you fret, ma'am, you won't be workin' for free this time. I wasn't spinnin' tales when I said I had the coin." Gale opened his wallet and upturned it next to Missus Smith's book on the countertop. Silver and copper coins spilled out and rolled every which way. Missus Smith's eyes widened. Gale grinned.

"There you have it, ma'am. Twenty silver. You owe me a necklace for my lover."

Missus Smith muttered something incomprehensible, herding the escaped money back into a neat pile. She counted the coins, separating and sorting them—then she sighed. "You must be serious about this girl, Gale."

He nodded. "Guinevere means the world to me. I'd save a thousand times over if that was the only way I could show her my heart."

"Guinevere, eh? That wouldn't be the Syren girl now, would it? Markus' daughter?"

"The very same. In all my life, I've never met a girl so—"

Missus Smith cut Gale off with a gesture. "Her mother was old money, Gale. Old blood. And her father's a wildcard and no mistake. I hope you don't expect a pretty bauble to impress her, boy. She probably owns trinkets worth twice what you can afford, an' if she's got half her father's spirit it don't matter to her in the least."

"That ain't the point, ma'am. It's not about the worth of the thing—it's about showing I love her. We've been talkin' a while—as near to courtin' as we can get while keepin' proper, an' I'm fair certain she loves me back. I reckon it's time I take it forward."

Missus Smith chuckled and drew a hand down her face. "You're a fool, boy. A blasted sun-baked fool. Does her father know?"

Gale gave a lopsided grin, smoothing back his salt-stiffened hair and shifting his weight from foot to foot. "Know I'm a blasted sun-baked fool, or know that I hope to marry Guinevere?"

Missus Smith let out a single barking laugh. "The

second option, boy—the first point is plain enough for anyone with half an eye to see."

Gale scratched his cheek, shifting his weight again and shuffling his feet. "I haven't quite told him my plan, yet, but I'm fair certain he knows Guin and I have been talking."

"And the gods only know what he thinks of that," Missus Smith said, shaking her head slowly. "I'll do the job I said I'd do as best I can, but I pray you don't wind up disappointed."

Gale shrugged. "A man's gotta dream, ma'am. And then a man's gotta have enough steel in his soul to chase that dream. Fish can't fill nets you don't throw—ain't you the one who told me that?"

"I swear, Gale—if I weren't retired, I'd give you the hiding you deserve. Throwing my words back at me... Hah! Who do you think you are? 'Cause to me, you don't look like more than a young fool." She sighed, her harsh edge melting away to something softer. "You listen to me now, Gale—don't ever get old. It ain't worth it."

"I'll try, ma'am." He chuckled softly.

Missus Smith sighed again and clicked her tongue in mock disapproval, shaking her head as she collected Gale's money. She gave him one last appraising glance, then stepped into her shop's back room to gather her materials. Gale crossed his arms and leaned against the wall to wait.

A few minutes later, Missus Smith returned, carrying a heavy-looking toolbox with both of her frail-looking arms. Gale stepped forward and offered to take it, but she shooed him away, thunked the box down on the counter, and gestured for him to pull up a stool and sit.

"So. Let's go over again: just what is it you want me to make, Gale?" Her flint-brown eyes pinned him in place.

"A necklace for Guinevere," he answered immediately, "something silver—but magicked up so it won't tarnish. I'd like it shaped like a sea flower, too—with all those delicate leaves and vines and such. Oh, and I'd like if you could work these in, too."

He reached into his pocket and pulled out a tiny drawstring bag, which he opened to reveal a slightly misshapen pearl and five tiny pieces of sea-polished glass ranging from blue to green. "I found all this on the beach over the course of the year. I thought if you could use 'em it'd make the gift more... I dunno. Personal, I guess."

Missus Smith took Gale's contribution, examining the glass and testing the pearl between her fingers. "I guess no one can say you ain't thoughtful. I'll see what I can throw together, and you give this mess your best shot. Guinevere's a lucky girl, to have your heart."

Gale grinned, and Missus Smith opened her toolbox to withdraw several lumps of dark metal. When she had four or five good-sized lumps, Missus Smith cracked her knuckles as she always did when she called her magic. The lumps of silver shivered as though alive. One by one, they shuddered and morphed, birthing tiny beads that pulsed and quivered with a rhythm like breath. Missus Smith closed her eyes, and the beads ran together to form tiny puddles on the countertop. Then the puddles stretched into strings and the strings wove together into a soft braid of living metal.

Gale watched as more shapes began to form. The

brightest silver pooled in the center, collecting into a brilliant sphere that exploded into the perfect image of a sea flower. The metal seemed somehow more alive and more real than the living plants that grew by the shore. Missus Smith opened her eyes and carefully pressed the pearl into the center of the flower, where it stuck. The bits of polished glass found their homes spaced equally along the braid, and then all at once the metal grew to encase the additions in a delicate network of gossamer wire.

Sweat beaded on the old woman's brow. The metal grew brighter—and like an image appearing through misted glass, the details emerged, growing and twining into delicate leaves and elegant vines until at last Missus Smith exhaled and the metal faded back to lifeless silver.

Gale exhaled as well. "Ma'am, you've outdone yourself. I'll never be able to thank you enough."

"Start by promising me you'll keep that head on your shoulders where it belongs, Gale. You get fair stupid when you let it float off into the clouds."

Gale nodded, gently scooping the necklace up from the counter and stowing it away. "On my honor as a child o' the sea, ma'am. I'll keep my idiocy to the bare minimum."

"Good," Missus Smith said, collecting her leftover materials and returning them to her toolbox. "That's a promise I expect you to keep. And you'll start by takin' this." The old woman extended her hand. Five pieces of silver and three copper coins rested in her palm.

"What? What do you—"

"Just take it, Gale."

"But you made me swear to pay the full cost—

you insisted I—"

"Aye, that I did. And if I know you, you were in such a hurry you didn't keep a single copper back, an' you probably haven't eaten. I didn't take you outta that home to watch you starve to death."

Gale smiled and clasped her hand with both of his, accepting the money and pulling Missus Smith into another hug. "I owe you too much, ma'am. Someday I'll repay you."

"Oh, belay that gushing, boy. It ain't proper."

Missus Smith could not hide the grin in the corner of her mouth. "You paid me with cold coin like everyone else and there's no call to get sentimental. Stop wastin' time with these old bones and go off to your girl. She's waitin', aye?"

"Aye!" Gale clasped Missus Smith's hand again, hardly aware of the faint breezes his joy stirred up in the room. "Aye, that she is! Thanks a million, ma'am—I'll stop by again 'fore I set to sea! Until then, wish me luck!"

Gale gave a small salute and a wide grin before he turned and fled the shop, taking the restless breezes with him.

He ran all the way down Palm Street, though the market, past the docks, and onto the streets where the sea folk made their homes. He cut through the slums to reach Molly Street, then followed that further into the city before a left on Keller Road took him back seawards. From there, Gale only had to hop a wall, climb a tree, edge through a back alley, and then he was throwing pebbles at Guinevere's window. The sun was down, sunk well below Alinor's high stone walls, but Gale knew Guinevere would be awake.

Sure enough, after the third stone she opened her

window and her smile lit up the world.

Gale's heart tripped, and his breath caught in his throat. Guinevere held up a finger, mouthed something inaudible, and disappeared from view.

Gale crossed his arms and leaned against the nearest tree. His face hurt from smiling, but he didn't care.

Two minutes passed. A faint breeze rustled the sleeping flowers in their neatly-ordered beds. Crickets chirped in the manicured hedge.

Guinevere reappeared at the window. She had a jacket on, now, and her long brown hair was braided over her left shoulder.

Gale smiled and blew her a kiss, sending a light breeze to carry it towards her. She laughed softly and blew a kiss back, before swinging her leg over the windowsill and climbing down the ivy trellis to meet him.

CHAPTER TWO
Guinevere

No sooner did Guinevere's feet touch earth than Gale swept her off her feet and spun her up and around into a warm embrace. He smelled like the sea breeze and his smile shone like the sun. Guinevere laughed and wrapped her arms around him, and the two of them shared a kiss.

When their lips parted, Guinevere caught her breath and spoke.

"I missed you, Gale. I'd be sitting there minding the shop, and all of a sudden I'd realize I'm staring at your ship on the horizon."

"And every moment I wasn't workin' I'd catch myself starin' at the shore lookin' for you, too," Gale replied, resting his forehead gently against hers. He had that look in his storm-grey eyes—the soft, vulnerable look that made her heart do flips. "I'd ask myself—is Guinevere standin' there, waiting? Does she miss me as much as I miss her? So naturally as soon as we made port I came as quick as I could. How've you been?"

Guinevere smiled even as she lowered her gaze. "Oh, I've been well enough. But... Gale? I have something I need to talk to you about."

She lifted her face again, just in time to catch the flicker of concern spark to life behind Gale's smile. She bit her lip as he took both her hands in his.

"As it happens, so do I," he murmured. "I have a... well, I have a rather important question, Guinevere."

"Oh?" Her curiosity was shadowed by a sneaking, almost dreadful suspicion. Gale was late, today. He was normally as reliable as the tide, but he was late—and there was no alcohol on his breath, which could only mean... "You go first, Gale. What is it you want to ask me?"

Gale swallowed hard, a pink blush coloring his tanned cheeks as he took a knee before her. He reached into his pocket and presented her with a beautiful silver necklace, never dropping her gaze.

"Guinevere... will you marry me?"

Guinevere choked back a gasp, her own face flushing hot. She'd guessed his intent, but the words were still a shock to hear.

"Gale, it's beautiful, but..." She reached out and closed Gale's hand back around the necklace, closing her eyes so as not to see the hurt on his face. "Though I would love nothing more in all the world, I can't accept it—not yet. My father... That's what I wanted to talk to you about, Gale. My father doesn't want us to see each other any more, and until we change his mind, I can't in good conscience..."

Gale opened and closed his mouth like a displaced fish; then he nodded. "I... I understand."

"And Gale—I want you to know that if it were

up to me and me alone, I would marry you in a heartbeat. My father... he worries. He doesn't know you as I do. Where I see a brave, devoted, kind man, he sees a penniless, drunken sailor."

Guinevere trailed off. Though he was sad, she could see the flicker of quiet rebellion flare to life in Gale's eyes. "I... I don't drink that much."

Guinevere chuckled, pulling Gale to his feet and stepping back into his arms. "You drink enough that he worries. Don't imagine for a moment that I intend to let this be the end of things, but... I want him to approve. I love him and I love you and I want us all to be family."

Gale was quiet for a long moment, his fingers gently moving to stroke Guinevere's hair. "We'll show him how he's wrong, then. Just tell me what I need to do, Guin—I wanna do this right. I'll bring your father the moon on a plate if that's what it takes."

Guinevere smiled, lowering her gaze. Her eyes traced the edge of the protective tattoo that poked up beneath his unbuttoned collar. "It shouldn't take anything quite so impossible as that. Father just... wants to be sure I marry a man who's good for me. Someone who won't lose his heart to the sea and never come home."

"Guin, you know I would never—"

"I know that, Gale—I know that beyond doubt. And I know we can make Father see it too. It's just... you know how he is about matters of blood and money. He won't let go of the idea that I should be looking to marry an enchanter who could help out with the family business, even though most of those cold-blooded stiffs have more ice in their hearts than a snowman. He thinks I should marry a—a

Spellcrafter, or a Wardweaver, but I couldn't care less about the Enchanters' Guild. I love you, Gale, and I want to marry you. I'm sure—if we can make him see you the way I see you, he'll come around."

"Aye…" Gale nodded slowly, and Guinevere felt a light breeze ruffle her hair. "Aye, Guinevere, but… what do I do?" Gale broke off with an awkward chuckle, and he gestured to the necklace in his hand. "This's… actually why I came to you, first, rather than goin' and askin' him if I could ask you like would be right. I want him to approve—I'd like his blessing—but I don't got a shot on my own. As things stand, he'd chase me off the porch before I got a word out."

Over the garden wall, the bells rang and the city watch—the Dogs, as they were known—called the hour, announcing curfew. A faint wind sighed through the trees at the sight of the rising moon.

Guinevere licked her lips and gathered her thoughts. "Well, I've been thinking, since he asked me to stop talking to you. I think—no, I'm sure—he simply doesn't know how to see the good in you. He's been blinded by assumptions, and we need to help him to change those. But if we can prove beyond doubt that you're not the man he takes you for…"

Gale leaned forward and gave Guinevere a kiss. The familiar thrill fluttered up within her chest and stole her breath.

"I'm going to buy you a house, Guinevere," Gale murmured, his gaze intense. "I'm gonna do it. I'll raise the money and get you a proper place with a view o' the sea. If that doesn't show Markus that I'm serious and worth your hand, I don't know what will."

Guinevere rested her cheek against Gale's shoulder and let out a slow breath. "I love you, Gale, but where do you hope to find that kind of money? Houses aren't cheap, and I know you don't get paid what you're worth. There's got to be a better way. If we work together we can find it and get married, and of course you can stay home with me when you're back on shore—you won't be paying rent, so you'll be able to save your money, and that'll be a point in your favor—and we can live together on your days off and everything will work out. We just need a good, rational approach."

Gale chuckled quietly. A light breeze swirled through the garden, gently caressing both their faces. Gale lifted his hand and pushed a stray strand of hair behind Guinevere's ear. "That's a pretty dream, Guin. But... do you know a more rational path? 'Cause I don't see one. Findin' an easier way ain't always the same as findin' a better way. But a house—crazy as it sounds, I don't think your father could discount it."

"But Gale," Guinevere said, pulling back to look him in the eye, "How would you get the money? I can't think of a single good way for an honest man to earn that sort of coin in any reasonable span of time. I don't think money is the answer, here—not for this. We'll find another way, and if money is a problem when the time comes and we're living together, I'll have my shop. Together we'll have enough to get whatever we need even without my family's money."

"I see what you're saying, but... even with the money aside, I don't know how else to show I won't turn into an anchor 'round your neck the moment we're wed. You said yourself I have to show your father he sees me wrong, and I don't got a better idea than this. Coming up with the cash to set us up with a home is bound to impress him. Even if we don't end up getting a place, having the silver set by wouldn't hurt. You know—for a rainy day."

Guinevere sighed softly. "That's all true, but... I still don't see how you plan to get this money within the next decade, Gale—and as much as I love you, I don't know if I can wait for you to hoard a sailor's pay until we're old and grey. I'd like to marry before I'm ancient. I just—I don't see how money can solve this problem, much less solve it fast enough."

"What if I signed up to sail the Rose Line?"

Guinevere's breath caught in her throat. "What?"

"I could do it, Guin. I'd say most of the ships that go out come back, these days, and I'm skilled enough—they'd take me. I could go before the trade season ends and be back with a profit this time next year. We could marry while the churches are in bloom."

Guinevere bit her lip. "Even assuming the money makes a difference to my father, Gale, please—let's think rationally. You want to risk your life for money that might not matter?" She took a deep breath. "It's bad enough to watch you leave each week with the fishing boats—I can't picture spending a whole year apart. Much less..."

"Guinevere..." Gale's voice was soft; his touch was firm and gentle as he ran his work-roughened hand down the side of her face. "I promise, nothing is going to happen to me. I... I don't want to be without you, either, but... what's a year, in the long run? It seems a small price to pay for a happy forever."

Guinevere looked away, over the wall and up at

the sky. "A lot can happen in a year, and worse things always happen at sea. So much could go wrong, Gale. I... don't want you to go." She turned back to meet his eyes. "Please, let's put these thoughts aside and think of some better way. There's got to be one, if we really apply ourselves to the problem."

Gale lowered his gaze for a moment, but the moment passed quickly and he raised his face again to give Guinevere a smile. "Okay, Guin. I'll let it be. I'd never want you to worry. Heck, I'll make a promise now—" he got down on his knees again and closed both of Guinevere's hands around the silver necklace, "—let this here stand as a token: no matter what happens, no matter what ill winds or cruel tides roll our way, our love will weather through. I promise I'll always come back to you, sure as I'm a child of the sea. So you set your worries to rest, Guin. My place is here, and here I'll stay."

Guinevere smiled, wiping the shadows of tears from her eyes. "Gale, you say the sappiest things, but I love you so much. Thank you. If... if it happens that the Rose Line is truly our only answer, I suppose... I'll live with it. But we really ought to explore other options, first, before we decide on something so drastic. The riskiest option ought to be left to last."

Gale nodded and murmured assent, and then in silent agreement the two of them made their easy way to the low concrete bench beneath the old oak in the corner of the garden. The stone was cold, now, under the stars, but Gale was warm enough beside her that Guinevere didn't mind. Together, they sat listening to the quiet sounds of the sleeping city—then Gale motioned to the necklace.

"May I?" he asked, his voice warm.

"Of course," Guinevere answered, holding her hair aside as Gale fastened the necklace around her throat. Then their fingers entwined again. Guinevere rested her head on Gale's shoulder.

"It looks beautiful on you," Gale murmured.

Guinevere laughed, careful to keep her voice soft so no one in the house would hear. "It's beautiful on its own, too."

Gale grinned and lightly kissed her forehead. "Well, it looks even prettier when you wear it."

"Thank you, Gale. For everything. My father will change his mind, soon. I'm sure of it."

"I hope you're right." Gale placed his arm around Guinevere's shoulders, holding her close. Though the night air was cold and the breeze made it seem even colder, Guinevere hardly felt the chill.

She cleared her throat. "Maybe we could get lunch, sometime soon. I know things didn't go well the last time you two met, but I'm sure we can change his impression, if we try."

Gale gave Guinevere a light squeeze. "If you think it'll work, I'll try it. You'll have to help me polish up my manners something serious, though. I stick out like a stone among pearls in polite company as I am."

"Don't sell yourself short, Gale. Though… I will admit, I don't know how I'd broach the subject. 'Yes, Father, that man you want me to stop seeing? He wants to marry me. Let's all get lunch sometime so we can get your blessing. Surprise!'"

"Well, I sure hope you wouldn't go and do it like that," Gale laughed, "I think he'd set the Dogs on me, if he thought I was out trying to steal you away behind his back. Which… well, does it count as going behind his back when I'm asking you how to talk to him? 'Cause I want to do this right."

"I think you're okay," Guinevere said, smiling. "I'm not being stolen away. Anyway… there's nothing saying we have to find all our answers tonight. We can sleep on these questions and maybe the Brother Gods will bring us solutions in the morning."

Gale agreed, and the two of them lapsed into comfortable silence, watching the stars together until at last Guinevere yawned.

"I should get back, soon, otherwise I won't be able to wake up on time. Will you come by the shop tomorrow, Gale?"

"Of course, Guin. I wouldn't miss seein' you for the world." He kissed her forehead again, allowing his lips to linger a moment on her skin. "You have yourself some sweet dreams, you hear?"

Guinevere laughed. "Of course, Gale. I'll be dreaming of you."

The two shared one last embrace, then parted, each making tiny motions to prolong the goodbye. Guinevere climbed back up the trellis to her window, and Gale climbed back up over the garden wall.

"Goodnight, Guin," Gale whispered, letting the breeze carry his words to her ear alongside a gently blown kiss.

"Goodnight, Gale," Guinevere mouthed back, blowing a kiss of her own. "Watch out for the curfew, okay?"

Gale nodded, smiled, and slipped back over the wall into the city beyond. Guinevere sighed quietly, slid back into her bedroom, and shut her window for the night.

* * *

"You were seeing that boy again, weren't you, Guin?"

The moment Guinevere's window was shut, her little sister's voice rang out, freezing Guinevere in her tracks.

"What are you doing in my room, Ell?" Guinevere turned around, forcing a calm smile as she undid her braid and fought the blush in her cheeks.

"I came to ask you a question, but you weren't here—but I knew you should have been here, so I looked out the window and I saw you with that boy again! Didn't Papa say you oughtn't talk to him anymore, Guin?"

Ell had that look in her eye, the mischievous little glint that only ever meant trouble.

Guinevere gave her sister a carefully careless glance, doing her best impression of nonchalance. "Yes, but we were… only saying goodbye."

"Goodbye?" Ell's eyes widened. "So you are gonna make him go away? I thought he was kinda cute. What's that around your neck?" She pointed.

Guinevere touched the necklace, cursing herself for failing to hide it. "It's… it's a token, Ell. Gale gave it to me so that I'd never forget him."

Ell's eyes went wider, and her overly innocent act got even more cloying. "But I thought Papa said you were *supposed* to forget him!"

"He did, but Gale didn't know that when he came by. I know Papa doesn't like him, but… Gale, he…" Guinevere trailed off. Though she didn't trust her sister with the truth of Gale's proposal, she couldn't bring herself to lie completely. "He knows Father doesn't like him, but he loves me enough that he's willing to go away for a while, if that's what it takes. And he gave me this necklace so that if something like that does happen, I have something to hold onto while he's gone."

Ell plopped herself down on Guinevere's bed and swung her legs childishly. "If he loves you, why is he going away? That doesn't make sense. He ought to stay, if he really loves you, and he shouldn't care what Papa thinks! Where's he going, anyway?"

Guinevere lifted her hairbrush from her vanity and ran it over her hair, sitting so that she could keep an eye on her sister through the mirror. "Have you been reading Mama's old books again? You know even she thought those tragic romance stories were silly."

"I know, I know—but silly or not, I love them. And she did, too! Otherwise why would we have so many?" Ell grinned. "Anyway, they're just so *romantic!* The boy and the girl love each other so much and nothing can tear them apart! Not their parents—not even death! They fight the world and defy fate and it's all so sweet it makes me wanna cry. I wish someone loved me like that. Guin, do you think that's how Gale loves you?"

"I should certainly hope not," Guinevere answered, chuckling. "Gale's a dreamer, but he has more sense than that. No—he loves me even more. He wants Papa to like him, because he doesn't want to come between me and everyone else I love."

"But what if Papa never likes him? What'll you do then, Guin? Will you make him go away? I don't think it's really true love if you can bear to make him go away."

"Ell, please. It won't come to that. You're twelve. I know how you think. I was twelve, once, too. But the world isn't like that. Papa isn't unreasonable, and I'm sure once he sees—why am I explaining myself to you? You're my sister."

Ell made her eyes wide again and pouted, asserting her innocence the way she always did when she wanted something. "You're explaining to me because I wanna know? Come on, Guin, please? I wanna know all about everything!"

Guinevere sighed and put down her hairbrush for a moment, turning to look at her sister directly. "Do you swear not to repeat any part of anything I say?"

Ell nodded, eagerly resting her chin on her hands for the tale. "I swear it!"

"Swear on your life?"

"On my life, Guin! I won't tell anyone!"

Guinevere raised an eyebrow. "You're making this promise awfully easily. I want to be sure you understand how important this is to me."

"Oh, come *on* Guinevere! Please? I swear—I swear it on my life, on every book I've ever read, and—and on my future love! Is that enough for you?"

"I guess so," Guinevere conceded, turning back to the mirror and lifting her brush again.

Ell cheered, rolling over onto her back to examine Guinevere from another angle. "So I wanna hear everything! How can you bear to let him go if you really love him? Where's he gonna go, anyway? How long will he be there? What's he gonna do? I want the whole story."

"It's nowhere near as dramatic or exciting as you

seem to think, Ell. I don't want him to leave, but if the only way we can be together is to wait a while, first, then I'm going to wait as long as it takes. We were talking about it, and he thinks leaving is the only thing he can do to prove to Father that we're serious about each other. That this is real love and won't wear away as soon as we stop talking."

"I guess that does make sense. After all, true love conquers all, right? Even time!"

Guinevere chuckled and shook her head. "You sound like Gale when you talk like that. Only when he says it, it doesn't sound near as silly."

Ell pursed her lips. "Why does it sound silly, Guin? Isn't it true? Why isn't it silly when Gale says it?"

"Because… because when he says it, he sounds as though he's working towards it. You just sound like you're quoting. If you met him, I think you'd understand what I mean. He's… got this way about him. This conviction. He dreams these crazy dreams, and he sweeps the world along with him to come and dream them too."

Ell gave a heartfelt sigh and rolled back onto her stomach, a sappy smile on her face.

Guinevere turned around and shot a confused glare in her direction. "What?"

"It's so cute! I've never seen your face do that before, Guin—that thing it does when you talk about him. Do you think I can meet him someday? Before he leaves? Where's he going, anyway? You still haven't told me."

"I suppose I have been avoiding the question, haven't I?" Guinevere chewed her lip for a moment, suppressing a sigh. "We're still figuring that out. He might not actually go—we're looking for another answer—but Gale... He mentioned signing up to sail the Rose Line."

"The Rose Line?!" Ell's eyes widened again, this time in genuine surprise. "But—isn't that dangerous?"

"Yes... he thinks the risk will impress Papa."

"Well, it will, won't it? That's impressive! It's like—like—I don't even know, but I *need* to meet him! Okay? So you're going to introduce me, Guin. I want you to introduce me to him tomorrow."

"Tomorrow?"

"Yeah! You said he might be leaving. And if he does, he might not come back and I wanna meet him so if that happens I can—oh. Sorry, Guin."

Guinevere turned away from the mirror, refusing to face the heartache in her reflection. "If he goes, he will come back. He promised me. He swore it. And anyway... anyway, we haven't actually made the decision, yet. There's got to be a better way to win Papa over, and we're going to find it. That way he won't have to leave."

Ell sighed again, practically oozing melodrama. "You say this isn't like the stories, Guin, but it *is!* Star-crossed lovers, forced apart by fate, drawn together by the inexorable force of—"

"Ell, if you insist on carrying on like that, you're going to have to leave my room. Please, this isn't a game. Gale and I aren't star-crossed, whatever that's supposed to mean. We're just trying to find the best way to make things work. No more tragedy talk, okay?"

"Okay..." Ell sighed again, but she straightened up and smiled. "Can you make me a promise though, Guin?"

"Yes, I can introduce you to Gale—if you help me mind the shop tomorrow. He said he might stop by."

"Yay! I can't wait to meet him! That isn't what I was thinking about, though. I mean, it is—but it isn't." Ell's face was an odd shade of pink, and she refused to meet Guinevere's eyes.

"What is it, then?" Guinevere asked, bemused.

"Well… When I'm a bit older, can you help me find a boy like Gale, too?"

CHAPTER THREE
Gale

Gale left the inn early in the morning, long before the sun peeked her yellow head over the horizon. The sea breeze was chill, at this hour, and heavy with a thick grey fog that rolled off the water in suffocating blankets. The moisture made Gale's shirt cling uncomfortably to his skin—it caught in his throat and made it difficult to breathe until he called his magic and summoned a gust of wind to sweep the street and blow it all away. He could not get rid of the fog completely, but he was able to shove it aside long enough to walk down the street without drowning.

Not that many people were out and about to drown, yet. Most of the sailors were sleeping off a week spent working and a night spent carousing, and everyone else had the kind of steady job that kept them in bed at the usual hours. Even the thieves were asleep, for the most part. Curfew would not lift for a few hours more, so there was no one on the streets to rob.

Gale smiled and began to whistle a quiet little

tune under his breath, tossing a breeze up to play among the eaves of the houses as he went. The whistling wind echoed his melody in its own haunting way.

He strolled down the empty cobbled street, wandered past the docks and the sleeping forest of masts and lines, and found himself walking alone across the bare stretch of beach just beyond the marina. The black sea-polished pebbles slithered pleasantly underfoot, and the ocean waves breathed softly, gently hushing the restless stirrings of the sleeping city.

Gale let a slow sigh escape his lungs as he settled back to relax on the dark stone beach. The rocks were damp and gritty beneath his hands, but Gale did not mind the texture. He knew no better place to sit and watch the rising sun.

There was something strangely invigorating about seeing the world come to life before him—the shrieks and cries of the awakening gulls, the gentle sighs of the tide, the way color slowly leached into the sky to chase away the predawn grey—it did something to his mind and left him breathless. The golds and silvers the rising sun cast over the blue-green water set Gale's soul alight with joy.

As the sky lightened further and the curfew lifted, the city behind him found its voice. The screams of the gulls bled into the back-and-forth shouts of people hard at work, and the roar of the tide was joined by the creaks of sailing ships and the songs of sailors just beginning their day.

Though he was happy to be ashore and more than happy to be able to visit Guinevere again, Gale couldn't shake the pang of longing as he watched the fishing boats sail out to the horizon to gather whatever fish fortune lured into Alinorian waters from the shifting Thousand Seas.

He stood, brushed off his hands, and let himself be drawn forward by the allure of the ocean. He didn't stop until the reaching waves lapped up around his feet—at which point he only paused long enough to pull his boots off and toss them back up onto the pebbled beach to wait for him while he waded out further. When the water was up past his knees, he decided it was time to stop.

On a whim, Gale cupped his hands around his mouth and shouted to the ships, letting the wind carry his voice out across the water. The sailors heard his cry, felt his namesake wind urging them out of the harbor, and whooped a reply. Gale grinned and waved them off, increasing the flow of magic to aid their way.

The strong burst of wind pushed away the last of the morning fog, whipping around the flags and banners at every merchant's stall and rocking every boat within Alinor's seaside domain. The sailors aboard the ships whooped again, and Gale called a breathless reply and flopped backwards into the cold water, exhausted.

He drifted for a long moment, grinning aimlessly at the sky. A sound caught his ear. A low, sweet sound. Gale sat up and shook water from his hair, wiped the salt from his eyes, and listened carefully. A laugh bubbled up from his throat. Unsteady as the burst of magic had left him, Gale wasted no time finding his feet and floundering back to the shore. He grabbed his boots by the laces, threw them over his shoulder, and strolled out to follow the sound.

It led him up to the edge of the seaside district, to Darrian Road, where the craftsmen worked and the charm-makers plied their trade. Guinevere sat in the shade of an open-air shop, singing over her work as she wove at an overlarge loom. The hanging curtains—samples of her craft—wafted in Gale's breeze as he neared. She matched her song to the rhythm of her rattling loom as her deft hands wove back and forth along the threads, and when Guinevere finished her verse, Gale saw fit to chime in on the refrain.

Guinevere started slightly in her seat, but she did not stop singing. Gale leaned against a wooden post within her view and passed her a smile. She returned it, her voice growing even sweeter as they finished the song together.

Guinevere's hands slowed to a halt as the last note faded. She examined her work, then turned to look at Gale.

"You know, I've noticed something, Gale. Even though there's no magic in your voice, I've noticed my enchantments come out stronger when we sing together.

"Aye? Do they really?" Gale laughed. "Fancy that. I was just thinkin' it's nice to share the melody."

Guinevere grinned and shrugged. "It's not a huge difference—the spell gets woven in exactly the same, but… I don't know. I feel when we sing together I can't help but put more heart into it."

Gale pulled up a short three-legged stool and sat adjacent to Guinevere, leaning in to plant a quick kiss on her cheek. "So what you're sayin' is that I bring out the best in you?"

Guinevere raised her eyebrow and grinned. "The

best in me? Oh, no—I could get a lot more work done if you weren't here distracting me, Gale. If mother were here, she'd have a fit to see me resting at the loom. But—I won't deny that you—" She cut herself off mid-sentence and reached out a hand to touch Gale's hair. "Why are you all wet?"

Gale chuckled, reclining as far as he could without tipping the stool. "You know me, Guin. I can't tear myself away from the sea. I know it's my day off, but I just had to pay her a visit this morning."

"Gale…" Guinevere clicked her tongue and shook her head, covering her grin with a show of exasperation. "One of these days, you're going to catch your death. Do you want a blanket? Or I could make you some tea."

"Thanks, but no thanks, Guin. I appreciate your offer right enough, but the sight of your smile is all I need to warm my heart and keep the chill from my bones."

A faint blush crept over Guinevere's cheeks. "You can say as many pretty things as you like, Gale, but it won't change the fact that you're soaked. Please, at least let me get you a towel?"

"If that's what'll make you happy, Guin, I'll take it, but I'm also fine without." Gale ran his hand through his hair. It was still surprisingly damp. He called a quick breeze to help blow it dry.

Guinevere sighed. "What am I going to do with you, Gale?" she muttered, half to herself.

"Marry me, I hope." Gale replied, his grin broad and sunny.

"I just might have to! I mean, I don't see any other way to keep an eye on you, Gale. And you know I worry."

"I don't mean to worry you," Gale said, taking both of Guinevere's hands in his.

"I know, but that doesn't change the fact that I worry. And let me just say this now: don't you dare give me a hug while you're still soaking wet. I know you're thinking about it, and I won't have that."

Gale laughed and released Guinevere's hands, holding up his own in a gesture of peace. "Aye aye, no hugs 'til I'm dry. Got it. Now—I don't mean to darken the day, but have you thought any more about—"

"Is that him?" A high, breathless voice interrupted from the street. A small girl with spattered freckles, large green eyes, and dark hair in twin braids down her back pushed aside a curtain and leered up at Gale. Though she was as tall standing as he was seated, the girl's bright eyes held a fierce enthusiasm that had Gale inching back as far as the small stool would allow.

Guinevere pinched the bridge of her nose, momentarily hiding her face behind her hand. "Yes, Ell, this is Gale. Gale, please meet my little sister, Elaine."

Gale nodded politely and held out his hand to shake. "Nice meetin' you, Miss Elaine. I've heard a fair bit about you."

Ell made a noise like a teakettle, her already large eyes going wider. Before Gale could blink, the girl sprang at him, wrapping her arms around him and almost knocking him from his seat.

"It's so nice to meet you, Gale! Guin's told me *all* about you! Oh, Guinevere! He's so—cold?" Ell released Gale and held him at arm's length. "And wet... why is he all wet?"

Gale opened his mouth to speak, but Guinevere answered before he could, her voice thick with exaggerated patience. "That's probably because he went for a swim, Ell."

Ell turned her attention back to Gale, and he got the distinct impression she was committing his face to memory.

"You went for a swim? Already? But curfew's only just lifted!" She cut herself off with a gasp. "You weren't out swimming before curfew, were you? Why in the world would you do that, Gale! Aren't you worried about getting in trouble? What about the—"

"Beg pardon, miss, but how can I answer your questions when you won't stop askin' em?" Gale asked, chuckling. Behind Ell's head, Guinevere mouthed an apology. He gave her an understanding grin and a slight shrug.

Ell blushed and released Gale, dropping a swift, demure curtsy and lowering her gaze. "I am so, so sorry, Gale. I was just so excited to meet you, I suppose I forgot my manners."

Gale looked to Guinevere. "What all have you been tellin' her, Guin? I ain't heard of a king gettin' a reception like that!"

Guinevere seemed even more bemused than Gale. "If I had a clue what was going through her head…"

Ell giggled. "I really am sorry. Here, let me try again: it's a pleasure to make your acquaintance, Mister Gale." The girl extended her hand, and Gale took it, pressing it to his lips in imitation of a gentleman.

"Nay, lass, the pleasure's mine. If you're Guinevere's sister, then you're my friend as a matter of course."

Guinevere laughed. Ell didn't seem to know where to put her face.

"So… why were you swimming, Gale? If you don't mind me asking, of course."

"Not at all. Y'see, Ell, I live most of my life on those waters. Stick me on land and I hardly know how to live. So each morning I'm ashore, I make an effort to get out and see the dawn over the sea. I was out there today, watchin' the sun, and I couldn't bear to see the other ships sail away without me givin' 'em a proper windworker's sendoff. Y'know—one good gust to send 'em off safe, get the breezes flowin' for those men doin' their hard day's work while I'm here lazin' away. And it really only seemed natural to do that from a few feet in—can't do a sailor's job on the land, after all."

Ell's brow creased. "That… almost makes sense. Wait—do you mean—was that gust of wind you? It blew the neighbor boy's hat clean off!"

Gale chuckled. "Well, you can tell him I say sorry for that. I can't say I was really thinkin', all told. I've been known to forget my own strength."

"Oh, no, don't worry about it. He's pretty annoying."

Guinevere ran a hand down her face to cover a laugh. Gale grinned and shook his head.

"Anyway," Guinevere said, her voice suggesting it was time to get back to business, "did you need something, Ell? Or did you just stop by to say hello? I know you too well to think you're here to help me work."

Ell paused and thought for a moment, then her face lit up and she nudged aside the curtain again to reveal a bag she'd dropped. "I got so distracted I almost forgot, but I remember now! You accidentally left your lunch at home, Guin. Also, Papa told me that he wants you to stop by, later. Something about singing at the shipyard."

Guinevere nodded, frowning slightly. "Did he say when he wants me to be there?"

Ell shook her head. "No, he just said later today. He's there now. Do you want me to go run and ask him?"

"No, thank you, Ell. It's fine, I'll go see him this afternoon. Was there anything else?"

Ell shook her head, then abruptly switched and started nodding.

Guinevere raised her eyebrows. "And what was that?"

"I had one question for Mister Gale, if he doesn't mind my asking."

Gale sat forward. "Aye? What question is that? No need to walk on eggshells around me, lass. You're welcome to speak freely."

That seemed to embolden the girl. A flush of color rose to her cheeks, and she regained the brashness she had shown in that first instant. "Do you love Guinevere? I mean—do you really love her?"

Gale blinked. "Aye, I do. With all my heart."

Ell nodded. "Okay, good. You're sure?"

"Aye, Miss, I've never been more sure of anything in my life. Guinevere has my heart. The sea and the sky might change daily, but my love for her never wavers."

"Would you die for her?"

"Ell!" Guinevere interrupted, "what kind of

question is that? Please, leave the tragic love talk elsewhere—I don't want to hear any more of it."

Gale looked to Guinevere and smiled. "It's alright, Guin. I don't mind. Ell, I would die for her, if the gods blew that fate my way. I'd rather not have to—I reckon it'd be a lot better to get the chance to live for her—but if that were the only way in the world she could live and be happy... Well, I love her more than life."

Though Guinevere's face was stern, a blush lit up her pretty cheeks. "Gale, please, stop. Don't encourage her—her head is full to bursting with silly romance novels, and if you play along, she'll never stop to talk sense. Empty words are one thing, but..." Here, her voice softened. "I don't like hearing *you* talk like that, Gale. I want you to live for yourself, not for me."

Gale met her eyes and nodded, letting a faint smile play at the corner of his mouth. "Guinevere, I—"

He was interrupted by the shrill cry of a teakettle. "Oh, you two are just too *cute!*" Ell squirmed on her feet, her eyes squeezed shut and her face filled with a painful joy. "The way you look at each other—the things you say—it's so lovely I just wanna die! How can you bear it, Guinevere? I'm not even part of this and I feel like I'm gonna explode! You should just marry each other right this second—if you don't, I think *my* heart will break!"

Gale and Guinevere exchanged a glance. Guinevere looked mortified, and Gale felt his own face heat. He cleared his throat and gave a quiet chuckle.

"Right this second? I reckon that'd be hard to

pull off, Ell. I mean, there's paperwork. Things to buy. We'd need a church, and though I'd like nothing more in the world than havin' Guinevere as my bride, there's still the matter of—"

"Excuse me, I'm not interrupting anything, am I?"

Guinevere went pale, and Gale's heart flipped and fell down to the depths of his stomach. Guinevere's father, Markus Syren, pushed aside the curtain on the other end of the shop and entered, his voice like ice and his face like the distant storm that rushed in from the sea. Gale dropped Guinevere's hand and stood, knocking over the stool in his haste. He offered Markus a handshake, but the man ignored the gesture—ignored Gale completely—and gave Guinevere a stern glare. Ell took one look at the scene and ducked behind the curtain and fled off to who-knows-where.

Markus stood with the sort of confidence that suffered no foolishness. He was one of the biggest names in shipbuilding, and it showed in every aspect of his being. He owned the largest share of the shipyard, he hired the best craftsmen, and his talent for singing enchantments over ships was as such that many sailors swore Markus' songs could turn a loose net watertight and turn stones seaworthy. Some people whispered that there was enough magic in the man's voice to stop a heart with nothing but a word.

Gale felt cold enough to believe it.

Markus let the silence brew for a moment before he cleared his throat and spoke again. His voice was soft, menacing and calm. "Guinevere, I'd like an explanation. I coulda sworn I just heard you and this... young man... discussing marriage. But that can't be the case. Not when you've gone and promised me you'd let the boy go. So I must be mistaken, aye?"

"Y-yes, Papa," Guinevere stammered, "Gale was—he was only joking around. Ell asked a silly question, and Gale was only answering in kind."

"Good." Markus swept his eyes around the shop, lingering on Gale for an uncomfortably long moment. Gale resisted the urge to shuffle his feet and stared back boldly, trying to forget his own damp clothing and tousled hair. Markus looked so clean by comparison—even though his red hair was ruffled and unruly, even though he dressed casually in workman's clothes, something about his straight spine and his calm face made Gale wish he'd remembered to shave.

"I trust," Markus continued in the same soft voice, "that you'll understand if I don't see the humor, Guinevere. I thought I'd asked you to stop…" He paused and glanced at Gale again. "I thought I'd made it clear that I'd rather you chose your company with a bit more care."

Guinevere stood to face her father. "Papa, I know. I know you don't approve of Gale, but… Well, I'd like you to give him another chance. I know you got off on the wrong foot last time, but—"

"Guinevere, I work with sailors every day. I know his kind, and I know the sort of lives they lead. I'd rather my daughter not throw away her future on a man already wed to taverns and drink."

"Please, Papa. Gale doesn't drink that much. If it's commitment you're worried about, you can rest easy. Gale is—"

"Guinevere, of all the conversations we could be

having in the middle of the street, this is not one I'd choose. Come with me, I'd like your help in the yard, today. Once we're done there, we can sort this out proper."

Gale sent a tiny breeze past Guinevere's cheek in silent support as she took a deep breath, gathering her voice.

"Papa, no. I know you want what's best for me, but I want you to listen for a moment. Gale… I know you want me to say goodbye to him, but he came here to say goodbye to me."

Gale blinked. Markus seemed taken aback. He looked almost relieved.

"He did? So… it truly was a poor joke, then? You weren't talkin' 'bout runnin' off behind my back, Guinevere?"

"No, Papa. You walked in before Gale could finish his sentence. While yes, he was saying he hoped to marry me someday, he was in the middle of saying he could never do so without permission when you interrupted. Gale and I want nothing more than to do this right."

Gale stepped forward, squaring his shoulders and setting his feet apart.

"Aye, sir. I know where we stand here, and I know that only a bas—only a… I'm not the kind of man who's willing to come between a father and his daughter. I know you have your doubts 'bout me— and I know you have fair reason to have 'em—but I'll do whatever it takes to prove 'em unfounded."

Markus raised his eyebrow. "I thought I heard you say you two were sayin' goodbye. This sure don't sound like goodbye."

Guinevere rested her hand protectively on Gale's

arm, "That's because that while it is, it also isn't. Gale came here to tell me he was leaving to sail the Rose Line. He's willing to go away—to leave Alinor for a whole year—just to earn enough money to give me a proper home before he asks you for my hand."

Markus's gaze hardened. "Is this true, lad? Is that what you're hoping to do? The Rose Line is quite the gamble."

Gale nodded. "Aye, sir. But there's no better way I know to earn the coin it takes to be considered an honest man. Way I figure, if the gods don't guide me home, if I don't make the journey, if I blow the money or lose my life or get back to find Guinevere don't love me the way I think she does—well, then it wasn't meant to be. I'll accept any risk, if that means we can win half a chance at being together."

"Pretty words, sure enough. Pretty promises and pretty ideas, but I'll be hanged if they're not all pretty empty, lad. I know this game. I know it's all naught but words."

"Papa, Gale means it. He means every word he says, and I love him. Please give us a chance."

Markus sighed, closing his eyes and pinching the bridge of his nose the way Guinevere sometimes did. "You know what? Fine. If he sails the Rose Line and comes back with the both of you still faithful to each other, I'll... consider. Maybe. But—" Here, he turned and glared at Gale again. "you listen good, lad: the ship I'm fixin' now—*The Morigana*—she sails at dawn tomorrow with a cargo of goods bound for Mikare. If you're not signed up for a full voyage by the time she embarks, there'll be hell to pay. And if I so much as catch wind of your presence in this city at any point over the next year after she leaves, I will personally see to it that you never set foot on a workin' ship again. You hear?"

Gale whipped off his smartest salute. "Loud and clear, sir! You have yourself a deal. I'll swear now in front of all of you and beneath the eyes of the Brother Gods—I will sign up, I will sail out, and—Gods willing—I will come back. I'd sooner die than lie to you."

Markus nodded—in acceptance, if not in approval—and left, stalking off without another word.

Guinevere looked after him, then cast a pained glance at Gale.

"I should go after him," she murmured, pulling Gale into a quick hug. "I'm sorry. I didn't expect this to happen. I didn't know he would stop by, today... I love you." There were tears brimming in her eyes, just below the surface.

Gale smiled and leaned down to give her a gentle kiss. "I love you, too, Guin."

"Visit me tonight?"

"Of course."

They embraced again, then Guinevere reluctantly closed the shop and left to follow her father.

CHAPTER FOUR
Crawford

Crawford awoke to screaming gulls, shrill shrieks that pierced his head like needles. Bright rays of sunlight stabbed through holes in the inn's ratty curtains. Crawford rolled over and buried his face in his flat pillow, but it didn't help. After a moment spent vainly trying to recapture sleep, Crawford gave up, stretched, rolled the crick from his neck, and disentangled himself from his coarse bedsheets.

Stifling a yawn, Crawford stretched again and turned his back to the window to block the light. He pulled on his clothes, tracked down his boots, grabbed his hat and ran his fingers roughly through his hair—all the while humming an old, repetitive shanty. He kept humming as he staggered out of his rented room, barely missed a note when he tripped over the drunk sprawled asleep on the staircase, and only allowed his melody to fade when he saw Gale seated at a table in the main room, eating from a bowl of tasteless-looking porridge.

Gale caught his eye and waved at him, gesturing

for Crawford to take the seat across the table. Crawford grinned and nodded a greeting in reply, hardly stumbling as he stifled a yawn and made his way over.

"Fancy catchin' you again, Gale. I ain't seen you since we hit land. Where you been, mate?" Crawford asked, motioning to the innkeeper for breakfast.

Gale filled his spoon with porridge, brought it halfway to his mouth, then let it fall again. "Crawford, I gotta leave."

"Say again, mate? Leave where? What the hell're you talkin' about?"

"Alinor, Crawford—I gotta go. Made a deal with Markus—he ain't crazy 'bout the idea of Guinevere with a sailor, but he swore to consider the thought if I went and signed up to sail the Rose Line aboard *The Morigana* for a year."

The innkeeper's son came by and set a bowl of porridge in front of Crawford, but for the moment, he left it untouched. "You—you're kiddin' me, Gale. Am I still drunk?"

Gale chuckled slightly, but he shook his head. "Nah, mate. The reason you're hearin' me talk crazy is 'cause I'm talkin' crazy. I'm gonna sign on today to leave at dawn tomorrow—it's set. I gave my word."

"I—What the hell did you do that for, Gale? What the hell were you thinking, doing a thing like that?"

"I was thinking of Guinevere, Crawford. Guinevere, and that distant horizon. Sure, it's short notice, but... I reckon this is my one chance to chase 'em both. I figured I should let you know 'fore I sail off and vanish. You're gonna have to be the best windworker in Alinor all by your lonesome, for a while."

Crawford lifted his spoon and brandished it at Gale like a knife. "You belay that talk, mate—I'll do no such thing. You think I'm about to let my best mate ship off for glory, girls, and grand old riches without me? Gale—I'm not about to sit back while you have all the fun." He punctuated the thought with a bite of breakfast and a pointed look. "What was it—*The Morigana,* you said? Give me enough time to properly wake and rise, and I'll sign up right beside you."

Gale laughed, a grin splitting across his face. "Crawford, you stone-cold son of a sea snake—you'd do that?"

"Aye, Gale, consider it done. I spent the better part of the past decade workin' beside you—why the hell would I wanna hafta seek out a new partner now? The thought of tryin'a quell a squall with some greenleaf rookie…" Crawford made a face. "Nah, better prospects out on the Line. What's a year? Without a mum or a steady sweetheart, I might as well just cast my lot in with you, ya bastard. Only stand to gain."

"Aye, I'll drink to that," Gale replied, raising his wooden spoon as though it were a glass.

Crawford raised his eyebrow. "You would, would you? Never known a man able to drink cutlery afore. That's some talent, Gale. You've been holding out on me."

Gale shook his head, chuckling. "Well, you know me, mate. Full of surprises."

"Aye, and the biggest one among 'em is that fact that you haven't gotten yourself killed yet, Gale, gamblin' the way you do. I swear, if it weren't for me, you'd be drowned in the sea already. Way I see it, it'd be murder not to keep an eye on ya."

"Oh, ye of little faith, Crawford. I'm not quite as blind as all that."

"Gods know you're blind enough."

CHAPTER FIVE
Gale

The sun was high when Gale strolled out towards the shipyard with Crawford to find *The Morrigana*. Though large, puffy clouds hung over the horizon, the sky above Alinor was blue and clear, and the warm sea air had lost its morning chill.

The shipyard bustled with activity—men ran about here and there and everywhere, hoisting crates of supplies, carrying away old growth, and painting elaborate enchantments on nearly every surface. A number of ships in various states of completion floated stoically, grand ladies awaiting the attention of their loyal servants, and one great galleon—*The Morigana*—sat among them like the queen of the lot. Every line of her build screamed power, grace, dignity—her three tall masts looked as though they were about to tear holes in the sky, and the strand— the white hairlike leaves that sprouted from the top of the mast—drifted and waved like proud banners in the wind. Her fresh coat of black paint shone in the sun like polished midnight, and the bright name-glyph on her side looked as though it had been written in shimmering gold.

She was the center of a hive of activity. Enchanters crawled over her surface with their special paints and tools, touching up the protective spells against the wind and the rain. Other men were busy polishing the deck and making sure every piece of equipment was shipshape, while a tall man with white hair and spectacles stood watching over everything, shouting at people and calling out orders to the men loading the cargo.

The sight of the ship, the activity, the looming adventure set Gale's heart pounding with a strange exhilaration. Though anxiety still had dull claws sunk deep into the back of his mind, Gale's cheeks hurt from grinning. He exchanged a glance with Crawford, who nodded.

Nearby, on the docks, Gale saw Markus Syren talking with a tall, dark-haired woman. Guinevere stood beside them, nodding politely every now and again, but it was clear that her attention was elsewhere. When she saw Gale, her face lit up and she waved him over.

Markus turned his head as Gale and Crawford approached, his expression darkening with every step they took. The dark-haired woman raised both her eyebrows and pursed her lips, placing her hands on her hips. She moved with an air of casual, deadly grace, her eyes were chips of bright steel, and her long hair was plaited down her back in one neat rope. On her left cheek, she bore a Captain's Mark—the pale, scar-like pattern identical to the name-glyph on the side of her ship—and at the sight, Gale found himself standing straighter.

"This the man, Syren?" the woman asked, looking Gale up and down.

"Yes ma'am, that tall one there's him," Markus answered, sighing. "And I know the other lad, too, but I can't say I'm right fond of him, either."

Guinevere stepped up, clearing her throat softly. "Captain Nimune, please meet Mister Gale Windworker, and Mister Crawford Breezebender—his companion, and my friend. Gale, Crawford, meet Lady Nimune Ironhide, Captain of *The Morigana.*"

"Pleasure to make your acquaintance, ma'am," Gale said, nodding a polite greeting.

"Aye, pleasure," Crawford echoed, tipping his cap from Gale's shadow.

"Markus didn't think you'd show," Nimune said, dismissively examining her fingernails, "I certainly didn't expect there to be two of you. And windworkers both, eh? How much experience you got, lads? You any good?" She looked up, her eyes sharp. Gale and Crawford exchanged another glance.

"Aye, Cap'n, the best," Gale answered, pulling himself to full height and clasping his hands behind his back. "I've been on and off fishing boats since I was old enough to totter, and Crawford's much the same. We've worked together most of that time—you'd be hard pressed to find a better team of windsmen anywhere in the city."

"References?" Nimune asked, stepping close and taking Gale's chin in her hand, twisting his face this way and that for a better view. Her grip was a vise, her eyes were chunks of sea ice, and her voice, though apparently disinterested, had enough natural command in it to make a limp noodle stand up and salute.

"Started aboard the *Red Gull*, with Captain Herald Strongarm back 'fore he retired, served five years with Captain Abrams Swift aboard the *Orange Glory*, before movin' on to work aboard the *Osprey* under Captain Jonesson Prophet. All of them were glad to have us and pained to see us go."

Captain Nimune released Gale and turned, squinting down at Crawford. "Same for you, lad?"

Crawford nodded. "Aye, ma'am, near about."

"Right then. I suppose I could do worse..." She stared back at Gale for another long moment. "You have that look in your eye. You're a gambling man, and stubborn, too. Markus might not like ye, but I happen to like a man crazy enough to risk everything. But I'll give you fair warning now: I don't put up with bastards and I never suffer fools aboard my ship, understand? I already got a set of tried and true windworkers who can handle themselves—so if you two prove more trouble than you're worth, I won't hesitate to have you thrown into the drink."

Gale and Crawford both saluted. "Aye aye, Cap'n!"

Captain Nimune nodded once and smirked.

"I'll see the both of you bright and early, then. We sail at dawn. I expect you to arrive well before that."

With that, she stalked off, shouting orders to the enchanters busy refreshing the protective spirals painted on *The Morigana's* bow. Markus followed, sweeping Guinevere up in his wake.

* * *

That night, shortly after dusk, Gale returned to Guinevere's garden. Her window was dark. Though he threw stones and waited, she never showed her face. The night remained as cold and bleak as ever, and Gale eventually had to go back to
the inn to sleep.

CHAPTER SIX
Guinevere

The next morning was grey and misty again, hazy and cloudy and colorless. Guinevere woke from a restless sleep with a bad taste in her mouth. Her body ached for no reason, and a sour knot sat in the pit of her stomach. Despite the warmth of her blankets, the heavy chill of nightmare had settled deep into her bones.

She shook herself and slid from her covers, untangled her unruly hair from around her neck, and went to the window. The grey touch of twilight was fading. The edge of the sky was already turning gold.

Dawn. Guinevere's stomach froze, churned, twisted. She fled her room and ran without bothering to grab either coat or slippers. By the time she reached the docks, *The Morigana* was kissing the horizon.

Guinevere screamed. She imagined she felt a soft wisp of wind caress her face in reply.

CHAPTER SEVEN
Crawford

Alinor was a toy town, foggy and fading against the black and green coastline. From his place in the crow's nest, Crawford could see it all—the tiny turrets of the Palace, the uneven spires of the Tower, the brown smear of the Seaside District, the lonely black beaches…

Beside him, Gale sighed.

"Gonna be a long year, eh, mate?" Crawford said softly, giving Gale a careful glance.

Gale nodded. "Feels like ages already, and we haven't even hit the Line."

"Well, you better get used to that, shipmates," a brown-haired man with a scar over his right eye said, grinning like a fox. "Though the trip's gonna get shorter, each passin' day's gonna feel longer than the one before. Right, Devyn?"

"Aye, how true that is, Daryl," his twin—identical, but for the scar—replied, laughing. "Y'know, lads, if you two greenhorn shore-huggers 're feelin' homesick already, you might be better off jumpin' into the ol' blue swell now. We're not far yet—swimmin' back'd be a fair sight safer than stickin' out, if you're heart's not in the voyage."

"Aye?" Crawford was quick to answer. "You think Gale an' I can't cut it, eh? Well, you better watch your back, boys, else my mate and I might just pinch your jobs out from under you while your backs're turned. We're some o' the best in the business."

"Oh, are ye?" Devyn answered, lifting his eyebrow. "Do you hear that, Daryl? This pair of Alinorian shallow-skimmers think they're the best. They think they're better'n us—what do you say we show 'em a trick or two here, before we hit the Line proper?"

"Only if they're up for it, Dev," Daryl replied, smirking. "What do you say, lads—the Captain told us to show you the ropes. Would you care to see some real windworkin', while you're here? Unless o'course you two ain't brash enough to handle the seaward gales."

Gale chuckled, though his eyes kept flicking back towards the shore. "Well, mates—how d'you think I got my name, eh? You want a squall, look no further. You want gales, I'm your guy. Sure, maybe Crawford'n I ain't as traveled, maybe we're green when it comes to a ship as big and grand as all this, but you just give us a chance, lads, an' we'll show you both skill and steel. Show us what you got—maybe we'll all learn somethin'."

The twins exchanged a glance and shrugged, sharing a smirk. "If you say so, mate," Daryl said.

Devyn closed his eyes and tensed his shoulders, and a strong wind filled *The Morigana*'s sails. Daryl leaned against the handrail as though he were on some kind of pleasure cruise.

"Y'see, mates," Daryl began, covering a yawn with the back of his hand, "the way things work out on the Rose Line, y' gotta be ready for anything. Out there on your fishing boats you just drift here an' there an' everywhere chasin' the fish. You're fine so long as you don't drift too far or bash into anybody, aye? The domain border's a whole big circle you can wander, and if a storm crops up or a lost sea monster pops by for tea, you got a whole crowd at your back to face it."

Crawford nodded. All around *The Morigana*, gulls wheeled and called. Fishing boats in all sizes still wove randomly together across the nearby waters, chasing the schools of fish that swam in from the Thousand Seas, but every passing second took *The Morigana* closer to the Rose Line and further away from the rest of the crowd.

Daryl stretched for a moment, then gestured starboard, curving a bit of the world's wind around the crow's nest and away from *The Morigana* before continuing. "The Line is different. First of all, it's a line. Straight. Narrow. Nearly no room to drift or fall astray. Lucky the enchanters got that colorful pink kelp growing to mark our way. And I'll say now—you lose sight of that lifeline, and you're gonna wish you'd gone and drowned yourself before you were born. So you gotta be able to push this fair lady forward, you gotta be ready to keep the world's wind from guidin' us off course, and you gotta be ready to jump up and quell a storm at any hour of the day should the Gods try to pull somethin'. You got that?"

Crawford and Gale nodded.

"Tell them more about the Domain shift," Devyn added, his eyes still closed, "city folk don't know a blamed thing about the domain shift."

"Ah, right, Domain shift. You two know much about that?" Daryl cast a critical eye over Gale, lifting his eyebrow as Crawford shrugged.

"We know a fair bit," Crawford said. "Back in the day, the gods got careless, shattered the world, an' now we gotta deal with the poor job they made of fixing it. All the bits and pieces move around randomly, 'cept our city."

"Our city, the Rose Line, and Mikare, by extension," Gale added.

"Aye." Daryl nodded. "So it's just about crucial that you understand how important it is that we keep from drifting, boys. The Thousand Seas aren't kind— sure, you go over the edge once, maybe you can blow us back on course in time to get on track afore the domain shifts away from the Line and sends us all to the back o' beyond—but there's a fair shot of ending up spliced. Or worse, adrift forever on the endless seas. A man can't get much more lost than that, and the chances of anyone ever even seein' your vessel again are slimmer than shadow."

Crawford and Gale exchanged another glance.

Gale cleared his throat. "Aye, sir, I think we get the picture."

"Yeah," Crawford added, adjusting the cap on his head, "we might be new to the Line, but we sure ain't new to sailin'. We got the message loud and clear, and we sure ain't about to forget it."

Daryl grinned. "Just what I like to hear, boys! Captain'll be glad to know you ain't a pair of idiots, though you may yet prove to be fools. Anyway, time's come we see whether 'best in business' is even close to halfway true. You up to put your money behind your mouth?"

"We're up for any test you care to name." Crawford straightened his shoulders and drew himself to full height, looking both of the twins full in the face. Though he was not quite so tall or broad as Gale, he was sure the effect was almost the same.

Gale nodded as well, his eyes drifting back over the horizon to Alinor.

Daryl looked at Crawford and grinned. "How about you first, mate? Looks like your pal ain't full woken up, yet."

Devyn snapped his fingers beside Gale's head to get the blond man's attention. Gale shook himself lightly and found his way out of whatever dream he had been lost in. "Sorry—what were you sayin'?"

"A test, mate," Devyn said slowly, exaggerating his patience. "We're gonna test the two of you. Starting with your pal, here."

Gale nodded. Crawford caught the almost imperceptible flicker of annoyance that flashed across his face.

"So. You ready, mate?" Daryl asked as Devyn allowed his magic to fade and let the world's wind take over.

"Just tell me what you expect, and I'll show you whatever skill you wanna see," Crawford answered promptly.

"That's talk I like to hear! Now listen up—your task is fair simple: just pick up the slack and guide *The Morigana* out to where she needs to be. For a windworker of your obvious talent it should be cake, aye?"

Crawford raised the winds in answer, refusing to rise to the twins' baited smirks. *The Morigana* was heavier than the *Osprey* had ever been, but she was a trade ship full of cargo, so he wasn't surprised. He summoned every drop of magic in his blood and threw the wind into the sails with all his might— straining until his body ached and his brain screamed in the agony of effort. *The Morigana* slid out towards the open water, building momentum and easing towards the Rose Line with a smooth and ponderous grace. Sweat beaded on Crawford's brow, his knees shook, but he gritted his teeth and held the wind in place.

Daryl set a hand on his shoulder. "'Hoy, mate, you know we're not on course anymore, aye?"

Crawford's concentration broke, and the wind broke with it. His shoulders slumped and he raised his head. Sure enough, he'd gotten the angle wrong. The direction was right, but if he'd held *The Morigana* to her course, he would have driven the ship past the Rose Line and out into open water.

Crawford growled, internally cursing himself.

"Not a bad effort, mate," Daryl said, shrugging. "You had a fair bit of power, there, though your technique could use some work. Too much bleed-off—not enough finesse. Gotta work on your stamina, too, but that'll come with time. Our grand *Morigana* is no little lady, and it takes a while before any sailor's grown enough to dance with her the way she deserves. You'll get there."

Crawford sighed and let himself sink down to his knees to rest.

Devyn looked to Gale. "So. You next. Time to get your head outta the clouds and work for a living, boy."

"Aye aye, sir." Gale rolled his neck and stretched his shoulders, loosening his arms. A fierce wind picked up almost instantly, filling *The Morigana*'s sails so that the white canvas billowed and was taut. The ship picked up speed, gliding over the ocean like a gull through the air. Gale hardly seemed strained— the way his eyes shifted lazily between the Rose line, the horizon, and the shore, he hardly seemed to be paying attention. But *The Morigana* never wavered from her target, and she never drifted so much as an inch from her course.

As if that weren't enough, Gale still had enough energy to divert a tiny, contrary breeze to keep his hair from falling into his eyes.

Crawford whistled under his breath.

The twins exchanged a glance, their eyes wide.

Devyn cleared his throat. "You're not—"

"—helping him, are you?" Daryl finished for him.

A moment of silence passed, with only the wind to fill it. Then both men burst out laughing.

"Okay—you can stop, lad. We've seen quite enough." Devyn said, clapping Gale on the shoulder.

Gale let the wind die down. His grin was broad. "Satisfied?"

"Aye," Daryl said, "more than that! Gale's a right title and they were right to give it to ya. Power— control—damn, boy, I wish I had your blood. Who're your parents? I bet they're proper legends."

Gale chuckled. "Wouldn't know—never met 'em. But I was trained by ol' Hamish Guster aboard the *Red Gull*, afore he died—he an' ol' Missus Smith got me started sailin' and taught me all I know."

"What d'you know," Devyn said, chuckling, "Hamish Guster was our uncle. Good man, he was. No wonder you're a proper talent."

Crawford gave a breathless laugh, still wheezing slightly from the strain of pushing the ship. "What did I tell ya, lads? Me an' Gale—we're the best.

The Thousand Seas ain't seen the like."

CHAPTER EIGHT
Gale

Gale climbed down the ladder from the crow's nest, his thoughts returning to Guinevere with every step.

Crawford and Daryl followed him down, while Devyn stayed above to manage the first wind shift. The moment their feet hit the deck, the pale, white-haired man with the spectacles—the first mate—started shouting orders.

"Alright, lads! Pile on every last stitch of canvas, now—prepare to hit the Rose Line! Windworkers—set course! We're away!"

The crew cheered and set to work, Gale and Crawford among them. Someone struck up a shanty, and soon enough the entire crew was singing along with the refrain, matching their work to the rhythm.

"Come all you young sailors, now listen to me
I'll sing you a song of the fish in the sea,
and it's...

Windy weather boys, stormy weather, boys
When the wind blows we're all together, boys
Blow ye winds oceanward, blow ye winds, blow
Jolly pink waters, boys, steady she goes.

Up jumps the eel with his slippery tail,
Climbs up aloft and reefs the topsail,
and it's...
Windy weather boys, stormy weather, boys
When the wind blows we're all together, boys
Blow ye winds oceanward, blow ye winds, blow
Jolly pink waters, boys, steady she goes.

Up jumps the kraken with his heavy claws,
Bites the main boom off with terrible jaws!
and it's...
Windy weather boys, stormy weather, boys
When the wind blows we're all together, boys
Blow ye winds oceanward, blow ye winds, blow
Jolly pink waters, boys, steady she goes.

Up jumps the fish-maid, with her tresses fair,
She'll kiss you then drown you, so sailors beware!
and it's...
Windy weather boys, stormy weather, boys
When the wind blows we're all together, boys
Blow ye winds oceanward, blow ye winds, blow
Jolly pink waters, boys, steady she goes.

Up jumps the whale—the largest of all!
He says, 'If you want wind—well, I'll blow ye a
squall!'
and it's...
Windy weather boys, stormy weather, boys

When the wind blows we're all together, boys
Blow ye winds oceanward, blow ye winds, blow
Jolly pink waters, boys, steady she goes.

Windy weather boys, stormy weather, boys
When the wind blows we're all together, boys
Blow ye winds oceanward, blow ye winds, blow
Jolly pink waters, boys, steady she goes."

Gale's spirits lifted with every refrain, and all at once the sky seemed brighter. The sun was warm and the water sparkled—sparkled almost as much as Guinevere's—

He cut the thought short. There was no reason to make a long year longer.

"You sure you're good, mate?" Crawford asked.

"Aye," Gale answered, "I am. I'll be fine. I'm doin' this for her, so I gotta make sure I stay focused. Otherwise why'm I makin' her wait?"

"That's sure one way to put it, I s'pose."

"Rose Line ahead! Crossing in two minutes!" Devyn cried from The crow's nest. He was a lookout as much as a windworker.

Gale and Crawford exchanged a grin and ran to look over the side of the ship. Daryl chuckled, joining them.

"Quite a sight, eh, lads?"

Gale nodded. "Aye, that it is!"

He leaned over the bulwhark, letting the world's wind ruffle his hair. Up ahead, the green water of Alinor's coastal domain—the safe sea upon which Gale had spent his entire life—ended in an unnaturally neat line. Beyond it, a long strip of rose-colored ocean stretched out to the horizon, surrounded on either side by thousands of shifting, shimmering patchwork pieces of ocean in every possible shade. Above, the grey clouds parted, driven away by the seas' own salted breeze.

Devyn gave a wistful sigh and mirrored Gale's grin. "I remember my first voyage. The thrill of the wide-open world, the sheer joy of sailin' out where most folk don't dare go... Makes you feel drunk, don't it?"

"Aye, better'n any ale!" Gale agreed, tossing his head back to give an exhilarated laugh.

"It's a heady draught, right enough, but I wouldn't go so far as that." Crawford chuckled, elbowing Gale in the ribs. Gale elbowed him back lightly, grinning.

Devyn laughed as well. "Nor would I. As it happens, I'm proper fond of the real stuff—Brothers both know there ain't enough to get drunk on 'twixt here an' Mikare, and the joy of a cast-off never lasts long enough. But one way or the other, Gale, you better keep a weather eye on that magic o' yours. You're a fair sight stronger than I've seen, and it looks to me like you ain't quite in full control, yet."

"What?" Gale turned to face him. "I don't catch your meaning, mate—I'm in complete control. You saw up before—I handled the wind exactly! Didn't even have overspill!"

Devyn raised both of his eyebrows and the corner of his mouth quirked into a half-smile. "Being able to control completely is a fair sight different than bein' in complete control. Sure, you got a proper talent for makin' the wind obey ye, and sure, I've never seen the like, but I'd bet you a pretty copper coin that you didn't notice yourself bendin' the wind as we speak. Did ye?"

Gale blinked. "Now? I'm not doin' anything, now. What makes you say I'm bendin' the wind now?"

"Your hair, lad. It's never once blown in your eyes, though it should have by now. It ought to be a right pain, but you sweep it away with a breeze. Not to mention when you were leanin' over the side just there, I felt all the air lean with ye. You better watch yourself, lad. A rogue breeze on the Rose Line's a fair sight more trouble than even proper talent's worth. I ain't about to get blown off course 'cause some over-eager grass-colored shore-hugger's drunk on the romance o' sailin'."

Gale paused, then nodded, forcing himself to relax his natural hold on the wind. "Aye aye, mate. Got it. No wild winds—no magic done unless I mean to do it."

Devyn clapped him on the back. "Good lad. Don't you worry too much—my brother'n I will slap you upside the head if we catch you slippin'."

"Aye, an' you can count on me to do the same," Crawford added, "an' if that ain't enough, I'll just have to keep you rememberin' that girl of yours. If you blow us all off course, you'll leave poor Guinevere alone."

"Point taken, Crawford. I'll be double sure not to let that happen."

"Captain on deck!" The white-haired man's voice rang out clearly, and all hands stopped what they were doing to salute. Captain Nimune emerged from her cabin, a stern, businesslike scowl on her face as she cast a critical eye over *The Morigana* and her crew. Her dark hair was braided back, and her long red coat swirled impressively around her muscular legs.

"What do you call this, Mister Kirk?" She asked, her voice cold.

The white-haired man pushed up his glasses. "I call this a sharp-lookin' crew on a sleek-lookin' ship, ready to face the world, Cap'n!"

A smile broke through Nimune's affected chill, and she nodded, her posture relaxing to become almost casual. "Aye, that's what I call it, too. Back to it, lads! It's a long way 'til land, and there's no call to start slacking now!"

The sailors all cheered, and *The Morigana* sailed on, leaving the green seas of Alinor behind her.

It wasn't long until the city faded completely into the haze.

* * *

Over the next few weeks, Gale and Crawford settled into the new rhythm of life on the Rose Line, living and working among the crew of *The Morigana*. They took turns on the wind shifts, spent several hours each day training under the supervision of one of the twins, and when they weren't working the wind, they were out hauling lines, out helping catch fish, or using what little downtime they had to eat, drink, and socialize with the crew in the galley. All other hours of the day were spent catching what sleep they could in the fo'c'sle.

It was hard work, but Gale loved every minute of it. He could feel himself getting stronger with every day that passed, and though he missed Guinevere enough to make his heart ache, though his dreams often returned to their last meeting and that final, futile night spent tossing pebbles at her window, the unbroken line of the horizon soothed his mind and eased his heart. There was nothing quite like sitting on a swaying mast at the center of the world, watching the domains waver and shift around him as he urged the ship onward towards the open sky. Sure, Crawford and the twins frequently had to cuff the back of his head to remind him to reign in his magic—but still, the first three weeks of the voyage were paradise.

Then the waters went black.

Gale was on the wind shift when he saw it. He was staring at the sea, daydreaming about Guinevere, when a patch of silver-blue water just off the starboard side of the ship shimmered and shifted and gave way to a section of sea as black as the midnight sky. As Gale watched, the blackness spread—dripping over the domain border to cover the pink kelp that marked the safe water. Gale halted the wind and brought *The Morigana* to a slow halt.

"Dark waters off the starboard bow!" he called down to the bosun. The bosun peered over the bulwhark for a look and gave a cry—and the next thing Gale knew, alarm bells screamed and the crew scrambled over the deck, shouting like madmen as they cleared the space.

"Somethin's swarming the ship!" they cried.

"All hands, get below!" the captain roared. "On pain of death—no one's to show their face 'til I say! Windworker—get down here! It's in the Brothers' hands, now!"

The crew cleared the deck. Gale swung himself down to join them, but he fumbled and slipped. His right wrist caught in the thin, hairlike leaves that grew from the top of the living ship's mast. Gale bit back a curse and tugged.

"Windworker! What in Chaos' name are you doing? Get down and take cover!" Captain Nimune shouted. She was the only person still on the deck—every other sailor was safe away, hidden in the depths of *The Morigana*.

"Aye aye, soon as my hand's free!" Gale called back. He pulled his knife from his belt and hacked at the silvery fibers, but they clung and tangled around the blade. Gale swore and wrenched at his arm, but nothing happened. He was trapped.

A low, rolling rumble filled the air, growing louder and louder until Gale could feel his soul shake with the thunder. The captain shouted something, but her voice was lost beneath the all-consuming noise.

Gale glanced down. The darkness beyond the ship thickened and deepened with every moment. The water roiled—the waves thrashed and bubbled with black, slimy bodies. The Rose Line was invisible under a living sea of eels.

Captain Nimune swung herself into the rigging.

Gale jerked his knife free from the hairlike strand and hacked again. Several fibers snapped, but not enough to free his wrist.

The cloud of eels reached *The Morigana's* keel. The whole ship shuddered to a halt. *The Morigana* groaned and creaked. Gale swore again, gritting his teeth and closing his eyes as he offered up a prayer to anyone who was listening.

When he opened his eyes, Nimune was at his side. Her teeth were bared, and her left hand was frozen into the shape of a claw—the skin of her arm gleamed silver under the bright sun. She cut the strand with a swipe of her hand and vaulted into the crow's nest, hauling Gale behind her.

He tumbled at her feet. Nimune peered over the handrail and swore softly. Gale pulled himself up to see, too.

The swarm of eels was dense, nearly a solid mass. Each eel wasn't swimming in water so much as it was swimming in other eels. The roar in the air grew louder. It dawned on Gale that the eels—the individually clicking eels—were responsible for the hellish noise.

Then the eels started to climb. They threw themselves at the sides of the ship, hurled themselves at *The Morigana's* hull until they'd squirmed their way up past the bulwharks to *The Morigana's* deck, a writhing wave of glistening black and purple.

Gale felt the bile rise in his throat.

The eels kept piling on, squirming up and over each other and climbing, always climbing. They tied themselves around the masts, wrapped themselves around every pin and pillar, and before Gale could blink, they'd drowned the deck in darkness.

"What do we do?" he asked Nimune, unable to tear his eyes away from the eels below.

Nimune didn't hear him. The eels were too loud. Gale had to repeat his question at a shout.

"Nothing!" Captain Nimune growled over the din, "There's nothing to do but wait and pray they can't come high enough to kill us!"

"Cap'n—can they do that?"

"These things are either magic or poison—and either way, one touch will stop your heart an' you'll be dinner! They're bloody locusts!"

Gale nodded, not trusting himself to speak. He

looked down again. The eels were halfway up the mast, close enough for Gale to distinguish individual forms within the writhing, roiling mass.

Each one was between three and four feet long, about a hand-span broad, and a third as thick. Their ribbon-like fins palpitated wildly as they thrashed and flung themselves up the mast—closer with every moment. The motion of the swarm was hypnotic—the noise was deafening—Gale could see jagged rows of mottled, needle-like teeth amidst the—

Nimune cuffed the back of Gale's head hard enough to send a flurry of tiny stars across his vision.

"You listening? I gave you an order! Wake up an' use that wind o' yers for somethin' worthwhile—move it!" she roared, her face an inch away from his.

Gale snapped to attention, nearly smacking himself with his own salute. "Aye aye, ma'am!"

He looked around. There was little he could use. He did not have the energy to blow them away with a gust—there were too many, and he was too tired from his shift. They'd keep coming and coming and he'd tire long before they stopped.

One slimy, rope-like fish squirmed its way up between the bars of the railing and wriggled towards Gale's feet. The captain sent it flying out over the water with a swift kick, but more were on their way. Dozens—hundreds—

"Gale! If you don't move this second, I swear I'll kill you myself!"

Gale took a deep breath, summoned his strength, and raised the wind. He grabbed the breeze and spun it, twisting it around and around and around the crow's nest—pushing it harder, faster—until the breeze was a wind, until the wind was a gale—until the magic was strong enough to sweep the eels from the ship and pluck them into the sky. They stayed there.

He fell to his knees and gasped for breath, but the wind kept spinning. Every eel that reached the crow's nest was sucked up by the growing cyclone until the wind was black with thrashing, writhing fish. Gale's brain pulsed in time with the wind's movement. His whole body ached and shook, but he pulled the cyclone down until it touched the deck below.

Everything not tied down took to the skies. Dark spots swam before Gale's eyes, blocking out the sun. Nimune shouted something, but Gale could not hear her. He held the wind for as long as he could—until at last it slipped from his grasp.

The cyclone flew apart, hurling eels in every direction. They fell back into the seas like so many raindrops, disoriented and half-dead from the flight. Gale's eyes stayed open just long enough to see the eels streak off into the black waters, then he kissed the deck and knew no more.

* * *

Gale awoke in a cot. A dim glass magelight swung freely on the end of a silvery rope, casting a cold, sterile light over the darkness. The smells of lemon and old blood mixed in the salt air. The ship creaked and groaned and swayed from side to side with the motion of the waves, and when Gale tried to sit up, he found himself groaning and swaying as well.

He felt as though something had crawled into his skull through his eyes and was trying to scoop out his brain with a rusty spoon. Someone had replaced his throat with sandpaper, and his arms, his legs—every muscle in his body ached and throbbed, heavy as iron and full of hot lead. Gale had never felt more tired in all his life.

A dark figure—an older, spindly man with a sharp, narrow face and pale eyes—leaned over from a nearby chair to peer into Gale's face.

"You're awake?"

Gale squinted at the man. Though the face looked familiar, it took far too long for Gale to recall him. "You're... the medical man?" His voice was hoarse—he started at the sound of it, barely recognizing the noise as having come from his own throat.

"Aye, lad. I am. Can you remember my name?"

Gale thought for a moment, letting his eyes wander up to the ceiling as he traced his way through his memory. "Uh... No, sir, I can't say I do."

The man huffed, frowning. "Not at all? I know I mostly spend my days down here below decks, boy, but we've met twice, now."

Gale shook his head, cringing as the motion sent sharp spikes through his eyes, straight to the back of his skull.

"Keep still, keep still. Move too much, and you'll only hurt yourself worse."

Gale closed his eyes and took a deep, calming breath. "Aye, sir."

The man nodded, satisfied, and settled back into his chair. "Good lad."

A moment passed, but the man did not offer any answers. He simply settled back, laced his fingers together in his lap, and closed his eyes as though to rest.

Gale cleared his dry throat, licking his lips in a futile attempt to moisten them. "Uh... what... what happened? I remember... Eels, an' the captain, and..." He frowned. A thick, slow fog seemed to have rolled in from the realm of unconsciousness to spread its damp tendrils over his brain. Nothing was free from the haze.

"You pulled a crazy stunt with the wind, lad. That's what happened. We got overtaken by swarmin' eels, and you blew 'em all to the back of beyond. I didn't see it meself, but that's what I hear. And from what I hear, you near about blew yourself out, too, lad."

"...Huh?"

"You're strong, boy. Strong enough to rival ol' Captain Johnny, from what I hear. But even you have your limits. You ever reached your limits afore, boy?"

"What?"

"Every man has his limits, lad. No matter how strong he may be, every man has his limits. From what I hear, you worked a long hard shift then blew all the eels out to the edge of oblivion. I won't waste words beaten' around my point—I was fair certain for a time there that we'd soon be singin' the Dead Man's Chant and tossin' you into the blue."

Gale opened his mouth, but before he could say anything, the thin man spoke again.

"You're blessed to be wakin' up. 'Specially this soon. It's only been about four days—most folk'd be sleepin' the long sleep after a stunt like that. Magical overload ain't a thing you can just up and run away from. Speakin' o' which, how do you feel?"

Gale blinked. The man was erratic—he tossed

the conversation around like a leaf on the wind. Gale's head was too full of fog to follow. "I—uh... I... Thirsty?"

"Is that a question or an answer, lad?"

"Answer."

"Right, well, you shoulda said sooner. I got fresh water right here."

The man bent down and lifted a wooden mug from the floor, lifting Gale's head so he could drink. All the while, the man rambled.

"I got nice fresh water, I got a bit of bread for ye, as well as a good fresh bit of shipfruit. Cap'n was adamant that I saw to ye proper. Normally I'd just give you a shot o' magic to patch whatever was ailin' ye, but magical overload is near about the one thing I can't go and cure easy. Can't cure it at all, actually. Don't know if there's a man on the sea who can. Not a knitskin or a boneweaver in all the world who can cure what ain't actually broke."

He tilted the mug a bit too far, spilling water over Gale's face and neck. Gale coughed and spluttered, almost convulsing from the pain it caused.

The man jerked the mug aside and pushed Gale's chest to keep him down. Thin though he seemed, the man was surprisingly strong.

"Shh, shh—none of that now, boy. The stiller you lie, the faster you'll be back out workin'. And the captain wants to have you workin' again long afore we reach port. If you can't work, you have no place here—and you can't work if you don't got magic."

Gale sucked in a deep, slow breath, forcing himself to be still. The last thing he needed was a worse injury. He was in quite enough pain already.

When the man was certain Gale would be still, he

released his hold. "That's a fair sight better. Now—you been able to recall my name, yet?"

Gale bit the inside of his cheek, carefully patient. "No, sir. Not yet."

"More's the pity. Guess I gotta remind you, then. I'm Edwin Patcher, ship's healer, though the lads all call me ol' Eddy. I'll be the one to fix ye up if you ever get yerself hurt again. Hopefully with a jolt of magic, next time. Now, you ought to rest, lad. You can't expect to get better any time soon if you're awake all night talkin' my ear off!" With that, the skinny old man threw himself back against his chair, closed his eyes, and began to snore. Gale waited, but the man truly seemed to have tossed himself into a deep, natural sleep.

Gritting his teeth against the ache in his bones, Gale hauled himself out of the cot and
    staggered toward the door.

CHAPTER NINE
Guinevere

"Guinevere, what are you doing?" Ell asked, her high voice ringing through the brightly-lit parlor like a funeral bell.

Guinevere did not turn to face her, instead choosing to keep her face to the window and her eyes on the distant sea. A squall had blown in from the water and the air was grey with drumming rain. "I'm sitting, Ell. Just sitting and... thinking, I guess."

"About Gale?" Ell sat herself down on the windowsill. Guinevere forced a smile.

"Yes, Ell, about Gale. I was wondering if he's safe, out there. If he's having adventures, and if he's thinking of me."

"Oh, I'm sure he is, Guin! He's having all the most exciting adventures, and he's never thinking of anything but you! When he comes back, he's gonna sweep you off your feet, and you'll both get married, and he's gonna have so many wonderful stories to tell!"

"But... how do you know, Ell? There are so

many things that could happen out there on the Thousand Seas... So many things could go wrong, and..."

"I know because he loves you. He told me. He promised. You love him too, don't you?"

"What? Of course, Ell! How could you ask that? I love him more than anything!"

"Then why don't you believe he'll keep his promise?" Ell was doing that thing with her eyes again—making them wide and innocent. She did that whenever she said anything she deemed particularly biting, as though it would keep people from getting mad at her.

Guinevere sighed, calling upon every ounce of patience she could muster. "I do think he'll try and keep his promise, Ell. It's just... sometimes things happen, and there's nothing we can do. That's how life is. I'm afraid something will happen out there, and Gale... I worry that it will be out of his hands."

"Well, stop worrying, Guinevere! Gale is strong and brave and I trust him to do everything he can to keep his promise to you! Anything is possible when two people are in love!"

The wind changed direction, blowing a fresh torrent of rain to beat at the window. "Ell... You do realize that this is real life, yes? Not one of your books? Gale is out there right now—out there on the Thousand Seas where anything can happen, and..."

"And what, Guinevere?"

"And..." Guinevere felt a tear leak from her eye. She scrubbed it away, drawing herself up and in. "And since Father wanted to talk that evening, I never got to tell him goodbye. I never got to tell him how much I—I never got to wish him—" More tears threatened to follow the first. Guinevere broke off, unwilling to release the flood. She bit her lip hard and fought back a sob.

Ell was by her side in a moment, her face the picture of concern. "Guinevere?"

Guinevere shook her head. Ell eased closer and wrapped her arms around her sister. Guinevere hugged her back tightly.

"I'm such a fool, aren't I? Worrying about things I can't help."

"No, Guin, you're not a fool. You're in love. And nothing causes greater pain than that which brings purest joy."

Guinevere's mouth quirked up in a slight grin, even though she had to release Ell to wipe her face again. "That sounds like a quote, Ell."

The girl looked away, shuffling her feet and grinning sheepishly. "It might be. But I still think it's a good line, even if you think the books are silly."

The wind changed direction again and the rain slacked—the pounding roar fading to a patter.

Guinevere nodded. "The books are unforgivably silly, but... I agree. That is a nice line. But... do me a favor, Ell?"

"Yes, Guin?"

"Don't ever fall in love with a sailor."

CHAPTER TEN
Crawford

Crawford awoke in his bunk to see a familiar hand dangling in front of his face. He stared at it dully for a long moment, then jolted upright.

"Gale?! You're back?"

A low groan floated down from the top bunk. The dangling hand twitched. Crawford rolled from his bed and leapt to his feet. Sure enough, there was Gale—back and very much alive. Crawford laughed.

"Gale, my ol' shipmate—what the hell're you doing back here so soon! I heard you weren't s'posed to recover for ages!"

Gale groaned again and opened one grey eye. "'Hoy, mind pipin' down, Crawford? A body's gotta rest."

"Gale, you been sleepin' for near a week solid. Twins an' I have been coverin' your shifts and we're sick of it!" Crawford grinned and poked Gale's forehead. "You've had enough rest. It's time for you

81

to be up an' at 'em again! Live your life an' your life'll come back to ya! What'd you say, mate? Come on, rise an' shine! The lads've all been waitin' to talk to ya—you know you're near about a legend, now."

That got Gale to roll over and open his other eye. "Legend, you said?"

"Aye, mate—you blew that bloated swarm o' blasted fishes clear to the Brother's Gate! I ain't seen a bit o' windworkin' fair as that in all my days, Gale—it was near about heroic! I'd say it were full heroic if you hadn't got yourself stuck out there to begin with, but a man can't go winnin' everything all the time."

Gale chuckled, wincing slightly and rolling back so that he could clutch at his abdomen. Crawford bit the inside of his cheek.

"Hey, hey—you alright, mate? Maybe you should rest up after all. I don't want you keelin' over now that you've finally gone and opened your eyes."

"Nah, nah—if I missed four days o' this voyage, it's high time I got back out there. I reckon you're right—sunshine's gotta be the best thing for me." Slowly, Gale dragged himself up and eased himself down from his bunk. He stumbled when his feet touched the floor, but Crawford was there to catch him.

"Easy now, Gale. Here—let's go down, get breakfast in the galley afore the rest of our shift's awake. Beat the rush, aye?"

"Aye," Gale answered, "that's a fair idea. I could use a good meal."

"I'll say. You're a fair sight lighter than I remember, mate. Last time I had to carry you, I'd have sworn you were made of stone."

Gale paused. "I... don't recall you ever havin' to

carry me, Crawford."

Crawford chuckled. "Well, mate, you wouldn't. It was that time—maybe two years ago—when you near about drank your weight."

"Oh, right… Hah—that was one heck of a night. Good times. I don't reckon I had *that* much, though."

"Gale, you sure as hell had quite enough. You shoulda seen yourself. Didn't you ever wonder why the folk down at the Blue Crab Tavern always smile when they see ya comin'?"

"I always figured they were just friendly people."

"Aye, well, they're special friendly when they see a guy who near about funded 'em for a year in the space of a night."

The two of them staggered towards the galley, occasionally bumping into walls as the ship rocked them back and forth. Gale laughed, and a weak breeze tousled his hair, barely twitching the yellow strands from his face.

"Damn… I really did wear out my magic, didn't I? Anyway, Crawford, you gotta give me some credit—I ain't done a thing like that in a long while. Not since Guin set me straight."

"Aye, lad, I know. The folks at the bar've started to miss your mug. Y'know, I meant to mention— back when we were still ashore, I had someone ask me if you'd gone and died."

Gale laughed again. "What'd you tell 'em?"

Crawford grinned. "I said that you were aiming to settle and get yourself married. I swear every sailor among 'em shed a tear for your loss."

They reached the galley. Crawford lowered Gale down at one of the low tables before leaving to fetch water from the ship's magically purified cistern. He paused on his way back to pluck a pair of large orange fruits from the thick web of vines on the ceiling. Each was about twice the size of a man's fist and gave off a tart, sweet smell that reminded him of sunrise during the bloom months. He passed one to Gale, taking out a knife to peel his own.

The rind fell away easily, revealing neat, even wedges of vibrant purple. Crawford deftly slipped the skin off of each wedge, baring the sweet, pulpy fruit.

"Only got one seed today," he remarked, picking out the small wooden teardrop and setting it beside the rind, "looks like fortune's winds're blowin' my way."

"Aye?" Gale did the same with his fruit, pulling two seeds from the mess. "Lucky you, mate! Got two pips here—bet it means Guinevere's thinkin' of me back home."

Crawford nodded, chuckling, and ate his breakfast. "You need a piece of shipfruit superstition to tell you that, mate? You're crazy enough to set to sea for the girl—she'd better be thinkin' of you."

Gale laughed and shrugged. "I know for a certain fact that she's missin' me like I miss her—but all the same. I got two pips together to reassure me."

As they ate, the rest of their shift trickled in to break their fast before the day's work began. Devyn was among them, and when he saw Gale, he let out a whoop.

"Look if it ain't the cyclone spinner! Blow me down, Gale—has crazy ol' Eddy let you out already? I didn't expect to see you for a few days yet!"

"I wouldn't say he let me go, exactly. More like I decided it was time I got outta bed and started pullin' my weight. Where's the fun in sailin' if you spend the whole voyage asleep?"

That got a laugh. Within moments, Gale was surrounded by a throng of people, clapping hands on his back and offering him praise. Crawford grinned, playing absently with the seed from his shipfruit as he downed the last of his water.

CHAPTER ELEVEN
Gale

"Captain wants to see you, lad." Gale was called from the galley by a quiet word from the pale first mate. As the rest of the sailors went to work, as Crawford ascended the main mast to take his place on duty, Gale knocked at the thick wooden door of Captain Nimune's cabin.

She bid him enter, and Gale opened the door to find the captain alone inside, sitting in a wickerwork chair beside her desk with a thick book in her hands. The cabin was surprisingly spacious and spotlessly clean—the only signs of human habitation were the few scattered charts on the table and the large family portrait on the wall.

Nimune read down to the end of her page, then glanced up. "Oh, it's you. It's good to see you're up and moving, Windworker."

Gale nodded, stepping inside and standing at attention.

"Aye, ma'am, it's good to be up and movin'."

"I'm sure." Captain Nimune set her bookmark in place and set her book aside, looking Gale firmly in the eye. "Do you know why I called you here, lad?"

"No, ma'am."

"That stunt you pulled with the eels…"

"Yes, ma'am?"

"Stop 'ma'am'ing me, boy—I'm your captain, not your mother. That stunt… Gale, though that was a fine bit of windworking you pulled, I'm going to warn you now: I can't have you floatin' along on my ship if you don't have the sense to watch yourself. Gettin' tangled in the strands—that's a rookie mistake. If you can't keep that head o' yours out of the clouds, boy, you'll find it won't last on your shoulders. I run a tight ship and I won't suffer fools."

Gale nodded slowly. He'd only slipped because he had been exhausted and terrified, but he held his tongue. "Aye aye, Cap'n. On my honor—no more rookie mistakes."

Captain Nimune nodded. "Good. Because I'm savvy to that bet you made with Markus. He an' I— we go way back. As it happens, he don't much like you, Gale. Now, I understand that he's a father, so reason ain't always a thing in his mind—always was a headstrong bastard, that one—but you ain't gonna prove yourself worthy of joinin' that family by screwin' up. He made me swear to come back with an honest report assessin' the cut of your jib, and I like him more'n I like you. That girl of his might be head-over-heels for ye, but I can tell you this as an honest woman: if you fail, if you fall, she will get over you. It's a rare day when there's only one fish in the net."

* * *

Days passed. Eventually Gale's strength returned, and he went back to work with new energy. On the fourth week out, the schedule shifted and Gale was placed on the midnight shift alongside Devyn.

He stood watch as Devyn worked, gazing wistfully at the ocean and trying to keep his mind on task. The ship's drifting leaves cast a faint white glow over the crow's nest, and below Gale, the various safety enchantments illuminated the deck with a soft red light and cast a pale gleam upon the shimmering pink water. The ocean beyond the Line was dark—black as tar, but for shimmering flecks of silver where the waves caught the moon. The stars above were an ocean of light, reflecting the glittering sea.

Gale sighed softly.

"Would you belay that, mate?" Devyn said, sounding harsher than usual.

"What?" Gale straightened, snapping back to the present.

"That sighin'—you been sighin' near once every ten minutes and I'm getting sick o' hearin' it. You know each time you been calling a crossways breeze? I swear, lad, I ought to have smacked your head by now! Stop dreamin' an' pay attention! You're on watch!"

"Aye aye, sorry, mate—lost focus. That's all."

"Lad, I don't know if you ever had so much as a drop o' focus to begin with. It's damn near amazin' you've made it this far."

Gale chuckled, apologized again, and took a deep breath to clear his head. He held the air in his lungs for a long moment, then he let out the breath in a long, slow, inaudible sigh.

His gaze drifted back towards the distant, near-invisible horizon. Though the world was black, he could sense a warm, natural wind blowing in from the port side, shorewards. Though the breeze was faint, it smelled sharp and heavy with moisture—like the forerunner to a storm.

"You feel that, Devyn?"

"Feel what?" Devyn's eyes were fixed on the sea—he seemed oblivious to all except the faint pink sheen on the water.

"I... It might be nothin', yet, but there's a storm brewin' out there. I can feel it."

"I don't feel a thing, Gale. Then again, I'm workin'. I ain't as attuned as you, and watchin' ain't my job, tonight. You think we'll have to take apart a squall? Or do you reckon we'll get off clean?"

Gale closed his eyes for a moment, casting a faint draft of air around to check the tides of the sky. "I reckon... I reckon it's young enough that we might scrape by clean, if the Gods see fit to shake the world and shift the Domain it's brewin' in. But if that patch of ocean out there stays where it is, we might have a problem or two comin' up ahead."

Devyn nodded, his gaze unwavering. "Jus' keep an eye on it, mate. Be ready to call alarm should it jump us."

"Aye aye, I'll watch it."

Over the next ten minutes, the sky down towards the edge of the world turned even darker as black clouds rose from the waves to blot out the twinkling stars. *The Morigana* rocked anxiously. Beyond the reach of Devyn's conjured breeze, the world's wind whistled low and began to howl.

Right on the horizon, a tiny light flickered and grew, like a star fallen down from the firmament to sail the Thousand Seas. Gale squinted at it. Though it was too far away to see clearly, the shape of it looked almost like...

"Devyn, do you see a ship out there?"

"You dreamin' again, Gale?"

"No, really, Devyn. Look, please. There's a ship out there—glowin' on the water off the Rose Line."

"Gale, if you think you're bein' funny, I swear, I'll—"

"Dammit, man—look! There's a ship off the Line, and it's comin' this way!"

Devyn finally raised his head to risk a sideways glance, and his face went bone-pale.

"Gale, belay all wind. We're becalmin' the ship. Now."

Gale knew better than to argue. He extended his power as far as he could and seized the wind, stopping it dead. When he spoke, he could barely bring himself to raise his voice above a whisper.

"Devyn—what is that ship? How is it—what's it doin' off the line?" He tore his gaze from the strange vessel long enough to glance at Devyn's face. The other man was shaking.

"Damn us all—that's... No. No, it can't be. That's a drifter, aye, lad? That's a drifter, or a wreck—an illusion—it... The stories can't be true. They *can't* be true..."

"What stories? Devyn—what do you know? What ship can't that be?"

"That ship, lad—that looks like the... No, I dare not speak its name on open waters. It'll only call her towards us."

Gale turned back to the distant ship. It was nearer, now, riding the waves of the brewing storm, and he could at last see it clearly. It was a two-masted Alinorian sailing ship, the kind built for speed and grown for trouble and trade, though he could see no trace of a crew. Tattered, salt-stained sails fluttered uselessly in the driving gale, and the ship's strand— those thin, ethereally glowing leaves—had grown longer than Gale had ever seen, to the point where they whipped about and trailed in the water like the bridal train of some forlorn and loveless phantom. When she twisted and turned on the rolling waves, Gale caught glimpses of the white-blue name glyph that shone on the ship's hull—but he did not recognize it, nor did he have the skill to read the plain common script printed beneath the magic sign.

Jagged lightning flashed in the sky, illuminating the distant towering clouds. The storm was still too far away to hear the thunder. Soft winds whistled through the rigging, and *The Morigana* creaked.

"Why?" Gale's voice was hoarse. He knew an ill-omen when he saw one, but his own macabre curiosity was too much to resist the question.

"Why? There's only one ship I can think to name that rides a storm like that, lad—only one damned ship in all the world that sails the outwaters without so much as a windworker to stave off the gales..."

A thick bolt of yellow lightning fell from the clouds, connecting sky and sea for an instant. A dread chill leaked into Gale's bones, freezing his blood and leaving him shivering despite the balmy air.

"What ship is that?"

Devyn passed him an incredulous glance. "You

don't know, lad?"

Gale shook his head. "I don't dare guess for certain."

Devyn took a deep, slow breath. "Lad, I reckon that's *The Tempest.*" His voice was hardly louder than the waves.

The wind howled, growing suddenly cold. Gale might have been imagining it, but it seemed the distant, unearthly ship aimed its prow at them. He shivered despite himself. "You don't mean—?"

"Aye, lad. That there—it looks to me to be none other than the lost ship o' Captain Johnny Zephyr, still wandering the endless waves."

"Why... why does she wander?"

Devyn seemed torn—Gale could see it in the man's face: the struggle between superstitious fear and the storyteller's natural urge. The storyteller's whim won out.

"I'm surprised you ain't heard the tale afore, lad. It's... Some years ago, when my pa's father was a lad, a man by the name o' Johnny Zephyr took to the seas. He was a right terror—a proper windworker, too—an' there hasn't been a better trader since. Brave an' bold an' fierce courageous. But he had a secret, they say. His ship—all ships 're alive, they look after their crews and give us what we need to survive the high seas—but his ship was somethin' special: she had the heart of a lady fair, and she was a jealous protective sort. Fastest ship on the Line, but from what I hear, she didn't half have a temper. They say that when ol' Cap'n Johnny took a wife, the ship got fair struck by envy. Couldn't bear to share him with another soul. So when he set to sea again, she kept him there. Days and nights—months and months—

even at the voyage's end, she refused to return to port in Alinor. No matter how hard they tried, they couldn't take her near the docks. She'd come in sight o' the city shore and then she'd stop, and the crew couldn't budge her an inch."

Devyn paused to stare out at the distant apparition. It was closer now, and glowing brighter. The man swallowed hard.

"Then what happened?" Gale prompted softly.

"Well, lad, y'see—the crew wasn't too keen on spendin' the rest of forever driftin' from port to port without ever goin' home. So one night, in the dark o' the moon when not even the stars were watchin', they hatched a plan. One of 'em found some spell to blind the ship for long enough to mutiny, and they attacked Cap'n Johnny, tossin' him clean over the side into the blue. Right outta this life an' into ol' Mother Ainsley's Keep, he went. An' the crew—they thought they'd finally be able to make port with him gone, but when the ship woke up… Way I hear it told, she pitched a right fit. Plucked all the crew right off the deck an' hung 'em in the strand, every Jack and Jane among 'em. Now, she wanders the waves, scourin' the seas in hopes o' findin' her lost Johnny. I hear tell o' men that've seen her—an' there's not a one that hasn't known some foul fate… Men've lost crewmates— whole ships to her vengeance and her grief. She takes 'em, you know. Legend says her strand'll sweep you up an' tie you aloft and you'll never be seen by a livin' soul again—though legend don't say what she does with them she takes. My guess is she hangs 'em, jus' like her cursed crew."

Gale nodded slowly. "An'… you think that ship there's her?"

"I pray to the Brothers that it ain't. If that's her, we can count ourselves damned as well."

Suddenly, the ship—the storm—the whole distant domain began to blur and swirl and run together, fading out and eventually vanishing to reveal a flat stretch of dark ocean, plain and blank as the void itself. The world had shifted. The dreaded, glowing ship was gone.

Gale and Devyn exhaled in unison.

"Praise be to the Orange and Violet!" Devyn cried, running his hand through his hair as his face broke into a grin. "Saved by the world shift! That's a stroke of fortune and no mistake! Thankee to Mother Ainsley, lookin' after the honest Jack Tar! Let's raise the wind back up, lad—we got fair ground to cover yet. 'S your turn to push it 'til next shift, I reckon. I... had more than enough for the night."

Gale saluted, letting his relief flood out into the world in the form of a strong, eager gust. "Aye aye, sir! Don't you worry, mate—I'm fair suited to cover the rest!"

Devyn nodded and drew a tiny flask from his jacket pocket. Gale tried not to notice how the man's scarred hands trembled and shook.

"Gale?"

"Aye, Devyn?"

"Word to the wise—I reckon... let's keep quiet about what we saw tonight, aye? Ain't no call to be stirrin' up ill winds among the crew. We don't want them thinkin' we're cursed or nothin'. A superstitious lot, sailors are. 'Specially on the Line. You take my meaning?"

Gale nodded. "Aye, mate. I do."

For the rest of the night, Gale worked the wind

shift, urging *The Morigana* further out to sea. Though he tried to keep himself on task, his mind kept drifting back to the strange, tragic tale of Captain Johnny, and his tired eyes kept imagining *The Tempest*'s ghostly form on the peak of every distant wave.

CHAPTER TWELVE
Guinevere

The sun was high in the sky as Guinevere set her basket down on the black pebbled beach and grinned at the blonde-haired girl beside her.

"This looks like a fine spot for a picnic, don't you think, Charlotte?"

"Oh, yes—this is a fine spot indeed!"

Together, the two girls spread out their thick quilted blanket and sat, carefully arranging their gowns so as not to soil them with the damp grit of the beach. The late morning sun was golden in the bright blue sky and a fair wind blew in from the sea, warm and pleasantly salted. Gulls wheeled high above and a flock of pelicans swooped low over the ocean waves like tiny, stately dragons in their precise formation.

Out on the water, the usual scattered horde of fishing ships darted to and fro like mayflies, driven this way and that by the windworkers' contradictory breezes. Guinevere tore her eyes from them and looked back to her oldest friend.

"I'm so glad you could take today off, Guinevere. It's been so long since we've been able to properly enjoy each other's company, and the weather is so nice, today!"

Guinevere laughed. "Thank you for insisting I take the time to relax! Brothers know I tend to forget. Alas, that's the trouble with loving my work."

"That's the trouble indeed! And I'm sure this business with your boy isn't making that any better. Is it true, by the way? What the rumors say?" Charlotte said, grinning as she unpacked their lunches from the cold-charmed wickerwork basket. There was a lovely array of fresh-caught shrimp, boiled and tossed in a bowl with a few slices of bright lemon and seasoned with a variety of herbs from Charlotte's own garden, along with a pair of bright red apples the girls had bought on a whim.

Guinevere selected a particularly pink-looking shrimp from the pile and delicately stripped it of its legs and tail. "That depends. What rumors have you heard?"

Charlotte lifted her apple and took a bite, passing Guinevere a knowing glance. "I heard from Selene who heard from Jenn who was talking to Gene when they overheard Cassidy say her father said that Markus mentioned you had an unfortunate suitor after your hand! Or something like that, anyway. You know how gossip is—it has a funny relationship to truth. Now that we're together, I'd like to get the story straight."

Guinevere lowered her eyes and chuckled. "It sounds ridiculous when you put it like that. Gale isn't an 'unfortunate suitor,' he's just... a sailor doing his best to do things right."

"Gale?" Charlotte's face lit up. "And he wants to 'do things right?' My! This is exciting! Why didn't you tell me earlier? What's he like? He's not the short one I met with you ages ago, is he?"

Guinevere allowed a small smile to sneak across her own face as she took a bite of shrimp. "No, though they're friends. Gale's the other one. I'm sure you've seen him around. Blond? Broad shoulders? Grey eyes? Always looks as though he just woke up from a beautiful dream?"

"Oh! *That* one! Yes, I have seen him, here and there. Guinevere, don't tell me *he's* the one you like?"

Guinevere bit her lip and nodded slightly. "He's the one."

Charlotte paused for a moment, looking pensive she bit into her apple again. "I can't say I blame you for falling for a man with a jawline like that, but... I can see why your father would be less than enthusiastic. I know my parents would be livid if I let a commoner court me. That—that isn't what this is about, is it, Guin? You're not just entertaining him to aggravate your father, are you?"

"No, Charlotte. I want to marry Gale as much as he wants to marry me."

"That is serious!" Charlotte cried, grinning, "Guinevere, of all my friends, I never expected you to end up marrying first! I didn't even know you were interested in dating at all! Is he... are you sure he's the one?"

Guinevere placed her discarded shrimp tails on the rocks beside her and met Charlotte's eyes, smiling. "As sure as I am of anything, Charlotte. I've never met anyone quite like Gale."

Charlotte bit her lip. "I'm sure that's true, Guin.

But… Okay, before I say anything more, I want to be clear that I'm speaking as your friend, alright? Because you are my dearest friend in all the world and you're probably not going to like hearing this."

Guinevere selected another plump-looking shrimp and peeled it, raising an eyebrow at Charlotte. "What have you got to say?"

"I can't help but think… even assuming all is as it ought to be, people will talk. I'll put rumors to rest when I hear them, but certain people always say the same things when something like this happens. They're going to think it's quite a shame that, after everything your father has done to elevate your family, you'd want to go and throw that away to marry a commoner—especially considering half the men in Alinor would die to have you look their way. I'm not saying that anyone's right to think that, but you ought to be prepared."

Guinevere shrugged. "They're not the ones getting married. They're welcome to say what they like, and they're welcome to miss the wedding."

Charlotte hid her laughter behind her hand. "I envy your attitude, Guin—I really do. I'd never hear the end of it if my mother were to hear of me trying something similar, and I doubt I'd have the heart to change her mind. I can hear her nagging now—" Charlotte adopted a rather shrill imitation of her mother and began to squawk and flap her arms like wings. Her mother was a bird-shifter, though Charlotte herself had inherited her father's ability to burst into flames at will.

Guinevere laughed. "I can't claim my father has ever said that, but he's come fairly close. We're going to convince him, though."

"I'm sure you'll do your best, Guin. But... again, I have to say—and know that I'm only saying because I care—are you sure this boy is worth it?"

Guinevere shot Charlotte a glance. Charlotte seemed sincere, so Guinevere nodded. "Yes, I believe he is, though I'm not entirely sure what you mean by asking."

"Well, Guin, a girl's got to be careful. I'm not going to be like my mother and claim that just because he's a sailor he's going to gamble and drink all your money away—"

"Good, because I'd be quite disappointed in you if you did claim that, Charlotte. Anyway, Gale doesn't drink nearly as much as he used to."

"—but all the same, I hope love hasn't kept you from questioning his motives."

"Questioning his motives?"

Charlotte nodded. "On two counts. The first, though I doubt your boy is the type, you do hear stories—are you absolutely, positively certain that he's not just after your money? Because Guin, you're a catch. You have a business and your father has a business and then there's your status—not to mention the fact that you're pretty—so if your boy is really the one I'm thinking of, he has absolutely everything to gain. Are you completely sure he's courting you for the right reasons?"

"I am," Guinevere answered without hesitation. "Gale's a good man. He doesn't think in those terms."

Charlotte nodded, though she pursed her lips. "That leads me to my second point. Aside from questioning his motives... have you taken the time to question... well... him? I only ask because I've seen him around. I remember I noticed him because— well, as far as looks go, you have excellent taste. But have you seen the way he flits about? The way he carries himself? I swear, I only had to watch him for five minutes and I could tell—he's a dreamer, and I don't think he's ever going to wake up."

"So? I don't see any problem with that, Charlotte. Yes, Gale is a dreamer, but if you only spoke to him, you'd see—he has this… this way. When you're with him, anything seems possible. Nothing seems out of reach. When he looks at the world… you can tell. He sees the beauty in things, Charlotte. Little things—raindrops and seashells and the way light sparkles on the water. When I'm with him, I see it all, too. I…" Guinevere trailed off, then shook her head, laughing self-consciously. "It all sounds kind of silly to say out loud, but I do—I love him exactly as he is."

Charlotte smiled and shook her head in wonder, brushing absentmindedly at her dress. "It's strange to hear you of all people talk like that, Guin. You've never been one for romance, and I never thought I'd see the day. I truly hope he's exactly as good a man as you think he is. But I'm going to argue against you for just another moment, alright? Just to ease my mind?"

Guinevere shrugged. "If you must, you must. Go ahead."

"I understand that you're head over heels and you want to think the best of him, but are you completely truly honestly certain that your Gale isn't the sort to go wandering off as soon as he finds some newer dream?"

"I've known him for more than three years. He's been… well, we've been serious two of those. He's not the type to wander."

"Three whole years? Guinevere, you've been seeing a boy for three whole years and you didn't even tell me?"

Guinevere chuckled. "I did tell you, Charlotte. Right when I met him. But you were distracted at the time, I think, and you must've forgotten. And then after that... I don't know. It never seemed important."

Charlotte laughed even as she shook her head. "I beg to differ, Guin! I still—all this time, I thought you weren't interested in love, and I could respect that, but then it turns out you've had a partner behind my back and I never knew! I feel I hardly know you anymore, Guin," Charlotte teased.

"Oh, yes. This changes so much," Guinevere replied, chuckling.

"At some point, Guin, I'd like to meet him. Officially, I mean. I've seen him around and I know his face, but you ought to introduce us."

Guinevere nodded and flicked a stray shrimp leg from her dress as her gaze was pulled back towards the sea. Gulls wheeled high above the fishing ships, snagging stray fish from the schools the sailors drove towards the nets. A soft, warm wind blew in from the water, and for a moment, Guinevere imagined she heard Gale whispering, imagined she felt his gentle hand touch her shoulder and caress her hair.

"I'd love to, Charlotte, but it will have to wait. Gale... is sailing right now. Across the Rose Line. It was the only way he could think to prove himself to my father. He's set to return some time within the Prominence of Fire, I think. So we've got some time to wait. As soon as he's home, I'll introduce you."

"Honey—he's doing what, now?"

"He's sailing the Line," Guinevere repeated, "to prove himself."

Charlotte clicked her tongue and shook her head slowly. "Well. That changes things. That changes everything. You need to promise me something, alright, Guinevere?"

"I suppose that depends on what you want me to promise," Guinevere said, mildly bewildered by Charlotte's sudden fervor.

"Please, Guinevere, I just want you to promise me you won't set your heart anywhere you can't pick it up again. Promise me you'll keep your eyes open. You're not obligated to give Gale anything, no matter what he does in your name, okay? Grand gestures don't entitle him to your love. Whatever happens, it's always your choice—and you have every right to change your mind, if that's what feels right."

Guinevere paused, then nodded, giving Charlotte a smile. "That's a reasonable promise to make. I do love him, and I spend every day he's gone wishing he were back—but I'll remember what you said, and I'll make sure my heart never overrules my head."

CHAPTER THIRTEEN
Crawford

Several weeks passed aboard *The Morigana* with little more to distinguish the days than the occasional drizzle of rain and the one odd sighting of a pod of sea serpents off in the distance.

Crawford and Gale were on day watch together again. While Gale pushed the wind, Crawford was left to scour the horizon for any sign of trouble. The patchwork sea was clear—blues and greens and greys all rested together without a sign of hardship amidst the sparkling waves, and the sky was clearer—a bright blue bowl resting atop the perfect horizon.

"This really is the life, ain't it, Gale?" Crawford asked, sighing contentedly as he leaned his elbows against the railing.

"Aye, mate," Gale said, laughing quietly even as he urged the wind onward at a breakneck pace, "that it is—not a soul on the sea could ask for a better adventure, with weather this fair. I shoulda gone and signed up to sail these waters years ago."

"Aye—you shoulda. I wager you coulda been

right proper famous by now, if you had. Though you know—if you'da gone and sailed off afore I met ya, you know what you'd be missin', Gale?"

"Besides you? What?" Gale was still doing that thing—somehow, despite sending a strong tailwind directly at *The Morigana's* sails, he still managed to steal a breeze to keep his hair in place.

Crawford adjusted his cap. "I'd have never gone and introduced you to Guin."

Gale paused, and the wind slacked for a brief half-second. "You know what, mate, you're right! Have I ever told you how much I owe ya for that? You near about set me down the path to the rest o' my life when you went and did what you did." A broad grin stretched across the man's face, and the wind picked up stronger than before.

"You really feel you owe me, Gale—buy me a drink next time we hit land. Gods both know I could use one."

Gale started to answer, but then he hesitated. "'Hoy, Crawford—do you see that?"

"See what?" Crawford looked at Gale, then followed the man's gaze out to the empty horizon.

"That—there's a bit of a smudge, right there, dead on front of us. You see it? Or are my eyes jus' givin' out on me from too long starin' into wind?"

Crawford leaned forward and squinted. The sun cast a bright glare on the spot in question, so it took a long moment for Crawford to find his answer. "Nah, Gale—I see it, too. What d'ya reckon it is? If I didn't know any better…"

"Aye, I'm thinkin' the same, mate. It looks to me as if that smudge out there…"

"An island?"

"Aye, an island."

"But that can only mean—"

"That must be Midway Point." Gale's voice was odd—both joyful and distant. Crawford glanced at him.

"You alright? You seem kinda... off."

Gale laughed and shrugged, shaking the shadow from his face and passing Crawford a bright smile. "Me? Off? Nah—I was just... it just hit me how long we've been away, an' how we've still got such a ways to go. But that don't matter right now. You want the honor, mate?"

Crawford chuckled and swept off his cap in an elaborate mockery of a gentleman's bow. "I'll gladly take the honor, ol' friend o' mine, thankee for providin' it!"

He leaned over the railing and cupped his hands around his mouth. "LAND HO!" he cried. "CENTER LINE, HALF A POINT STARBOARD!"

Down on deck, every hand who was not either asleep or aloft rushed to the bulwhark to peer out at the ocean. The captain called orders to the bosun, the bosun called orders to the rest of the crew, and the crew leapt to work while the shantyman struck up a song to aid the labor.

"When I was a little lad
So my mother told me,
Way, haul away, we'll haul away Joe,
That if I did not kiss the girls
My lips would grow all moldy,
Way, haul away, we'll haul away Joe.
Way, haul away, we'll sail across the Rose Line,

Way, haul away, we'll haul away Joe.

There was a king of Midway Point
Before the revolution,
Way, haul away, we'll haul away Joe,
He went and got his head cut off
Which spoiled his constitution.
Way, haul away, we'll haul away Joe.
Way, haul away, we'll sail across the Rose Line,
Way, haul away, we'll haul away Joe.

Oh the cook is in the galley
Making duff so handy
Way, haul away, we'll haul away Joe,
And the captain's in her cabin
Drinkin' wine and brandy
Way, haul away, we'll haul away Joe.
Way, haul away, we'll sail across the Rose Line,
Way, haul away, we'll haul away Joe."

Gale and Crawford both joined in the song, punctuating each verse with a strong pulse of wind that nearly had *The Morigana* taking flight and soaring across the sky. In no time at all, the crew brought the ship in close enough to properly see the strange island in the center of the Thousand Seas.

It was not really an island—at least, it was not really land. Midway Point was a floating mess of lopsided buildings, spindly turrets, and bizarrely angled docks and wharfs tossed haphazardly together and precariously perched atop stilted platforms connected by narrow bridges. It looked rather like a nest of giant sea urchins floating on the surface of the water, attended to by thousands of circling seabirds.

"Ah, ain't that a sight to see, Crawford?" Gale cried, his eyes wide and shining.

Crawford grinned and agreed.

Together, the two of them helped guide *The Morigana* to port, and the crew brought her in safe just as the sun began to set. Then, Captain Nimune called all hands on deck and announced that they would have one day ashore to rest and resupply before *The Morigana* sailed off again with the sunrise.

CHAPTER FOURTEEN
Gale

Hundreds of ships rested at the docks. Big trading ships, small fishing ships, massive Mikarean galleys, and tiny Alinorian sloops all floated together, bound to the artificial island of Midway Point. It was like a hive—a humming, vibrant mass of ships and sailors coming and going from both sides of the Rose Line in search of wealth and commerce, intent on drowning themselves in gold.

The Morigana's crew disembarked with the setting sun, eager to stretch their legs, see the sights, and meet what company they could in the local taverns. Crawford wasted no time following the others to a dingy alehouse under the sign of the Travelling Tern. Gale, however, hung back, and soon found himself walking alone through the slatted wooden streets.

The whole city echoed and shook with the roar of the waves beating against the city's tall, enchanted stilts, to the point where Gale imagined that he was not strolling the streets of a proper port, so much he walked across the deck of a massive ship that had been anchored in place to grow houses like other vessels grew barnacles. The buildings were haphazard and crooked, leaning together like old gossips, and numerous sprawling bridges and precarious archways stretched from one impossible structure to the next in a tangled nest of twisting streets and slim alleyways.

Everyone Gale passed seemed rough, as hard-worn and weather-beaten as the buildings themselves. Ragged sailors swaggered around in tattered sea coats, bearing all manner of scars from life spent on the water. Waifish thieves darted between lopsided houses, scrambling up walls and whistling secret signs to one another to hail the coming night, and everywhere, in every nook, cranny, and slightly sheltered eave, someone had set up a covered stall to hawk whatever wares they could get away with selling.

Weather-worn men and wizened women called and beckoned to Gale, offering him everything from sea-safety charms and hand-crafted fishbone jewelry to pearl necklaces and dragonscale pendants. Stalls sold painted earrings of dangling shark's teeth, special pouches made from serpent skin, and one man even claimed to be selling feathers from the gods' wings. Gale thought they looked more like albatross feathers, but he did not have the heart to raise the issue and so excused himself as politely as he could manage and continued down the street.

The boardwalk creaked ominously with every step, and the wind whistled strangely through the rickety wooden structures. Gale whistled back, cheerfully imagining how he would describe the place to Guinevere when he returned home. He wanted to commit every last scene—every sound and smell and exotic image to memory for her. Every instant would become a story to make her smile.

Gale took a random left turn and found himself strolling along a picturesque pier. For a moment he thought he saw a strange shadow out of the corner of his eye, but nothing was there when he turned to look.

The ocean sparkled under the light of the waning moon, and the stars were only just beginning to peek out from beneath the purple veil of dusk. The boards creaked behind him as he ambled to the end of the dock, and Gale gave a happy sigh—which was cut short by a small, sharp pain between his shoulder blades and a harsh voice in his ear.

"'Ere, boy—Gale, innit? You're lookin' pretty lost. What'd ye say you an' me—let's go on a walk, yeah? My pals an' I'd like to show ye 'round our lovely little city. For a light fee."

All wind stopped dead as Gale froze. His right hand drifted slowly towards the knife at his belt. "I— uh... I reckon I can find my own way, thanks. Though I'd appreciate hearin' how you fellows learned my name."

The dagger at his back bit a little sharper. Gale stopped reaching for his knife.

"I'm a Prophet, Gale. I know all about'cher destiny—right like the Gods wrote it. I know who ye are, I know where yer from, I knew where ye'd be, an' most of all—I know exactly what ye've got in that wallet o' yours. Give it here."

Two other voices murmured in gruff agreement. Gale started to turn his head, but a small jab kept him in place. He swallowed hard. His feet were uncomfortably close to the edge of the pier.

Gale raised his hands submissively, closing his

eyes as he secretly called the wind to gather below, just above the surface of the water. "Pardon me, mates, but… I ain't got much on me—no more than what I thought I'd need for a good night out ashore."

"No lies!" the Prophet said, jostling Gale so that he almost toppled, "I know ye got money—it's destiny! Ye got a purse full o' gold right now, an' ye're on yer way to buy a fancy trinket for yer lady fair! Like she needs another one."

Gale kept his voice from shaking and set his gathered wind to spinning. "I don't have a clue what you're sayin', mate. I wasn't on my way to do anythin'—I was just out for a walk, an' I'm broke as any other—"

"Enough blabbin'! Wallet! Now!" The Prophet jostled Gale again. Gale stumbled a half-step forward. His toes went over the edge.

"Aye aye—I'm gettin it—stop shakin' me! I can't give you a thing if you go an' drown me!"

The Prophet grabbed Gale's arm and jerked him around, cruel eyes leering out from a mess of rope-like scars. He stood about a hand's width shorter than Gale, though he was much broader, and his sharp grin gleamed nearly as bright as his wicked-looking dagger. Two other men stood behind him, thoroughly blocking Gale's escape. The one was tall and narrow, his face almost hidden by a mess of dark brown hair, and the other had the sort of sturdy bearing that suggested a lightning strike would be little more than an inconvenience. Gale divided his wind into three and willed it to spin faster.

"No funny business, lad," the Prophet growled, gesturing with his knife, "I know you got a set o' tiny twisters blowin', but it ain't gonna work. Reb's a

Shieldman an' he can stop yer gusts easy as breathin', then I'll have yer throat cut 'fore you can wink twice. I see yer destiny an' I know what you'll do long afore you even think o' doin' it. There's no use fightin'. Hand over your gold so we can all get back to our merry lives."

Gale released a breath and his winds dissipated. The Prophet sneered and held out his hand, beckoning for Gale's wallet.

Gale sighed and reluctantly fished it from his pocket. He tossed it forward, where it hit the dock with a depressingly tiny clink.

The Prophet snatched it up, his face darkening into a confused scowl. He weighed the little purse in his hand, then waved his knife at Gale.

"Where's the rest of it?"

Gale's breath caught in his throat. "I don't know what you mean—that's all I got."

"Don't lie to me, boy! I saw it—I read yer destiny—you oughta be loaded by now! Where's the rest?"

The man waved his knife around again, gesturing all the more frantically at Gale. Gale lurched back. His left heel crossed over the edge of the pier. The Prophet's cronies exchanged a worried glance.

Gale endeavored to make his voice soothing. "I ain't lyin'. I don't have the first clue what you're talkin' about. This—I gave you all I got on me, mate."

The man stepped in so his nose was three inches from Gale's face and the tip of his knife brushed Gale's chin. "I saw yer destiny, 'mate.' I know ye're holdin' out on me. I'll give you to the count of three—unless you hand over the rest, yer never gonna see your pretty girl again."

Gale didn't dare nod. The knife tip tickled his chin. He inched his hand towards his pocket again as though to grab some second wallet—then struck out at the Prophet's knife hand, snatching his small purse from the man's white-knuckled grasp.

They grappled for an instant, until Gale's foot slipped and he fell, hitting the cold, dark water with a heavy splash.

Struck by an idea, Gale allowed himself to sink. He counted to ten, then emptied his lungs. Bubbles billowed to the surface, and Gale swam beneath the pier.

Barely audible above the rushing waves, one of the Prophet's companions spoke.

"Is… is 'e comin' back up?"

"I reckon if he were, he'd 'a done so by now."

The Prophet hissed. "That bastard—he—that ain't how it was s'posed to go! Destiny was—he weren't s'posed to…." He trailed off and sighed. "Dammit. Hang it all. The swab was gonna die at sea anyhow. Tempest take 'im."

Gale held his breath as the heavy footsteps stomped back up the pier. When they were gone, Gale heaved a sigh and floated up onto his back. He rested like that for a moment, thinking quietly, until the water's chill leached into his bones and he decided it was best to get out.

Thankfully, it was only a moment before he found a ladder reaching down into the waves. Though his hands were numb, he climbed out of the sea and hauled himself onto the street, trailing saltwater behind him.

CHAPTER FIFTEEN
Crawford

Crawford sat at the Traveling Tern's bar with a drink in his hand, laughing and telling tales with the rest of *The Morigana's* crew. He was halfway through telling a pretty blonde girl how he singlehandedly saved *The Morigana* from a swarm of ravenous serpents when the door to the tavern swung open and Gale slipped inside. The man was dripping wet and shivering, and had leafy seaweed tangled in his hair.

Crawford interrupted his own story with a curse. "Gale—mate! What in all hells happened to ya? Where you been?"

Gale gave a sheepish grin and came to the bar, ordering himself a drink. "Oh, nothin' much. Just went for a walk, met some o' the local folk."

The blonde giggled, and Crawford raised his eyebrow. "And... you went for a swim along the way?"

"Aye. It... They... Well, if I'm tellin' the truth, they thought they'd like to try and wring me for all I'm worth."

Crawford raised his drink halfway to his lips, then paused. "Meanin'?"

"Thieves. Muggers. That manner of folk." Gale shrugged, nonchalant. The bartender handed him his drink, and Gale took a swig.

"Wait, wait—you done got yourself robbed, Gale? What the hell'd you do that for?"

Gale chuckled. "Well, I guess I jus' wasn't payin' attention. The one guy was a seer o' some sort. Knew I was comin' and knew what to look for. Claimed to know my whole destiny."

Crawford sighed and cast his eyes heavenward in a silent prayer. "Gale… Of all the people on the street out to get mugged, of course it'd be you. What'd he get off ya?"

Gale grinned, pulled his wallet from his pocket, and jingled it. "Not a thing. I got it all back without a drop o' blood spilled either way. All it took was a quick dip in the drink—bastard thought he knew my whole fate, but he didn't guess I'd be able to swim."

"Sounds like that seer's shortsighted," Crawford laughed, shaking his head. He turned back to the blonde and made to resume his story, but he was interrupted again by a quiet curse from Gale.

"What's wrong?" Crawford asked, passing the man a sharp glance.

Gale nodded towards the tavern door. "See those three that just came in?"

"Aye?"

"That's them. The one with the scars—he's the seer. The other two are pals o' his."

Crawford swore.

The three newcomers stalked in. The scar-faced one stomped in like he owned the place, and the other two seemed subdued as they followed.

Gale set his cup down on the counter and rubbed his face with both his hands. "'Course they had to come here…"

Crawford glanced at his friend, then at the three strangers, before turning back to give the blonde girl an apologetic smile. "Maybe we'll get lucky an' they jus' won't notice ya, Gale. If we just act natural an' go back to what we were doin'…" He grinned. The blonde giggled and batted her eyelashes. Crawford leaned in for a kiss.

The three thugs sat at an empty table beside the door. The tallest one came to the bar for drinks, and Gale hid his face in the depths of his tankard.

Crawford ignored them all. The blonde girl's arms were soft around his shoulders and his hands found their place at her waist. He smiled at her and was about to lean in for another kiss when a harsh voice rang out from the table.

"You! You flamin'—of all the—what the hell are you doin' alive?"

"I was jus' sittin' here enjoyin' one last pint afore I shove off for good, mate. From what I hear, ol' Mother Ainsley don't have much in the way of booze down at the bottom o' the sea, so I reckoned I oughta come back an' get good and drunk 'fore I commit to somethin' so permanent as drownin'," was Gale's calm reply.

Crawford sighed. He knew that tone—it was the calm before the storm. He reluctantly advised the blonde to leave.

The scar-faced man opened and closed his mouth a few times, then seemed to reach a decision. He beckoned to his cronies, and the two men stepped forward to stand on either side of Gale.

Gale cast a languid glance at both of them and sipped his drink again.

"Something the matter?"

The scarred man's face contorted into an ugly scowl, and he grabbed the front of Gale's shirt, nearly lifting him out of his seat. "You have the gall to ask that, boy? You have the gall to ask me what the matter is?"

"Aye." Gale lifted his tankard again and drained it. "It seems I do."

The scarred man's face turned red and his eyes bulged. The barkeeper exchanged a glance with Crawford and began to casually stow away the more expensive-looking bottles.

"Why don't we take this outside, boy," the scar-faced man growled, "Just you, me, and my mates here. Get this over nice and easy."

The barkeeper cleared his throat. "Aye, why don't you lot take this outside? That's a grand idea. Elsewise I might just have to call—"

Too late. Something in Gale's expression must have set the scar-faced man off, because before the barkeep could say another word, the thug lifted Gale bodily from his chair and punched him in the face. Gale took the hit admirably and flashed a grin despite his bloodied lip.

"'Oy, ain't that one of our guys?" A voice called from one of the other tables. Crawford looked and saw a deckhand from *The Morigana* rise in his seat, looking less than sober and more than a little irate.

"Aye, right enough, that's our Gale!" another man—either Devyn or Daryl—answered. A murmur passed through the rest of the crew as the men took notice. Crawford drained his drink, clunking it down on the countertop and baring his teeth in a grin.

Realization dawned slowly for the scar-faced man, and he released Gale with exaggerated care. His expression was dark.

Crawford stood and tapped on one of the cronies' shoulders. The man turned. Crawford slugged him in the jaw. The man went down.

"You ain't the only one 'round here with mates, mate," Crawford said, shaking out his hand and grinning like a shark.

Gale got to his feet and drew himself to full height. The scar-faced man backed away, then turned, only to find himself hemmed in by members of *The Morigana's* crew.

"You—you wouldn't be defendin' that flea-bit son of a sea snake if you knew what I know 'bout him! I seen his fate! He goes 'gainst destiny! He's cursed! Marked! *The Tempest* is huntin' him an' he'll bring her down on the whole crew!"

"Aw, will you quit with the crap an' turn tail already?" Crawford groaned. "Fight if you're gonna fight—get outta my face if you're not!"

One of the local men got similarly impatient and smashed a chair over Daryl's head. Devyn whirled around and slammed his fist into the guy's gut. Within a moment, the Traveling Tern was in chaos. Crashes, smashes, shattering glasses—metal clashed on metal, and the air was filled with shouts and cries and discordant, rowdy laughter as everybody in the building set to fighting everybody else within reach. For the most part the local folk fought the crew, and the crew fought the locals, but several people—both sailors and civilians—were far too drunk to care who they hit with what.

Someone threw a fireball, missing Crawford's head by inches. The fireball exploded into sparks against the tavern's wall, fizzling out under the anti-fire wards. A man halfway in the shape of a dog snapped at Crawford's face, but Gale smashed a bottle over the shifter's head and knocked him to the ground. Crawford nodded thanks, then spun around to swing at a woman who was midway through drawing a cutlass. His hand collided against an invisible forcefield, and he only barely ducked in time to avoid the woman's sword. A gust from Gale knocked the woman a step backwards, inadvertently flinging the door to the Traveling Tern wide open and depriving several people of their hats. Devyn stepped up and elbowed the swordswoman in the gut, then whooped and disappeared back into the throng.

Someone struck the back of Crawford's head and knocked him down, but Crawford kicked the person from the ground and jumped back to his feet just in time to see Gale lay out the scar-faced man with a well-aimed punch. The bastard hit the ground like a felled tree. Crawford and Gale exchanged a grin and a nod, and the pair of them seized the man by both his sides and hauled him up easily between them. They carried him to the door, and Crawford grinned. "Count of three?"

"Aye, mate, on three!"

"One!" They both called, hefting the man in preparation for the throw. "Two! Thr—"

Captain Nimune stepped into the doorway, her face impassive. Crawford and Gale dropped the scar-faced man on the ground without a second thought and saluted, both instantly sober.

The captain sauntered into the Traveling Tern, and the brawl died as quickly as it had been born. Every single person in the place stopped what they doing, several halting mid-punch. The sailors all saluted, and some of the locals got caught up in the spirit of things and saluted as well.

Captain Nimune flashed an icy smile and examined her nails, strolling back and forth and barely sparing a glance at the damage.

"What, may I ask, is going on here?"

Someone in the back of the tavern accidentally dropped a cup. The tiny thump was thunder in the hush.

"Because," Nimune continued, her voice deadly soft, "this looks to me like a regular ol' tavern brawl. But my crew—my crew's a well behaved, disciplined lot. They ain't the kind to go about pickin' fights or causin' havoc their one day ashore. No siree, they jus' ain't that kind o' low. Now, I'm gonna ask again: what the *hell* happened here? Ten seconds to answer, or I swear on both Brothers above, it will be the cat for every Jack and Jane in this whole damn establishment!" By the end of the sentence, her voice was a roar.

The silence deepened. No one came forward. Gale cleared his throat.

"Cap'n Nimune, it… This mess's my fault. I ran afoul of some of the local folk. I'm afraid things got a fair sight outta hand."

Crawford glanced at him in alarm. The captain whirled around and strode up to Gale, looking him in the eye despite his height. "'Course it'd be you," she muttered under her breath, before adding in a much louder voice, "Explain. Now."

Gale kept his eyes straight forward, his spine straight. "I went walkin', Cap'n. This jack here tried to mug me." Gale glanced down to the scar-faced man at his feet. "When I came back here, he followed. Was annoyed I didn't care to give him my pay. He tried to shake me down again, but my shipmates had other ideas 'bout crime against a brother."

"Is that so?" Nimune arched her eyebrow, her voice as warm and forgiving as steel.

"Aye, Cap'n."

"An' the rest?"

"Just… Jus' a bit of high spirits all 'round, Cap'n. But I ain't gonna say it was any man's fault but mine."

Captain Nimune turned her back to Gale and glared around the room again. "Is this true?"

There was a prompt chorus of 'aye's. Crawford added his voice in half a beat late.

"Barkeep?" Nimune turned to look at the man. He nodded as well.

Nimune paused, as if leaving a space for the sigh she suppressed. "Then it falls on your head, Gale. It's high time this crew remembered consequence." She raised her voice again. "You can consider your shore leave rescinded, boys—we're back on the ship tonight!"

With that, Captain Nimune flipped a couple of coins at the barkeep and stalked out of the tavern, fully expecting her men to follow her.

They did.

CHAPTER SIXTEEN
Gale

The following dawn saw the entire crew of *The Morigana* lined up, smartly dressed and standing sharp at attention. Gale stood nearby, apart from the rest of the crew. His throat was dry, and his stomach twisted in anxious knots as he waited for Captain Nimune to come on deck. The whole world was covered in a thick, clinging, white haze, and not even the slowly rising sun could melt the clammy chill from the air.

Gale fidgeted, resisting the urge to blow the fog away. He was under orders to stand still and do nothing. The crew mumbled among themselves quietly, and in the distance the slow, ringing peal of Midway Point's bell welcomed the sunrise. *The Morigana*'s bell tolled in reply.

Then the drums began. Rolling, pounding, deliberate—each beat shook Gale's bones and made his heart stutter. The crew straightened their spines. Gale held his breath.

Captain Nimune emerged from her cabin, carrying with her a length of waxed rope bound to a thick wooden handle. The rope was partially unraveled—the thin strands had been untwisted and rewoven into three smaller cords, each of which ended in a small, tight knot. Gale's stomach soured and sank. Every sailor in the crew removed their hats as she passed.

Captain Nimune approached Gale and cleared her throat. "Gale Windworker—you stand here for the crimes o' rowdy behaviors against the local folk o' Midway Point, startin' a brawl in the Travelin' Tern, an' destruction o' property in that same place beside—not to mention excessive drunkenness the like o' which ill suits a member of my crew. Anything to say in your defense, sailor?"

"Aye, Cap'n: I wasn't that drunk."

A few sniggers drifted up from the crew, but Captain Nimune did not so much as twitch a smile. "You think this is funny, Windworker? You laughin' at the shame you brought down on me, on my ship, an' on your shipmates with your conduct?"

Gale shook his head and dropped his gaze. "No, Cap'n. I ain't laughin'. I'll take what I got comin'."

Captain Nimune nodded. "Very well, Windworker. Remove your shirt."

Gale's arms felt like stone—his fingers may as well have been lifeless rock, for all the use they were to him. After an unpleasantly long moment spent fumbling with his buttons, Gale discarded his shirt and braced himself.

At a word from Captain Nimune, the bosun stepped up, turned Gale around, and bound Gale's hands to the rigging above his head. Gale took a deep breath.

"Bosun's mate, do your duty. Twenty strokes,"

Nimune barked the order, handing the whip—the cat o' nine tales—to a strong, sturdy deckhand.

The drums fell into a slow, regular rhythm. One beat, two beats, three beats—

On the fourth drumbeat, the deckhand brought the cat down across Gale's back. The knotted cords bit into his skin, leaving long, red welts across his flesh. Gale hissed in pain, fighting the urge to scream.

Three more beats passed, marking sixty seconds, and then the cat clawed at Gale's back again, welts crossing welts and abrasions drawing blood. Still, Gale held his silence.

This continued, minute after minute, agony after agony, until Gale's back was a mess of cold fire. He writhed under the lash, bearing the pain as best he could with thoughts of home and Guinevere.

After ten strokes, the captain called for pause. She called Eddy Patcher forward, and the man touched Gale's neck and checked his eyes. Captain Nimune barked something that Gale could not understand, and Patcher nodded. The man laid his hand on Gale's raw, pulped back, and Gale felt a cool jolt of magic rush through his system, soothing his injuries and closing his wounds.

Gale exhaled. His body went limp. Then Patcher retreated, and the drums began again.

The last ten lashes were harder than the first. By the end, Gale had given up on not screaming. However, despite the pain, despite the blood, Gale never once asked to be cut down.

CHAPTER SEVENTEEN
Guinevere

Guinevere sat at her loom in the drawing room, humming to herself as she worked. Her back was to the door and she faced the wide window, listening contently to the rush and the whisper of the rain against the glass. With the weather as it was, her shop was closed, so Guinevere had plenty of time to herself to work on whatever she pleased.

She shifted on her padded stool and leaned back for a moment to check the consistency of her weave. The fine, pearly threads all came together wondrously well—there were no lumps or bumps or unfortunate rough edges anywhere in sight—and the half-made cloth shimmered with a faint iridescence that only a Syren's magic could provide.

Guinevere smiled, running a finger over the barely translucent, faintly purple fabric. It was perfectly smooth, pleasantly cool, and perhaps one of the finest pieces of cloth to ever take shape on her loom.

A gentle knock sounded from the door behind

her. Guinevere turned in her seat.

"Yes?"

Markus opened the door, poking his head in and clearing his throat softly.

"Ahoy, Guinevere... Mind if I come in?"

Guinevere turned back to her work and resumed her weaving. The clack and clatter of the loom nearly disappeared under the hush of the rain.

"Not at all, Papa. You're more than welcome. Was there something in particular you wanted?"

"Does a father need a reason to come spend time with his girl, Guin?"

Guinevere smiled. "I suppose not. I guess I'm just so used to you always being busy with some job or another—it isn't often we get to simply chat."

"Aye," Markus laughed ruefully, sinking into a large, overstuffed armchair of which he was particularly fond, "it's been work day after day, lately, hasn't it? I s'pose we should be near about thankin' this weather for a reprieve. Been too long since I've had the time to... I dunno, to catch up with what matters. What's that you're workin' on, Guin? It's fair pretty."

Guinevere hesitated for a half-second before answering. "It's... I figured that it was about time I start on my bridal train, Papa. For when Gale comes home."

She did not turn to see her father's expression, but she heard the way he shifted in his chair.

"You're still on about that boy, Guinevere? It's been near half a year—there's nothin' wrong with... with lookin' around for someone a bit more suited."

"Gale is suited, Papa. I know you've yet to see it, but he is. He's... I could go on and on about his virtues, but I do realize that words are words and they're easy enough to say without meaning. When he comes back, you'll see. That's what this whole mess is about, yes?"

"He's impressed you that much, Guin? You still have that much faith, even with him this long away? You don't think he's... wandered off at all?"

"No, Papa. I know Gale better than that."

Markus whistled under his breath. "Then maybe I judged wrong."

That made Guinevere pause. She halted her weaving long enough to turn and look her father in the face.

"You don't mean..?"

"Aye, lass. You're makin' a bridal train. You're set and workin' and... Well, the more I get to thinkin', the more I realize I didn't raise a fool. If we're standin' here half a year later still talkin' about this lad, well... I reckon it ain't right of me to expect you to forget him. He's serious enough to work, you're serious enough to wait... I reckon if I don't consider changin' my stance on the lad, you'll start to consider changin' your stance on me. If he comes back to Alinor safe an' faithful... I s'pose... I will. I'll let past impressions pass, an' I'll give you two my blessing."

Guinevere leapt up from her seat and hugged her father. "I knew you'd come around, Papa! Thank you so much! When Gale comes home, he'll be absolutely delighted!"

Markus nodded and cleared his throat gruffly, the way he always did when he was hiding happiness. "He still has to come home faithful, though—if he drifts outta line an' loses our bet, well, there ain't nothin' I can do about that, Guinevere."

Guinevere smiled and returned to her seat and her weaving. "Yes, of course, Papa. But I'm not worried—now that you've agreed to give him the chance, I don't think there's anything in the world that can stop him from coming home. It's—as silly as this sounds to say, I truly believe it's destiny."

Markus chuckled, running his hand through his hair. "Have you been readin' Ell's books, Guinevere? Normally she's the one I hear this stuff from. You know, for those first two weeks after your boy sailed off, she glared at me like a villain an' I hardly knew why."

Guinevere laughed. "Did she really? I'm so sorry, Papa—she does get these notions in her head... I'm sure she'll grow out of it, someday."

"Oh, aye, I'm sure she will. She'd better—else Brothers save the jack she finally does set her eye on. I don't think there's a man alive who can match her standards. I love the fact that she's readin', but sometimes I wonder... Then again, your mother didn't half have the same taste, and yet she found herself happy with me. Speaking of which—I was thinkin'—once the wet season ends, what do you say you come down to the shipyard a sight more often to help out? I know you've got your shop to run, but I could use the company, an' it's high time I start training you to follow my footsteps proper, assumin' you still want to cast your lot after me an' inherit the place. What do you say?"

"I'd love to," Guinevere said, turning to face her father again. "I'd like to keep my shop running at least part time, but I'd love nothing more than to help make my mark on the family business."

Markus grinned, nodded, and stood, going back to pause in the doorway.

"Guinevere... I'd like to thank you for bein' so... mature, about this. About everything. You're a good kid, an' I want you to know... Whatever happens with that Gale, I'll always love you."

"I know, Papa. And I love you, too. Family is family and I never want that to change."

CHAPTER EIGHTEEN
Crawford

Months passed aboard *The Morigana,* and things quickly returned to normal. Crawford covered Gale's shift until Gale was fit to return to work, and eventually the shifts were switched again. The twins got night duty together, and Crawford and Gale were assigned to the day.

One night, in the small hours before the day crew had even begun to wake, the ship was roused by the frantic clamor of alarm bells. The sleeping sailors tumbled from their bunks and hauled their boots on in a hurry, fighting gravity as *The Morigana* pitched and rolled from one crazy angle to the next.

Gale seized the ladder up the main deck and forced open the hatch to the upper world, and Crawford followed behind with the rest of the crew. Within minutes, every man was soaked through. Rain pelted Crawford's face, driven in all directions by the writhing winds. Waves crashed all around the ship, splashing over the bulwharks and smashing against each other to shatter into sheets of spray.

The saturated air was thick enough to drown out *The Morigana's* safety lights and render all eyes useless. Even the glowing pink water of the Rose Line was nearly invisible in the chaotic storm.

Captain Nimune stood on the rear deck, roaring orders to the deckhands that scuttled around like ants in a flood. The first mate was at the wheel in the form of a great white bear, using all his strength to fight the waves and keep *The Morigana* on course.

"'Oy, windworkers!" Nimune roared, "get aloft now—grab your lifelines and get the twins safe!"

"Aye aye, Cap'n!" Crawford and Gale called back in unison.

Crawford battled his way across the deck, slipping and sliding on the slick wood as he fought to grab the rigging. By the time he'd secured a lifeline around his middle and started to climb, Gale was already aloft—twisting the cutting, freezing gusts so they bent harmlessly around as he climbed.

Crawford followed, fighting for his life. His hands were numb, his face felt frozen, and the strong, tearing winds would barely obey his commands. The ship's motion grew more intense the higher he went—the mast swung drastically as the ship careened, and it was all he could do to cling to the lines and pray not to be swept away.

Lightning crashed between the thrashing seas and the roiling skies, strobing and flashing and burning like curses from heaven, but thunder's roar was lost beneath the screaming ocean and the howling wind. When Crawford clambered into the tiny basket that was the crow's nest, he found Daryl clutching Devyn and fighting to keep them both anchored to the wildly careening ship.

Crawford shouted a question, but his words were lost to the wind. Daryl shouted a reply, but Crawford couldn't glean past the phrases "out of nowhere" and "worn out."

Gale nodded as though he understood perfectly and raised his hand to the wind. He squinted, closed his fist, and the fearsome gust slackened enough to allow Daryl to speak clearly.

"Worldshift called a squall!" he shouted, wrapping his arms more tightly around his unconscious brother. "Too strong—drained Devyn flat, an' I can't go like this much longer!"

"Aye aye!" Crawford answered, keeping a white-knuckled grip on the handrail as he helped Gale work the winds.

The storm was a mess of spiraling motion, violently swirling every which way without rhythm. Horizontal rain stung Crawford's face, *The Morigana* rocked between waves taller than buildings, and the wind howled with unmatchable fury. Crawford reached his magic out and grabbed a gust, pulling and curving it so the brunt of its wrath pushed out over the open sea.

Another fierce downdraft swept in from the sky, and *The Morigana* careened dangerously far over the water. People screamed, and Crawford found himself mouthing prayers he hadn't said in years. Gale waved his hand and the wind curled, spiraling in to urge the ship back upright.

Lighting crashed beside *The Morigana's* mast—thunder shook Crawford to the bones and filled his face with the smell of frying air. He shouted a curse and forced an unruly updraft away, past *The Morigana's* prow. The ship shuddered and groaned piteously as

Gale grabbed the same wind and pulled it aft-ward.

"Y' half-brained swabs!" Daryl yelled over the shrieking wind, "work together!"

Crawford glanced at Gale, who nodded.

"I'll carve if you push!" Gale shouted.

Crawford nodded back. "Aye, aye!"

Together, they both adjusted their magic. Gale turned his face to the sky and bent his attention to the whirling gusts among the clouds, and Crawford set his mind on *The Morigana*'s sails.

He gritted his teeth and threw himself at the wind, taking the wild, swirling eddies and shaping them to guide *The Morigana* forward. Gale, meanwhile, grabbed the violent gusts and shaped them around the ship, forcing them away to fight each other in the sky. Every so often an errant wisp would slip through his fingers and Crawford would curve it away from *The Morigana* or else wrestle it into submission to fill *The Morigana*'s sails.

Before long, Crawford's back ached, his legs trembled, and his arms shook from the effort. He could hardly breathe—he could hardly keep his eyes open—but the wind still gusted and pounded and writhed like a trapped animal. It fought and struggled and it was all Crawford could do to keep it from sending the ship to the depths. He bit his lip and strained to keep his hold.

One gust escaped his grasp, spiraling out across the water with a vengeance and spinning up into a terrific cyclone—a towering waterspout that stretched towards the sky.

"Gale—look out for—"

"Got it!" Gale had the vortex under control before Crawford could finish his sentence. He tossed the cyclone out over the water carelessly, as though the twisting funnel of wind was no more troubling than a bit of string he didn't care to keep. And to top it all, the bastard still had a breeze keeping his hair from his eyes like always.

Crawford groaned, and his knees gave out. His face hit the handrail. At that same moment, Gale summoned his magic, twisted the winds, and parted the skies—and the world went calm. The stars shone through the gap in the clouds, pale and fading as darkness lightened to dawn.

Gale wobbled and sank to his knees. The crew below raised a cheer.

Crawford started to laugh.

CHAPTER NINETEEN
Guin

"Charlotte, I don't know how I feel about this," Guinevere said, wincing as her friend tugged her hair back into a tight, elaborate braid.

"Guinevere, honey, it's fine! It's only a party. You've been working yourself so hard lately, it'll only do you good to have a little bit of fun." Charlotte smiled at Guinevere through the mirror, her blonde curls tamed and woven into a fashionable net of braids down her back. Guinevere made eye contact with the girl's reflection and grimaced.

"Charlotte—"

"No, Guinevere—I won't hear another word of it! I can't bear to see you waste away like this! You're young and beautiful—do you really want to let that all wither away while you sit and wait for life to pass like bad weather? No! You're coming to this party with me, you're going to forget your troubles for at least a few hours, and we're going to have fun. The matter's settled, and your family agrees. You've been moping for far too long!"

Guinevere gritted her teeth as Charlotte tugged her hair again, twisting the strands of brown into some unknowable pattern. "I haven't been moping, Charlotte—I've simply been busy. I've been practicing my craft, and father's grooming me to take over the shipyard, and beyond that, there are side projects I'd like to finish, and I simply don't have time for—"

"Guinevere—you're working yourself to death! What could be so important that you can't spare one evening to accompany your dearest friend to the most prestigious birthday party of the century? If you won't go for you, then at least think of me—my mother simply refuses to let me go on my own, and for some reason she doesn't believe it proper that my Jamison escort me." Charlotte finished restraining Guinevere's hair as she prattled, twisting a length of green ribbon around the final braid in one last ornamental touch. She lifted a hand mirror and held it up so that Guinevere could see the back of her head reflected in the larger mirror. "My, don't you look lovely!"

Guinevere chuckled and gave Charlotte a smile, running her fingers over her friend's handiwork. "Thank you, Charlotte, I must say—you have a gift for hair. Even with all the weaving I do, I never quite got the knack for pretty braids like this. They're lovely. Now remind me—which one is Jamison? Was he the tall boy with the dark hair? Or is Jamison the one with the scar?"

Charlotte laughed, tittering gently as she covered her mouth with a delicate hand. "Neither, honey! The dark hair was Isaac, and it was Kendall who had the scar. Jamison is new—and my, if he isn't sweet. He's an illusionist, you know—he calls up the prettiest pictures for me. I truly think he and I have a chance together, provided my mother can forget the fact that the poor boy's brother ran off to join the Thieves' Guild. The whole family's mortified. But Jamison's sweet."

"A brother in the Guild? My, and you worry about me and my sailor," Guinevere teased. "Anyway, didn't you say the same thing about the last boy you dated, Charlotte? Not the Thieves' Guild part, of course—but the other bit. What was his name—was it Carlyle? Whatever happened to him?"

"Carlyle—oh, don't get me started on Carlyle. If I ever said that, it was before he turned out to be such an awful bore. I'm not sorry to say, we drifted apart. He wasn't interested in me, I think. Only last week, we were having lunch at that quaint little tea shop on Green Street, and I swear, his eyes *lingered* on every other woman who walked by, and he barely spared a glance at me the entire time we were talking! Needless to say, I let him go right there."

"Right there?" Guinevere asked, turning in her chair to face Charlotte directly. "Perhaps the poor fellow simply had something on his mind."

Charlotte shrugged, setting the hand mirror back down on the vanity. "If he did, he should have told me. I'd have listened. One way or the other, I'm not about to buy lunch for a man who can't look me in the eye. But enough of that! I'm *so* looking forward to this party. You know, I heard the birthday boy is single?" The blonde girl grinned, flashing her teeth in a look Guinevere knew meant mischief.

Guinevere laughed. "Brothers help the poor man—he doesn't know what he's gotten himself into, does he?"

Charlotte gave her grin again. "Honey, he's about to! Jamison's sweet, but if I get the chance, I intend to flirt my heart out."

Guinevere shook her head slowly, chuckling under her breath. "I don't doubt you. One question, though: whose party is this, again? I know you told me earlier, but I fear I've forgotten."

"You know the Cleanser family?"

Guinevere nodded. "The ones who do the drinking water?"

"That's them! Honey, it's marvelous—Shiro's the heir to that whole empire, and it's his birthday, and we're all invited! Wouldn't it be simply wonderful to marry into a family like that? Even setting aside the rumors about Shiro himself, his family—do you know how much influence they have?"

"Only vaguely," Guinevere said, again patting the lattice of braids down her back, "I don't hear as much gossip as you, Charlotte. Well, I suppose I do, but I walk in different circles. The sailors I chat with are generally less preoccupied with Alinor's most eligible bachelors."

"Well, you're missing out, honey—"

"Oh, I don't know about that. I rather like the stories I get. Adventures in Mikare, strange things seen at sea—betrayals and murders and all manner of drama. One of these days, you should come and spend some time with me at the shop. I think you'd enjoy it."

"Murders? Really? That does sound exciting. But for now, just listen to this: the Cleanser family is big. Not in that they own a lot of property or anything, but they do *all the water*. I heard that not even the king himself would tell them no, if they asked for something! The influence they wield is *phenomenal!*"

"It sounds as though poor Jamison has some serious competition, then," Guinevere said dryly. "The Cleansers are quite a family to get involved with."

"They're absolutely fantastic!" Charlotte laughed, covering her lips for a moment with her hand. "And Shiro himself—I hear he's beyond handsome. Tall and dark and regal—it'd be like marrying a prince, only without all the tiresome responsibility that comes with royalty!"

"He sounds perfect for you, Charlotte," Guinevere said, letting a touch of irony trickle into her tone.

Charlotte raised her eyebrow a fraction, her mouth twisting into a wry grin. "Oh, I know—it'd be absolutely lovely. I could wear whatever I like and eat whatever I please—and never have to work or worry again! The position would be divine. And I hear he's so kind and polite, too—in fact, I can't recall hearing a single bad thing about the man in all my time as a gossip! If that's not a statement towards his character, I don't know what is. Don't get me wrong—I do like Jamison a lot, but if I can get Shiro to look my way…" she trailed off with a dramatic sigh.

Guinevere nodded, and smiled. "I don't know what I can say, except 'good luck fishing,' Charlotte. Well, that, and 'Brothers help the men you meet.' I think they need just as much luck as you."

* * *

The sky was dark with rain by the time the party started. Raindrops exploded against the stained-glass windows of Cleanser House, and though the musicians played a lively reel, Guinevere could barely follow the tune over the sobbing wind.

Charlotte still danced, whirling from partner to partner across the ballroom floor, but Guinevere sat to the side, watching the ebb and flow of the party. She was almost grateful the heel of her shoe had given out—she did not have the energy to keep up with Charlotte's boundless twirling, and a broken shoe was a legitimate excuse to sit down early. Though she appreciated that people kept thinking to invite her to rejoin the celebrations, she was perfectly content to sit and watch the happy crowd.

Guinevere smiled, her foot tapping along as one reel flowed into the next and the dancers passed each other from hand to hand in intricately woven circles across the ballroom floor. Their breathless laughter was infectious, and Guinevere was almost disappointed when the song ended and the musicians took their rest.

She settled back in her chair, toying with the heel of her shoe again as the dancers scattered, dispersing across the floor now that they were no longer bound together within the patterns of the dance. Charlotte spun off to chatter with a group of other young men and women—people Guinevere vaguely recognized as heirs and heiresses to several high-born families— and after a split-second debate, Guinevere decided she did not care enough to join them. Her chair was too comfortable, and her feet still hurt from dancing.

One young man happened to meet her gaze from across the room. He, too, stood apart from the crowd, his smile simultaneously charming and aloof. His long black hair was neatly braided, his clothes had clearly cost a great deal to make, and he seemed to have taken the moment's shared glance as an invitation to approach.

Guinevere suppressed a sigh and summoned a smile.

The man stopped beside her chair and cleared his throat. "Hello."

"Hello," Guinevere replied.

A moment passed. The man shifted awkwardly, lifting his gaze to the rain-spattered window. "Are you enjoying the party?" he asked.

Guinevere nodded amicably. "Yes, everyone seems to be having a great deal of fun."

The man paused again before responding. "Are... *you* having fun? I beg pardon for my intrusion, but I hate to see you sitting here all alone, when everyone else is..." he glanced over his shoulder at Charlotte's giggling group.

Guinevere gave a polite smile. "I appreciate your concern, but don't worry. I'm sitting by choice and having plenty of fun watching. I like taking the time to appreciate the ambiance—and here, I can listen to the rain."

The man nodded, and his smile grew a touch more genuine. "I understand completely. There is something about the rain—especially against a window. The sound, the way it grays the light and makes it waver... I'm sure others find it dreary, but I find the melancholy this weather evokes to be positively cathartic."

"Ah, I do agree," Guinevere said, chuckling, "though I don't know if I would put it quite as such."

"Really?" the man looked her straight-on for the first time since approaching, raising an eyebrow and letting the corner of his mouth quirk into a grin. His eyes were blue. "How are you inclined to phrase it, then? I can't help but wonder."

"To begin, I would shy away from being quite so polysyllabic. My fiancé, you see, is not a man of letters. Something to the effect of 'it makes me feel a sort of beautiful sadness' would be far more quickly understood."

Guinevere was not surprised to see a shadow of disappointment cross behind the man's eyes at the phrase 'my fiancé,' but to his credit, the man hid it well. "A fair point. Is—wait... I do beg your pardon—where have my manners gone? I nearly forgot to introduce myself. I am Shiro Cleanser, at your service. May I ask your name, my friend?"

"Oh, allow me to wish you every joy on your birthday! I'm Guinevere Syren—it's a pleasure to make your acquaintance." Guinevere cast a glance towards Charlotte. The girl was too busy flirting to realize that the catch she was after was on the hook elsewhere, ready and waiting for her.

"The pleasure is mine," Shiro replied, oblivious. "Syren... You're not by any chance related to Markus Syren, are you, Guinevere?"

"Yes, actually. He's my father."

Shiro nodded. "I can't say I've met the man in person, but I respect his work. He's made quite a name for himself, these past years. You must be very proud of him."

"Oh, yes." Guinevere nodded. "He works very hard, and he's done a lot of good for Alinor. I hope to be able to follow in his footsteps, someday."

Shiro gave another slight smile. "From what I hear, it seems you're well on your way."

Guinevere raised her eyebrow, carefully wry. "Have you heard much?"

"Only rumors, here and there, and most in the form of praise." He glanced around. "Do you mind if I sit?"

Guinevere shook her head, resting her chin on her hand as Shiro pulled up a chair. "Forgive my interest, but I can't help but wonder—what all have you heard? I don't walk these circles often enough to know the gossip. Charlotte—my dear friend—seldom repeats the things she hears about herself and me. She says it's not worth minding."

"She sounds wise," Shiro said with a soft chuckle. "I'm in much the same situation, actually—I know people must talk, but it seems they're loath to discuss my business to my face. Would you like to trade? We could exchange whatever rumors we've collected and set the record straight. I certainly wouldn't mind some plain, honest talk at this point in the evening."

"That's fair enough," Guinevere said, raising her voice slightly as the musicians again began to play and the dancers resumed their spinning. "Though I'm afraid I don't have much for you. Only that you're a wonderful man from a wonderful family who must be in want of a wife. They say that's what this party's for, actually. Though I suppose that rumor might just be wishful thinking on the part of those social climbers seeking to rise. Aside from that, I haven't heard much."

Shiro's lips tightened, and he sighed. "Is it all that obvious? Alas. I hate to admit it, but that rumor is unfortunately true—though it's less for my benefit than my mother's. She seems to believe that if I don't marry soon, I won't marry at all." He leaned in conspiratorially. "Between the two of us—she's already scheduled the wedding in the Kingsown Church, and if I don't have a bride by then... Gods only know what she'll do, because she insists it's impossible to cancel."

Guinevere shook her head in sympathy. "She's scheduled the wedding before there's even a couple to marry? I wish you the best of luck, Shiro—it sounds as though you need it. At the very least, you have plenty of options. In fact, if you'd like, I know some nice girls I can personally introduce." She glanced at Charlotte again—but the girl was still busy giggling with her flock of other friends.

Shiro laughed half-heartedly. "Yes, so many options... Though I won't deny I have much to be grateful for, I just... Ah, but that's enough about me and my problems. I suppose I ought to share your rumors now, oughtn't I?"

Guinevere smiled. "If you'd like to, I won't pass up the knowledge."

Shiro cleared his throat. "Well, people never fail to mention your talent, when they speak of you. And... the fiancé you mentioned—he's a sailor, yes?"

"He is."

"I'm afraid I haven't heard many nice things. According to rumor, he's low born, with magic above his station and habits to suit his class. Though... they also say he's set across the Rose Line to prove himself worthy of you."

Guinevere settled back in her chair and grimaced. "It's odd to think that my personal affairs should be of such interest to those outside my family... Regardless, yes. The bones of that are true. Gale is a sailor. I suppose you might consider him common, but I've never met another man so in love with life, and we understand one another in every way that matters. He's already 'worthy,' but..." she trailed off, reaching to touch the silver pendant at her neck. "It's true not everybody sees it. He agreed to sail the Line on a bet. So long as all goes well, Father will give his approval. So at this point, it's only a matter of waiting."

Shiro nodded, going quiet for a long moment. "I'm almost envious, to see how devoted you are to him, and to hear how devoted he is to you. I hope it all goes well for you—truly, I wish you both the best of luck, and I'll pray for his safe return. Please," he said, grinning suddenly, "I hope you'll see fit to invite me to the wedding."

CHAPTER TWENTY
Gale

"Gale, that was absolutely crazy—I can't believe the way you blew those blasted clouds all out to oblivion, mate! When the hell'd you get that strong?" Daryl sat across from Gale in the galley, a mug in his hand a broad grin on his face. "I knew you were a proper talent right enough, but I never dreamed in all my years I'd get to see a show like that! An' now the world's wind is blowin' us in the proper direction at a fair speed—how lucky can we get? How the hell did you do it, boy?"

Gale chuckled and set down his half-empty tankard, rubbing the back of his neck with his hand. "Well, y'know, mate—this voyage's pushed me harder than I've been pushed all my life. It's only natural I'd come out stronger. Truth be told," he paused for a moment to search for the proper words. Though he was proud of himself, it felt unnatural to say so. "I didn't have a flamin' clue what I was doin' 'til I did it."

"Aye, an' I'll attest to that!" Crawford laughed,

sitting down beside Gale with a plate of salt cod and his daily ration of shipfruit. "Mate, up until that last stretch, I thought fair certain we were gonna be kissin' hello to Mother Ainsley! I'm gonna count the fact that we're still here an' on course as a right proper miracle."

"Miracle?" Gale raised his eyebrow and grinned. "Nah, mate—that was all skill, right and proper. You an' me—we're the best, remember? I part the clouds, you push the boat—there's nowhere we can't go, an' nothin' we can't do!"

Crawford chuckled slightly, rapping his knuckles twice against the table. "Talk too cocky, Gale, an' ol' Mother Ainsley'll take you down to the deep. We don't want her thinkin' your head's gotten too big for your shoulders, do we? She might go ahead and take it off."

"Aw, don't be a killjoy, Crawford!" Daryl laughed, playfully punching Crawford's arm, "let the lad celebrate—what he did was somethin' proper special, an' there ain't two ways about it."

Gale shrugged, grinned, and spread his arms wide. "You flatter me! But you all know I wasn't workin' alone—we all played a part. I just... I just sorta... kept it smooth. That's all."

"Oh, you just gotta talk like a hero, don't ya?" Crawford said, chuckling as he rolled his eyes.

Gale grinned and mimed a little bow.

Daryl laughed along, taking a swig from his mug. "Aye, mate, that's because the lad's done some proper heroics! First the eels, now the storm... I swear, Gale, you're a gift! Brothers praise!"

Gale swept another mock-bow, then raised his glass and drained it. "An' I'm right proud o' what I do, and ready an' willin' to do it again, if Ainsley blows us another squall! The sea's my mother, the sky's my father—an' I'm—"

He was cut off by a cry from above. On the deck, the hands began to cheer. "Land ho! Mikare's in sight! Bring 'er in to port!"

Gale's heart skipped as every sailor in the galley leapt to their feet and scrambled up the hatch. Gale followed, squinting into the shining day.

Everyone was crowded at the bow of the ship. Gale jostled for a place. Someone's elbow dug hard into his side, but he hardly cared—the sea glittered and gleamed like liquid silver, and the sky was clearer than crystal, untouched by so much as a single puff of cloud. In the distance, scraping the perfect blue, a city of spires and domes broke the smooth horizon.

Gale's breath caught in his throat, and he wished Guinevere were beside him to share the sight. Though he could only make out the buildings in silhouette, they were like nothing he had ever seen—all curved lines and sharp points, twisting and spiraling together like so many ribbons into the sky. Even though he was not technically on duty, Gale called up a wind and urged the ship on faster.

"Wow, that's a sight, mate," Crawford said behind him.

"Aye," Gale answered, speaking slowly so as not to disrupt his own reverie, "here we are after half a year waitin', an' somehow I never quite imagined we'd get here. What do you reckon it's like?"

"I dunno, mate. But you'd better not go wanderin' off explorin' on your lonesome again—you get mugged a second time, an' I swear, there'll be no helpin' ya."

Gale laughed. "Fair's fair—I'll stay put with the rest o' the crew. Wouldn't mind swingin' by the market, though—if you ain't opposed to comin' with me. I'd like to pick up a trinket for Guin. Nothin' too fancy, jus'... Somethin' to say I been thinkin' of her."

"The fact that you went to sea for her hand ain't enough?"

Gale turned around and looked at Crawford, raising his eyebrow. "You know that ain't the point."

"Aw, c'mon, mate, don't make that face—I'm only jokin' an' you know it. You get her a gift. I'm sure she'd like a souvenir."

Gale nodded, turning his gaze back towards the sea. The water bound to the city domain was bluer here than it was back home—it shone like sapphire, rather than like murky emerald. The distant city was larger now, closer, and less a shadow on the water. Gale could make out colors on the blotchy shape—dusty reds and yellows, faded blues and bright, bright oranges all gleamed under the golden sun. The closer they got, the more distinct everything became—the smudge of dirty yellow became a sandy beach, the sparkling dots of red grew into shimmering clay tiles on the roof of some grand building, and the blues and oranges became bizarre swirls and intricate patterns on the walls of every building in sight.

"Damn," Crawford muttered under his breath, "I've never seen so much color in one place. 'S like a two-year-old got hold of a paint can and went crazy."

Gale grinned and nodded. "It's fair marvelous. Look at that—look at that tower! D'you reckon it's made o' real gold?" He pointed to a particularly tall, shining building with a swirled, conch shell roof. It glittered brightly enough to make his eyes water and leave glowing purple afterimages across the center of his vision.

"Eh, I reckon not," Crawford answered, speaking slowly. "It's prob'ly just brass or somethin'. There ain't enough gold in all the world to go 'round wastin' it on rooftops. Someone'd find a way to steal it."

Gale paused to picture a thief trying to carry the tower away in some overlarge bag, and the image made him laugh. "Steal it, Crawford? Steal a whole rooftop?"

Crawford shrugged. "I'm sure some bastard'd find a way to trim a little off the top, if they ever got the chance. I reckon a man could shave off a touch or find a metalworker o' some kind to magic it down without thinnin' it enough to notice. That's what I'd do, anyway."

Gale chuckled. "A right criminal mind, ain'tcha, Crawford? But I reckon you're right—real gold'd cause a world o' problems… But it wouldn't be half amazin'."

"Sure, but that's ain't how the world works."

"Always the voice of reason, you are. Now here—wanna help me bring the ship in on the sly? I reckon the cap'n'd appreciate a nice fine-tuned wind for her sails, instead of this breeze we got blowin'."

Crawford chuckled. "Help? You don't need my help, miracle boy. I reckon you could handle it all on your lonesome, if you wanted."

"Aye, I've no doubt I could—but it'd be easier with the pair o' us, an' you know it. Come on—I'll push, you steer." Gale grinned, and Crawford sighed.

"Alright, alright—I'm all for lettin' the world's wind do the work since it's blowin' our way for once, but if you gotta get there faster, you gotta get there faster. I can't believe you ain't dead after that squall last night. I'm damn near outta magic, an' Devyn still hasn't woken up."

Gale shrugged, flashing a quick, slightly apologetic grin as he called his magic to push the wind a touch harder. "Can't help the way we're made, mate."

Crawford ran a hand down his face, seeming somehow tired. "I know."

* * *

The sound of windchimes followed Gale and Crawford as they strolled together through the Mikaren marketplace. Gale knew the disrupting breeze was his fault, but he hardly cared to hold himself back in the face of the strange sights and smells of the vibrant city.

Mikare was a mess of color—every building was painted and patterned like something out of an artist's fever dream. Brilliant silk banners and ribbons hung about the city, fluttering ethereally as Gale swaggered past. Tiny silver windchimes dangled beside every door, and every street and alleyway seemed to sprout at least one twisting spiral staircase up to who-knows-where. The staircases twisted in random, dizzy circles, connecting together into high, cloth-draped archways, to the point where Gale imagined he was strolling through a loosely defined tunnel.

He grinned, allowing a tiny breeze to sweep the street and rustle the banners and make the windchimes sing. There was so much going on—so many interesting market stalls with bizarre wares, so many strange faces wearing strange dress, so much new, exciting culture to absorb—Gale hardly knew where to look.

Crawford elbowed him lightly in the side. "Ahoy, Gale, would you stop doing that? Jus' 'cause we're not on the ship anymore doesn't give you the right to go blowin' everything all over the place. Control, mate. You need to tame that habit o' yours."

Gale reluctantly reigned in his power and allowed the questing wind to fade. "Habit? I don't have the faintest clue what you mean, Crawford. You makin' stuff up? That's slander, mate. I'm wounded."

Crawford laughed. "You want slander? Slander, mate, would be goin' home and tellin' your fair Guinevere that you went and blew the place sky high on a whim for bein' drunk. This is just me keepin' you in line."

"I'm not drunk," Gale replied, lifting his chin in slight defiance. Though his face was warm and the world wobbled, he still felt perfectly clearheaded.

"Uh-huh. All that celebratin' you did on the ship don't count for nothin'. Do you even know how much you've already had?"

Gale shrugged and grinned. "Not enough to get drunk off, that's fair certain. You know me, mate—it takes more than that to cloud my head!"

"Aye, an' I know that you ain't binged since Guinevere told ye to stop. You been slackin' an' now you're worse off than you know—I guarantee it. Just wait 'til it hits ya proper."

Gale rolled his whole head around on his neck in addition to his eyes, exaggerating the motion to exaggerate his sarcasm. "Aw, mate—what are ya, my mother? I'm fine! Jus' trust me! Now—what do ya think—d'you reckon Guin'd like a scarf or somethin'?"

Crawford blinked, pausing a moment before responding. "I don't know."

Gale crossed his arms over his chest and nodded to himself. "I'm gonna get her a scarf. A nice colorful thing. Green, maybe. To match those lovely eyes of hers. Yeah, that's what I'll do—I'll buy her a nice scarf. I bet she'd like a thing to see how the Mikarens weave their stuff."

Gale strode forward to examine the nearest stall, not bothering to wait for Crawford's reply. The noontime sun glared down from on high, casting golden light onto the shimmering silken merchandise. The man in charge of the stall—a wizened, grandfatherly figure with bristly hair and clouded eyes—gave Gale a wide grin and began to chatter at him in strangely accented Common.

"You, sailor. You see something you like? Come on, come on, let old Sam show you his wares, there's a good boy. What is it you seek, come on, a gift for a lady, maybe? You look like a fine boy, I'm sure it's a gift for your lady. Maybe a dress, perhaps? See here!"

The man whirled around and brought out a bright pink dress, slim and slender and sparkling with all manner of glittering threads. Gale's eyes widened slightly as he shook his head. "No, sir, though I—"

"No? Wrong color, then. Perhaps the boy's lady would enjoy something of this style?" The man reached behind himself and pulled a soft blue gown from beneath a red one. "This—this is the height of Mikaren fashion, boy, your lady friend will love it dearly, I know. You can trust old Sam."

Gale shook his head. "Any scarves?" he

interjected before the man could say another word.

"Yes, yes! Old Sam has many, many scarves. You, boy, have good taste! How about this, come on, touch! See? This is a scarf suited for a fine lady!" The man reached up and pulled a long strip of translucent fabric down from one of the many pegs. The scarf looked as though it had been dropped into a puddle of rainbow.

"How about that one?" Gale asked, pointing to slightly heavier scarf in forest green. The man made several sounds of approval and brought it out with the air of reverence.

"Ah, yes! Fine choice! You have wonderful taste, boy! Look, touch, see—this is the one you want, no?"

Gale took the scarf lightly between his hands and examined it. The fabric was light, yet sturdy, strong, yet smooth, and the intricate pattern that covered it came not from dye or from embroidery, but from the texture of the cloth itself. And the rich, vibrant green matched Guin's eyes exactly. It would be lovely on her.

He nodded to himself. "Aye, this one ain't that bad. What's it cost?"

The man grinned wide. "For that one? Ah, that one is the height of fashion—very, very popular, here in Mikare. I cannot bear to part with it for less than... say, six silver coins, sailor."

Gale nodded and was about to reach into his wallet when Crawford stepped up.

"Here, mate, you don't want that one. That's not very... pretty. Your Guin deserves better. Let's go down the street—I saw some right fair scarves over there."

Gale shook himself out of his reverie and looked

at Crawford. "What?"

Crawford raised both of his eyebrows. "This ain't quite right, mate. I mean, six silver coins? For that... bit of cloth? Think about this—use that thing in your skull for once in your life."

"Oh, ah, right, right. Thanks, mate. You got a fair point, there. Let me see this stall o' yours."

They turned as if to leave, but the wizened man raised his voice. "No, no! Please, stay, there's no call to be so harsh on old Sam. Surely you do want this scarf—it is high quality and perfect for any lady!"

"Oh, I dunno, six silver's quite a price. I don't think it's worth more than... Eh, say, two an' three copper, right, Gale?" Crawford prompted.

"Definitely," Gale agreed, nodding along. Haggling—he had completely forgotten to haggle. Maybe Crawford wasn't *entirely* wrong about the drink...

"Two!" The man's voice went high with exaggerated outrage. "You boys will beggar me! I could never let the price drop below five silver—five silver is only barely enough to keep old Sam in business!"

"I don't think that strip o' cloth is worth payin' more than three for," Crawford argued.

"Four," the man countered.

"Three an' two bits, or we're walkin' away, mate," Crawford said, suppressing a yawn.

Gale looked back and forth between Crawford and the salesman for a long moment. The man gave an almost imperceptible shrug before turning and addressing Gale. "You have good friends, sailor. Your shipmate knows well how to drive a bargain. Give me three silver and two copper, and you may take the scarf."

Gale nodded, thanked the man, and made the exchange. He tied the scarf tightly around his own waist to keep from losing it and turned to grin at Crawford as they both walked away.

"Thanks, mate—you near about saved my wallet. I don't know what I was thinkin', takin' the first offer like that."

"It's simple—you flat out weren't thinkin'. Too busy dreamin' on 'bout Guin, aye?"

Gale laughed. "You ain't wrong, mate. I owe you one, I really do. How'd you know you could bring him down so far?"

Crawford gave a barking laugh and shook his head. "Have you seen yourself, mate? Your sea legs have you swayin' all over the street like you're half-dead drunk, you look as Alinorian about the face as we come, an' you near about stink of booze. If it were me tryin'a sell to you, I'd have gone and charged triple."

"Good—good point," Gale chuckled, rubbing the back of his neck, "I s'pose I do stick out 'bout as much as any man can."

"You can sure say that again, mate. I swear—you wouldn't know how to lie low if I put you six feet under." Crawford grinned and elbowed Gale in the side.

Gale stumbled a bit further than he felt he should have. "Aye, well, I have many skills, even if bein' incon... incon... Blast—what's the word? Inconspicious? Ah, you know what I mean. Even if that ain't one of 'em."

"Stay away from the big words, mate. They don't much like ya even when you're sober."

Gale gave an exasperated sigh, correcting his posture and taking pains to walk without swaying. "Really, Crawford, I'm not drunk. Jus'... I'm a still carefree from all that celebratin' we did on the ship. That's all. No more or less or anythin'."

"Aye, right. That's the reason, sure." Crawford said, nodding the way he only did when he was rolling his eyes.

Gale let exasperation slip into his tone. "I am, Crawford. I'm still sober. I could stand to be drunk, though. What do you say, mate? I owe you at least one good drink, prob'ly more by now. I have an extra coin or two I wouldn'ta had otherwise, an' I have enough cash saved by, stored up, an' comin' my way that I don't feel bad buyin' you a nice cold tankard of somethin' strong."

Crawford paused for a moment, then nodded. "Aye, sure, mate. I'll take you up on that—a drink or two at your expense sounds like just the kind of thing I need today. You may've celebrated more than a bit already, but I ain't celebrated anywhere near enough."

Gale laughed and clapped his friend on the back. "Come along then, mate—I think I saw a fair lookin' tavern back this way!" Without waiting for a reply, he turned and led them both down to the spiraling stairs that led back to the docks and the bars.

CHAPTER TWENTY-ONE
Crawford

Crawford leaned both his elbows on the bar and massaged his head. Gale was singing. Loudly. Again.

The man had drunk enough to drown a whale, and Crawford felt that he himself would have to drink twice as much before he'd be able to relax and ignore the noise. Though there were other drunks in the tavern, no one was being quite so loud or obnoxious as Gale. The other sailors, though rowdy, all seemed to sing quieter, and the group of well-dressed native Mikarens in the corner was positively silent as they watched the rest of the crowd. Crawford did not know anyone there besides Gale, so of course Gale was being as loud and embarrassing as any honest man could possibly be.

Crawford lifted his glass and took another sip. The drink tasted funny, here. It was too bitter, too hot as it raced down his throat, and it only seemed to be making his headache worse. The more he drank, the worse he felt, and the more he desired to drown his sorrows and sleep.

To his annoyance, Gale stopped spinning arm in arm with some other drunk and flopped down in the seat to Crawford's left. Crawford suppressed a sigh and forced a grin.

"Ahoy, mate—how's life treatin' ya so far?"

Gale laughed loudly and signaled for the barkeeper to pour them both more. "Life's just divine! I'm on the edge o' the world with the best crew an' the best mate, an' once we sail, I'll be on my way to wed the prettiest girl in all the blamed world! The Gods smile, Crawford—they're smilin' on me— they're smilin' on you—they're smilin' an' it's all gonna be smooth sailin' from here on out! Maybe— maybe when we all get home, I'll have money, an' you'll have money, an' Guin'll be there—an' you can find someone, too! Then we can all get married, an' it'll be great!" Gale laughed again, as though there were some great joke.

Crawford bared his teeth in an expression that almost might've been a grin. "Aye, mate. That's… that's an idea. Now how 'bout you give it a rest? You're drunk. You're drunk and you don't have the grounds to even try denyin'."

"So what if I am?" Gale grinned wide and spread his arms, leaning back as if to embrace the world. "It's been ages since I've been drunk—an' you, mate—you shouldn't be askin' me that. No, no—you should be askin' yourself, Crawford—you should be askin' what you're still doin' sober!"

Crawford rubbed his face again. "I'm lookin' after you, mate. I'm lookin' after you same as I have been every damn day o' this voyage. Hell, same as I have been near about every damn day since we met— you know that, Gale? I've been lookin' out for you near nonstop, an' I don't think all the booze in the world can repay the debt you're owin' me. An' you don't even have the faintest clue why."

Crawford took his hand from his face to look at Gale, but the blond man was obviously not paying attention. Gale's back was turned, and he was regaling the barkeeper with vivid descriptions of Guinevere's beauty—in excruciating detail.

Sighing, Crawford let his head thump down onto the bar. If only he were a braver man...

Gale slid down from his seat and swaggered back to shout cheerfully with some men who were striking up another song—some grating shanty about riding a donkey. Crawford groaned quietly.

Someone tapped lightly at his shoulder. "Hello, friend. You don't seem to be having much fun, today. May I ask why?"

Crawford lifted his head and turned, coming face to face with a tall young man with pale blond hair and a politely smiling face. He was one of the native crowd—his accent was clearly not Alinorian, but he spoke differently from all the other Mikarens Crawford had met on the street. He must've been a noble or something—he was too soft-spoken and too richly dressed to be anything but. His cloak alone looked to be worth as much as a year of any fisherman's pay.

Crawford cleared his throat before answering, taking pains to speak clearly as he waved vaguely towards Gale, "Eh, I got a drunken moron for a shipmate—that's all."

The stranger eased himself onto the stool next to Crawford and nodded at the barkeeper. The barkeeper nodded back and handed the man a drink without a word.

"He is… quite the lively man, isn't he? I've been watching him for a while now. You know him well?"

"Aye, well as any man. Gale's nearly… he an' I been workin' ships together longer'n I care to remember. I don't reckon any man knows that bastard better."

"Ah, I see… you don't seem incredibly fond of him, friend… may I ask why?"

Crawford lifted his drink and took a sip, using the moment to ponder the question as seriously as his aching head would allow. The motion made the world spin dizzily, but Crawford barely cared.

"He's… He's…" Crawford took a deep breath and sighed. "Gale's jus' too damn much, sometimes. He's—he's got… near everythin', actually. All the luck. I mean, look at him. I can't keep a girl for more'n a month, an' he has to beat 'em off with a stick. I gotta scrape and take what I get, an' he just walks in an' they give him whatever job he wants— pay him whatever he wants, too. I work honest hard and try my damned best, an' he just waltzes on up to the scene an' jus' cause he's a 'proper talent,' he's got every other windworker near about bowin' in the streets as he passes. It ain't fair, I say. 'Specially not… this whole damn trip, I've been lurkin' in his shadow, an' he just won't quit rubbin' the whole mess in my face."

The stranger nodded, frowning compassionately and furrowing his brow at Crawford's dilemma. "Yes… I can see that is cause for unhappiness. He flaunts his power, is it? Is that what makes you angry, friend?"

"Aye." Crawford took another swig of his rum,

his tirade gaining momentum the longer he continued. "Aye, he flaunts his flamin' power, an'—an'—he flaunts the rest o' it, too. He won't freakin' stop flauntin' everythin'."

"What else does he have to flaunt beside his power, friend? Is he rich? Perhaps he has a wealthy family? Magic like his… I've only ever seen it among the nobility."

Crawford snorted. "Gale? Money? As if. Rumor says his pa might've been a lord, but we ain't got a clue and he don't care. Nah, in that respect us two're equal. He jus'—he's… He's even worse. He won't quit flauntin' the fact that he went an' won Guinevere's heart 'fore I could go an' get the guts to try an' make her mine. I saw her first. I saw her first an' I went an' met her an' I even intro—introduced them. I introduced them an' the both o' them went an' fell in love before I could do a damned thing about it."

The stranger nodded and offered a smile. "That is rather unfair. It seems that your friend has put you through quite a lot, over the years. You know, it almost makes me want to—oh, no, never mind…"

Crawford paused with his glass midway to his mouth and lifted an eyebrow. "Makes you wanna what?"

"Well," the stranger smoothed his hair back and straightened his shirt. "I was only thinking, your story, it touches my soul. My heart goes out to you, friend, and I was thinking, maybe there's a chance I could help to end your troubles."

"Huh? How? What'd ya mean?" Crawford squinted suspiciously, but the man only smiled. It was a friendly smile. Crawford found himself smiling back.

"Allow me to introduce myself. I am Gaston Magesight, a merchant from the upper quarter. I deal in all sorts of goods and trade primarily throughout this city, though I also have dealings in Midway Point."

"Aye? An'… what's your point? What's this about endin' my trouble?"

Gaston inhaled deeply and released a delicate sigh, splaying both his hands on the bar and examining his fingers as though they held some great invisible secret. "How to phrase this… I often deal in… exotic commodities, here in Mikare—things of which Alinor has no idea. One of these things is… fortune—yes, fortune—we'll call it that. Fortunes and futures. Your story has touched my heart. I want to help you. Consider it an act of charity from a fellow long-suffering friend."

Crawford took a long sip of his drink, staring at Gaston all the while. "An' what exactly're you offerin' to do, mate? You're talkin' in circles an' I ain't followin'."

Gaston lifted his hands from the bar and looked Crawford directly in the face. "I'm offering to buy your trouble, friend. I trade in fortune and future, and I can give you the change you seem to need in your life. Do you find that agreeable?"

Crawford set down his cup and started to laugh. "Mate, if you can change my lot in life, I'd be damn grateful. Fortune or future or whatever the hell it is you're givin' away… I'll take whatever luck I can get."

Gaston nodded and smiled, raising his glass in a toast. "Then we have a deal. Here's to our brighter tomorrow."

* * *

Crawford awoke the next morning with a legendary headache and a tongue like old leather. His bones ached, his teeth hurt, and when he forced his eyes open enough to take stock of his surroundings, he found himself propped up against the bar with an empty mug in his hand and the sticky remains of a puddle beside him. Crawford shut his eyes and groaned.

He waited for the world to stop spinning before he opened his eyes again. The bar was mostly empty now that the too-bright sun was in the sky. The Mikarens were all gone, the barkeeper had vanished, and the only other people left around were sprawled somewhere between unconsciousness and possible drunken death.

Crawford sat up, holding his head in his hands as he sorted through his muddled memories to piece together the events of last night. He'd been... yes, he'd been drinking with Gaston. They'd drank, then drank some more, then Gale had returned and prompted them all to join in singing some shanty or other, then they'd all drank together, then... then Gale had passed out, Gaston had pressed something into Crawford's hand before leaving to disappear off to who-knows-where, and Crawford had pocketed the thing and gone to sleep.

He shielded his eyes against the sun and squinted over the room again. Was that man—no, wrong height... Maybe that guy in the corner was—no, wait, he was too fat... The one slouched against the opposite wall had the wrong hair color... Crawford rubbed at his eyes and blinked repeatedly, bringing the world into sharper focus. He stood up unsteadily, clinging to the counter and fighting nausea as he looked around the room again.

His stomach sank, doing a slow flip. A green silk scarf trailed over the dirty ground, caught in the legs of a nearby stool. Crawford crawled over to pick it up. His fingers were numb—his whole body was numb with an ache that went deeper than mere hangover.

Crawford reached into his pocket and withdrew three bright and shiny golden coins.

CHAPTER TWENTY-TWO
Gale

Gale awoke to shouting and a slap in the face. Not a light slap, either, but a full-on bruising blow from someone with a hand like a brick. Gale's head rang like a bell and he moaned—it felt as though death itself had wrapped its bony fingers around his brain.

"Come on—wake up you lucky lads an' lasses! Today's the first day o' the rest o' your miserable lives!" a gruff voice roared. There was a fearsome clanging—like someone beating a pot with a spoon—and the sound of a distant opening door.

Gale forced his eyes open and found himself face to face with a very ugly man. Runny eyes, misshapen nose, scar-pocked complexion, missing front teeth, and stringy, dirt-colored hair—with breath that stank of rotten fish.

Gale recoiled, groaning as his whole body screamed. Metal clinked against metal, and his wrists jolted to an all-too-sudden stop. The ugly man grinned and walked away to harass someone else—a woman lying asleep on the floor a few feet away, chained to the wall.

Gale glanced around, frantic and nauseous. The ceiling was rough, tan stone—not the wood slats of the tavern. Weirdly dressed Mikarens were chained beside disheveled sailors, and the air was stale and stagnant—everything was wrong. This wasn't the bar—this wasn't where he'd gone to sleep. Gale furrowed his brow and struggled to think.

A well-dressed man approached him and knelt, gently taking Gale's chin and twisting his head around to better view his face. "You hit him too hard, Rolland. You left a mark. You do realize that marks will lower his value, yes? This is the find of the century—I'd like to get full price for him."

The ugly man ceased his banging and clanging and cleared his throat. "Yessir—but I figure we can get a healer in here no problem, if it's naught but a bruise or two."

"Well, Rolland, did you think to figure that I might not wish to let the whole city know my business? I find that doubtful. I know you enjoy your job, but I would appreciate if you left the thinking to the professionals from now on. Cease that noise and go fetch... fetch Cecil. He's a good man."

Though the well-dressed man never raised his voice, Rolland flinched and nodded, retreating without a word.

Gale blinked and watched him go.

The well-dressed man released Gale's chin and smiled. "Do you know where you are, friend?"

Gale shook his head. "No, uh... sir..."

The man nodded amicably, apparently pleased by the response. "Very good, you're already assessing your position and submitting appropriately. That shows the kind of mental processes ideal in a good slave. You'll earn me a pretty coin or two indeed..."

Gale opened and shut his mouth a few times, but there were too many questions surging up at once—they blocked his throat and choked his voice.

The well-dressed man gave another soft smile. "I suppose you have some questions, don't you? You're wondering what happened, how you got here, where you're going, and so forth. Yes? Of course you are. Well, my friend, I purchased you yesterday for the price of three gold coins, my men retrieved you after you fainted from... overconsumption, I suppose we'll say, and now that I own you, I intend to sell you to the highest bidder. Does that account for everything?"

He was so... so polite about it. Gale did not know whether to spit in the man's face or thank him for his time. He rejected both ideas, instead moving to recover his voice.

"Purchased..?" The word came out as more a croak than a question.

The well-dressed man nodded. "My magic allows me to see your magic. When I saw your soul shining bright and strong out among the common rabble, I knew I could not let you go. I approached your friend in the tavern, and he sold you to me without a second thought. I got a surprisingly good deal, too. I was expecting to have to haggle, and I do hate negotiation. It slows the process down horrendously."

Gale opened and closed his mouth a few more times before speaking. "You're—you're lyin'. Crawford—Crawford'd never do a thing like that."

"I'm sorry, friend, but it turns out your shipmate had some rather serious grievances against you. Something about a woman? I don't know, it's really not my business what bad blood lies between the pair of you. It's all water under the bridge, now."

Numb. Gale felt numb. His limbs were dead and his mind was gone—he was entirely numb. "Crawford... Crawford wouldn'ta done that. He's—he's near like family."

The well-dressed man chuckled under his breath, plucking a stray thread from the sleeve of his jacket. "No wonder, then. No one gets under the skin quite like family. My own brother was the bane of my existence for years, until I sold him off to a man on Midway Point. There's something about a brother... But I digress. Back on the topic, now—I've answered your questions, so, naturally you shall return by answering some of mine. This is agreeable?"

Gale said nothing. He stared at the back wall, still trying to find his mind and wrap it around his situation. The well-dressed man frowned slightly and waved his hand in front of Gale's face.

"Excuse me, hello? I asked you a question. The polite thing to do is answer."

"Wha—" Gale shook himself, glancing briefly at the well-dressed man before returning his gaze back to the wall. "Uh.... aye... right... sorry."

The man smiled and nodded, apparently satisfied. "Very good. Now, my questions. Your friend mentioned that your name is Gale. Is this true?"

Gale nodded slightly. Crawford had... he'd gone and... but why?

"Good lad. Now, I'm aware you're a windworker of uncommon talent. What is your family magename?"

"Dunno..." Gale answered, his mouth moving without his conscious direction. "Never—I'm jus' a windworker."

Crawford had left him. He'd left him—and now Gale was on his own. No ship, no crew, no way home. No way back…

The well-dressed man sighed. "A pedigree would fetch a higher price, but I suppose that can't be helped. You're strong enough, and that shall simply have to make up the difference. So, Gale, my friend, how old are you?"

"Not sure. I reckon somewhere near twenty-two."

No way back to Guinevere. There was no way back to Guinevere. Crawford had stolen it, and now Gale had no way back to Guinevere.

"Good, good. That's very good. A perfect working age—old enough to be strong, but young enough to bear many years of labor. That's wonderful. Now, my last question—are you listening, Gale? It's important that you pay attention when I speak. It's impolite to—"

"You know what else is impolite? Slavery is impolite. Now would you give me half a second o' quiet? I'm tryin'a think, an' your talk ain't helpin' in the least."

The well-dressed man blinked, inhaling slowly and biting his lip in a clear show of disapproval. "Defiance is not appreciated, friend. This will be easier for everyone if you simply go with the flow and accept your new fate. Otherwise, I will have to break you, and that would lower your value considerably. I don't believe either of us wants that now, do we?"

"I want to get back to my life. I want to get back to my life an' get back on my course—I'm—I'm s'posed to get married—I'm s'posed to go home an' get married, an' it was all gonna work out for once!"

"I am sorry to say that your plans have changed, Gale. You're with me, now, and I intend to sell you to a trade ship, where you will likely work until you die at sea. I know it's not fair, and I know it isn't legal, but I'm afraid that's life." The man flashed a grin. "Some of us win, some of us lose, and I'm afraid you've lost. I expect your lover shall find some way to carry on without you, so I wouldn't be too worried. Actually, yes! I expect your shipmate shall take care of her in your absence! And with you out of the picture, I'm sure they will be very happy. Isn't that lovely? They'll be happy forever, and all it costs is… well, a little sacrifice on your part. Isn't it noble, though? You're nearly a martyr for them. I think it makes for a lovely story."

Gale refocused his eyes on the man's face and stared at him for a long, slow moment. The man stared back calmly, refusing to be intimidated. Gale took a deep breath, resenting his chains.

"I… I understand what you say," Gale said slowly, pronouncing each word carefully, "But I do not accept it. That ain't my destiny. That ain't my future. That might be your plan for me, mate, but that ain't gonna happen. I won't accept it."

The well-dressed man smiled and stood, dusting off his pants and straightening his jacket. He smiled down at Gale again and stuck his hands casually into his pockets.

"Oh, don't worry, friend. You'll learn to."

Gale felt his heart harden to stone as the well-dressed man turned his back and walked away.

CHAPTER TWENTY-THREE
Crawford

Crawford spent the rest of his week ashore looking for Gale. He combed through every tavern on the docks, asked everyone he met, searched every alleyway and climbed every last flight of stairs in the city—but he found nothing. No one had seen Gale. No one had heard of Gaston. It was as though the city had swallowed them both. If it weren't for the green scarf and the three gold coins, Crawford would have thought that neither man had ever existed in the first place.

When the time came to board *The Morigana* and head for home, Crawford did so with a heart of lead and a roiling stomach. He wanted a drink, but he knew it would not help—the dread was too deeply settled in the back of his mind.

He kept his head down all throughout the loading process, working in silence with his cap as far over his eyes as he could manage without blinding himself. Every time the captain—or anyone—glanced his way, his stomach twisted and tied itself into sour knots. He wanted to melt away, to sink into the deck and never rise again. The world was too much to face.

He nearly jumped out of his skin when Devyn laid a hand on his shoulder.

"Ahoy, Crawford! You wanna take the first shift outta here, mate? Daryl's still drunk, the fool, an'—what's eatin' you, lad? You look fair green—you ain't sick, are ye?"

Crawford swallowed hard. His throat felt as though it were full of sand. "I—I—uh—no, I'm fine. Jus'… Jus' a bit tired, is all. Hungover. That's it. Jus' a bit tired an' hungover."

Devyn frowned, raising an eyebrow. "You swallow somethin' too strong for ye, lad? If you ain't feelin' it, that's fine by me. Gale can do it, 'less he's worse off than you are. Where is he, anyway? I ain't seen him 'round, yet. He'd better not be passed out under a table or he'll miss the boat."

Devyn clapped Crawford's shoulder companionably, and Crawford nearly fainted.

"Gale's—Gale's—dead!" he blurted, the words jumbling incoherently as they dove from his lips.

The other man blinked, opening his mouth to retrace Crawford's words. "Dead—? What do you mean, dead, lad? What happened to Gale?"

Crawford's mind raced, tripping over itself as he stumbled around for answers. The truth? No—he'd end up keelhauled for sure. Even if he said he was sorry, the captain would not forgive him—no one would ever look at him the same if they found out he'd betrayed his best mate for a couple of gold pieces. So what if he'd been drunk?

"He—he—uh… there was a… another—another fight. In a bar. There was another fight, an'—

an'—some guy was comin' at me. Gale went an' took him down an' got taken down for tryin'. Didn't get back up. Couldn't get back up. 'Cause he was dead."

Devyn's mouth fell open further, and his brow furrowed. "What..?"

Crawford nodded, weaving his story tighter. "Aye... He—he died savin' me in a fight, an'—an then afore I could do a thing, someone went an' threw his body in the sea. Dunno why. But... But that's how it went."

Devyn gave him a long, slow stare, and Crawford fidgeted uncomfortably.

"That's... that's quite a blow, mate... No wonder you're under the weather. You're... You're... sure, that's what happened?"

Crawford nodded, nearly swallowing his tongue.

"Well... someone'd better tell the captain... Lady Nimune won't be pleased to have lost a good sailor. I reckon Gale's girl's gonna be heartbroken, too... Shame about that. Real cryin' shame..."

Crawford nodded again, more slowly this time. He could taste the guilt in his mouth—cold, slimy, and bitter. He turned a strangled sob into a ragged cough. Devyn patted his back and turned away. "I'll get Daryl up an' sober. You better go an' report to the captain, lad. She'll be wantin' to know."

* * *

Crawford approached Captain Nimune as she stood beside the ship's wheel, shouting orders to all hands. Before he could so much as clear his throat, she turned around and pinned him in place with a cold stare.

"What is it, sailor? This'd better be fair important to come 'twixt you an' your job."

Crawford bobbed his head, licking his lips and willing his heart to stop pounding in his throat. "Aye, Cap'n, ma'am—this is. I—er—I have to… I have a report. It's… It's—"

"Out with it, man. Time an' tide don't wait—and neither do I. Speak your piece and return to duty, Crawford. Every hand needs to pull his share."

"It's—it's important, ma'am," Crawford said, taking a deep breath as he prepared to dive headfirst into his lie. "Gale is dead. I thought you oughtta know that, afore we set sail, Cap'n. I'm sorry."

Captain Nimune paused, looking directly at Crawford for the first time. "Dead? How?"

Crawford swallowed hard and told his story again, unable to look the captain in the eye or even raise his face from the deck. He felt cold—heavy. His tongue was dead in his mouth as he spoke; his voice could barely drift above a hoarse mumble.

When he finished, Nimune sighed.

"An' the poor fool was doin' so well. More's the pity. May the Brothers have mercy on his soul. Thankee for the report, Crawford. I'll see that we hold a proper send-off after we're away at sea."

Crawford nodded once and turned his back, thoroughly ashamed of how much better he felt.

CHAPTER TWENTY-FOUR
Guinevere

At last, the rain cleared, and the Month of Water gave way to the Prominence of Darkness. When the wet season ended and the sun finally saw fit to peek through the clouds, Guinevere and her father went down to reopen the shipyard.

The place was more crowded than it usually was after the off season—a large trade ship had blown in from the Rose Line after an unfortunate storm, and the poor vessel was in dire need of repair. The ship's foremast had snapped, her strand was ragged and tangled, and half the enchantments painted on her bow had been scoured away by the harsh ocean waves. Everyone agreed the ship was lucky to have made it back to port at all.

Guinevere stood beside her father on the upper deck and suppressed a flash of worry as they both surveyed the damage. She had never helped with something so broken before.

Markus placed a hand on her shoulder. "Thanks for comin' out with me, Guin—I'm fair glad of the extra hand."

Guinevere gave her father a smile. "I don't mind. I happen to enjoy the work. Now—what exactly are we in for, today?"

Markus chuckled. "That's what I like to hear. We're looking at a complicated fix, today. Not only do we have to sing for all the usual charms, but we also have to handle the repairs. Which means the enchanters are working double hard, and we gotta be double sure we don't blow anyone's head off with a wrong resonance by accident. We also gotta make sure the ship don't reject the new growth they're prompting—it's our job to keep her calm while they patch her. Sounds simple enough, aye, Guin?" His eyes twinkled.

Guinevere laughed. "Yes, Papa—about as simple as untangling my loom after Ell's played with it. But I'm sure we'll manage. Which part shall I sing?"

Markus grinned. "Think you're up to take the charms?"

Guinevere nodded.

Markus grinned and began tapping the side of his leg. Together, the both of them counted a beat, and the song began.

There were no words to this old melody, only patterns of sound and rhythm and magic. Markus crooned a low, soothing lullaby as the builders went to work on the ship's new mast, and Guinevere accompanied him with the high, soaring notes of the classic shipwright's charm. First came the lilting melody that was the prayer against rain, then came the slow, strong notes of the spell against ill wind. A fluttering fall in pitch served to ward off monsters, and the strong refrain repeated again and again through every part, binding the ship to itself and willing her to always stay fast to her course.

Magic resonated through Guinevere's voice as she sang, pouring from her soul into the ship. When it came time to repeat the body of the song and reinforce the enchantment, she was struck by a thought.

Gale's homeward journey should be starting any day, now.

Her voice wavered, and suddenly the ship became so much more than it was. She saw her task and imagined Gale, tossed about the Rose Line—and she lifted her voice, bringing new meaning to her music. Guinevere did not know what her father sang for, but she found herself pouring her own longing into every breath. She wanted nothing more than Gale's safe return, and that desire melded into magic and cast itself over the ship as a prayer for all sailors' safe journey home.

Markus caught her eye and nodded encouragement, adding flourishes to his tune to match and echo hers.

The other hands finished securing the new mast in place, and the Syrens' song faded to a gentle end. Guinevere allowed her shoulders to fall as she panted, exhausted and drained, and her father smiled, though he seemed just as tired.

"I'm right proud o' you, Guin. This ol' girl ought to be patched somethin' proper, now."

Guinevere nodded, still catching her breath. The wounded ship looked as though it had never been broken at all: the mast was in place; the bow had a healthy gleam—it looked brand new. Once the enchanters finished painting their glyphs, the ship would be ready to sail again.

Markus surveyed the scene, then nodded to himself. "We did good. Now, Guin—you have anything else goin' on this afternoon?"

Guinevere shrugged. "Nothing more pressing than finishing a few minor commissions. Why?"

"I'm meeting with the Cleanser family this afternoon, and I'd like you to come. I figure it's high time you got more involved in the business side of things. What do you say, lass?"

Guinevere grinned. "How could I say no?"

* * *

The meeting was to happen in a little restaurant where the Seaside District joined with Merchant's Way. It wasn't a large place, but it was clean, well-run, and politely quiet—perfect for leisurely meals and pleasant conversation.

Guinevere and her father had only just sat down when a familiar, black-haired figure strolled in, followed by a stern-looking woman in an immaculately tailored steel-blue suit. Her dark, grey-streaked hair was swept up in a tight, conservatively stylish twist, and her eyes were hard and sharp, flashing with a cool, collected authority that had Guinevere half intimidated and half inspired to someday command the same confidence.

As the pair approached, Guinevere and her father both stood, and handshakes were exchanged all around. The woman had a grip like a sailor.

"Evelynn Cleanser, it's a pleasure to finally be meetin' ya," Markus said.

"Likewise," the woman said with a curt nod. "My

son speaks highly of you and your family."

The group all sat, and Evelynn laced her fingers together on the table, barely giving the waiter a glance as he took their orders.

"Let's not waste time. My son and I are working to develop a new technology—something that will better our fair city and coincidentally bring considerable profit to all involved. We have the opportunity and the funds—but we lack a team. We need experts, we need craftsmen, and we need tools. We need honorable partners who will take initiative and give the best—and from what I hear, Mister Markus Syren, you and your company fit the bill. What do you say?"

Markus placed his chin on his hand, thanking the waiter who brought his drink. "I say 'what's the job?'"

Evelynn nodded to Shiro, who cleared his throat. "As you know, the Cleanser family is singlehandedly responsible for maintaining most of the city's drinking water. Though our current methods are good, we can do better. As things are, exploration to the Outlands is severely limited due to the limitations on supply in the shifting world. Settlers make due, but innovation in the water industry is just what the city needs to bring Alinor and her settlements into the future. We wish to create a portable water purification device—possibly similar to the methods used on ships of the Line—to benefit travelers and improve the overall quality of city life."

"And maintain monopoly 'fore someone else snatches it," Markus muttered so that only Guinevere could hear. In a normal voice, he added, "You know you're askin' for trade secrets, aye? Knowledge of how the water works has been passed from master to apprentice for years—guarded carefully so that we don't get a wash of swabs thinking they know better an' messin' the whole thing up."

Evelynn gave a tiny smile. "Which is why you'd remain as primary manufacturer once the device has been developed. Your secrets would remain in your hands—you'd simply be applying them differently."

Markus nodded slowly. "Guinevere, what do you think?"

Guinevere thought for a moment, then answered, "Let us imagine for a moment that we're interested in this new venture. What projections do you have? As far as cost and profit and timeframe, I mean. How long do you expect this to take, how much shall it cost—and what recompense can we expect for our time? Because I feel it's worth saying— my father and I have our own business and our own obligations. No matter how noble your cause, the ships must be built and time spent toying with new designs is time not spent securing the safety of our sailors. Are you prepared to balance those needs with your own?"

"Of course we are," Shiro said. "Your commitment to quality and public welfare is in part what drew us to you. If you would, I brought notes."

Shiro reached into his jacket and pulled out a small stack of papers, which he unfolded and slid across the table. Markus took the sheets, and Guinevere looked over his shoulder. It was all there, neatly scrawled in immaculate, spiraling print. Markus nodded to himself, and as the food came, the true conversation began—a long process of haggling and polite debate, which Guinevere found she rather enjoyed. By the time they'd all finished eating, they'd negotiated their way to a consensus, and both parties shook hands and agreed to have their lawyers meet to draw a contract.

Guinevere caught Shiro's eye as they all stood, and Shiro grinned.

"I look forward to working with you, Miss Syren. I have no doubts that our partnership shall lead us all to good things."

Guinevere dropped a slight bow and answered with a smile of her own. "And I with you, Mister Cleanser. I cannot wait to see what we create."

CHAPTER TWENTY-FIVE
Gale

Three days passed before Gale saw the sun. Rolland, the ugly man, brought him his meals—weak soup—and every so often Gaston would stop by to check in and chat. Once he brought a healer with him to ease Gale's bruises, but for the most part, the man only seemed to want to exchange pleasantries and discuss the weather.

On the morning of the fourth day, Gale was unchained and led out of the stone hole in the ground, but his time under the sky lasted only as long as it took to walk up two flights of stairs and into a large, multi-spired building the color of a conch shell.

"Welcome to my humble home," Gaston said, sweeping a bow as they passed the threshold. But as Gale was led up to a small, bare room at the top of a tower and left shackled to the wall, he felt that welcome was perhaps not the most appropriate word.

For the next five days, Gale was left alone with his thoughts, little though he could bear to face them. Guinevere's tears—Crawford's betrayal—they echoed in his head, rebounding and reverberating inside of his skull until Gale was half-certain he was going mad. Finally, when the desperation built up in his chest to the point where he knew it was scream or die, Gaston appeared with a too-wide smile on his too-smooth face.

"Gale, my friend, you'll be pleased to hear I have some good news to share with you."

Gale stared out the single, tiny window, refusing to give Gaston so much as a glance. "What—has someone finally tracked down your human soul?"

Gaston laughed—a genuine, cheerful sound. "Good one, friend! But I'm afraid that's not at all what I've come to share. No—you see, I'd have to have had a soul to lose before anyone could find it, and I assure you: I've never owned one of those. But I don't really mind—I own you, and I figure that's the next best thing. Especially considering I've found a potential buyer. I'm already rich, but I expect that I shall soon be even richer—and you'll live out the rest of your days singing and working away on those fair blue seas. Isn't that just lovely, Gale? I'm so happy for us both."

Gale gave a strangled sort of laugh. "Oh, aye, I'm damn delighted, mate. I'm damn delighted. Oh—wait, no—actually, I reckon I'm just damned. Has anyone ever told you you're a right cold bastard, mate? Because you need to grow a heart."

Gaston laughed, smoothing back his hair and brushing a bit of imaginary lint off his shirtsleeve. "My brother used to express similar sentiments, as it happens. They tell me he's what passes as a good man. I'm not certain I would agree. Nevertheless, this is all rather irrelevant, my friend. Your fate is the matter at hand. In three hours, your visitor will arrive—and I would appreciate if you were on your best behavior, as your demeanor reflects back upon me. I'm sure you understand.

"After all, what has a man got, if his reputation has been tarnished? No, no, I don't need your sarcastic answer. I know you have one—I can see it on your face—but it was a rhetorical question, and if you must see it answered, take this one I supply: without his reputation, a man has nothing, and if a man has nothing, he is nothing. I suppose he has his health, but even that will someday fade. So allow me to be clear: you will not tarnish my name and my honor, and I shall allow you to keep your name and some degree of dignity. Do you understand me, Gale?"

Gale sighed, pushing a faint breeze past his tiny window so that the wind sighed with him. "I understand."

Gaston smiled. "Very good. However, you are forgetting something important, Gale. Need I remind you of your place?"

Gale sighed again, fantasizing vaguely about what he could do with a knife. "No, *sir*. You don't."

"Very good! I've grown rather fond of you, Gale. You're so cooperative and intelligent. It's a nice change of pace from the usual rowdy, imbecilic crowd I deal in. I'm almost sorry to see you go. But then again, I have always found that money makes for the best company. But I digress. We were discussing your behavior for our guest, weren't we?"

"Aye aye, sure. I won't… I won't kick him or anythin'. I get it."

"Wonderful, kicking people is very impolite.

Positively barbaric, actually. I expect so much better from you, my friend. Now—permit me to elaborate on my expectations—"

"No," Gale interrupted, his voice flat.

Gaston paused mid-word, blinking rapidly and looking like a fish caught in the air. "Excuse me?"

"I said 'no.' I don't wanna permit you. I've listened to you babble for long enough, mate. My ears need a rest."

Gaston licked his lips, and Gale could nearly see thoughts billowing up behind the man's eyes like so many thunderheads. Gaston's face was ice for an uncomfortably long moment, then his cold visage cracked to reveal an warm smile.

"Well pointed out, Gale. I did ask your permission, didn't I? That was my mistake. However, you must trust me: it's for your sake that I ignore your wishes. This behavior is precisely what I hope to warn you against, you see. When our guest arrives, you will address him from a position of appropriate subservience, you will reign in your wit and your individualistic will, and you shall stand calm and demure and obey whatever request is made of you without question, comment, or hesitation. Am I clear?"

"No, sir, you're opaque."

There was another frozen pause before Gaston smiled again. "Why, Gale, I'm surprised! That's quite an advanced word, for a sailor. I'm impressed. And such an astute observation too—I am indeed completely opaque. However, allow me to be quite clear—which is to say, I intend to make myself understood without room for creative misinterpretation: I would hate to have to damage you. From what I understand, a sub-par windworker aboard a ship is a liability. There's no market for the purchase of liabilities. If all else fails, I suppose I could find you a job based on your looks, but prostitutes are already a dime a dozen and I feel that would be a waste of talent, in your case. Don't you agree?"

Gale opened his mouth and inhaled as though to speak—then he closed it again. After a few moments spent searching for a response, he gave a quiet, frustrated sigh. "Aye. That I do. I don't much fancy that manner of life."

"I wouldn't think so," Gaston agreed, laughing as he smoothed back his hair. "No, no, you're a mariner in your soul. I can see that. And that's why, if you look at it, I'm doing you a wonderful favor. You'll never have to leave the sea! It doesn't appeal to me personally—I'm rather fond of my home here, and I finally have it decorated the way I like—but you sailor-types always speak of the water as your truest love, and this way, you'll be with it forever, and you'll never have to choose between this and some mere human. Isn't that grand? It should all be so simple, now!" The man beamed in the manner of a child bestowing a gift upon a treasured friend, and for a moment Gale almost forgot how much he hated Gaston's face. But only for a moment.

"Aye, right—simple. The same way drownin's simple. The choice is mine to make, mate. You don't get a part in it."

"And in that, you are entirely wrong. The choice has been made. The matter is resolved. This is what's best for you, friend. I've simply removed the barriers between you and what you love. Now, would you care for some tea, Gale? I fear this talking has left me rather parched."

"No, I don't want your tea, I want—"

"More's the pity. It's a rather lovely blend. Are you sure?"

"—I want to go home! I got a life to get back to!"

"'I had a life,' you mean," Gaston said, standing up to ring the bell for his servants. "Your grammar is atrocious, and you'd best remember to use the proper tense when referring to that which you no longer possess. Otherwise, people might accuse you of trying to steal from those who own what you've lost, and trust me when I say that could be the last accusation you ever hear. And in my experience, that sort of thing tends to end with a mess, and blood does have that incredibly unfortunate tendency to stain. Quite inconvenient all around, believe you me."

Gaston gave a knowing nod, then a broad smile as a quiet woman in a cornflower-blue dress slipped into the room bearing a tray laden with two teacups and a kettle. She bobbed a slight curtsy, set the tray down on the floor, then exited again without once looking Gale in the face. Gaston gave a small chuckle, lifted the tray, then sat down cross-legged on the floor across from Gale.

"Marianne is such a dear. Look—she brought a cup for you even without being asked! The poor woman works ever so hard, it's actually quite adorable. Since she went out of her way to accommodate you, I feel like it's only proper that you take tea with me after all, my friend. Here—try it—it truly is quite good."

The man poured two cups of tea and slid one

towards Gale. Gale looked at it, raising both his eyebrows and feeling ever so slightly ill. He reached for the teacup, cringing at the gentle clink of chains. The tiny piece of porcelain looked terribly fragile in his tar-stained, sea-roughened hands.

Gaston nodded encouragingly. Gale took a small sip. The tea was good.

"There we go. That's much better. No questions, very little hesitation—perfect! You learn so well, Gale. When our guest arrives, I expect you to continue this good behavior and remain appropriately silent. As much as I appreciate friendly banter, not all men have my taste. Likewise, you are not to frown or scowl or make any of those unpleasant faces. I don't demand a smile—there are few things as ugly as a forced smile—but I will insist that you keep your demeanor reasonably pleasant. Oh—and please, though I understand that this is a lot to take in, you mustn't forget to finish your tea, my friend. It's far too expensive to waste, and I'm afraid it's not nearly so nice-tasting cold."

"If it's expensive, then why the hell're you givin' it to me?"

Gaston blinked. "Because you're my friend, Gale. Naturally I rather prefer to be a good host, when I can."

"Then... If we're... friends, then why are ya sellin' me?"

Gaston took a sip of his tea, never breaking eye contact. "Because I'd like to make a profit, Gale. I'm an ambitious man, and I can't become governor without the funds to run a proper campaign. I know Alinor has a king—at least, you had a king. From what I hear, it's been long enough since anyone's seen him that I'd be questioning that use of tense, if I were you. Regardless, though I know Alinor has a king, here in Mikare we elect our government officials, and if a man wishes to climb his way up to the top of the social staircase, he needs enough gold to keep his shoes clean. Though my job does pay quite well—I'm a government labor official, you know, which means I help to allocate people towards the tasks best suited for them—I've found that one can never have too much money. Especially not when one has dreams like mine. Would you care for a bit more tea, friend? It looks as though your cup is empty."

Gale shook his head slowly, and Gaston shrugged, pouring himself another cup. Gale set his own cup back on its saucer and stared at the abstract pattern of leaves at the bottom.

"I ain't gonna stand for this," he said, halfway lost in thought. "I ain't gonna stand by and let you take my life from me, Gaston. I have my own dreams, too, an' they ain't worth any less than yours just 'cause they're mine."

Gaston smiled over his teacup. "Of course not. However, while you're here under my roof they are completely irrelevant, while mine are the order of the day. What you do once you're out of my possession, well, that's not my business. But so long as you are my business, I aim to manage you appropriately. I'm sure you understand?"

Gale nodded, though midway through the motion, he realized that the gesture was a lie. "No. No I don't. I don't have a damned clue."

"Well, that's perfectly alright. Ignorance is bliss, or so they say. Truthfully, it's not my business to educate you. I'm simply the middleman, uniting those who want with those who have. And those powers you have—it's quite tragic. Your kind are in such high demand, and yet have this awkward habit of drowning before you're out of your prime. It's quite tragic. Which is part of the reason I want to encourage you to consider the benefits of my offer. I promise you— it really is for the best."

"Maybe for you, but not for anyone else." Gale felt a twitch deep in the pit of his soul, a dark little swirl as helpless frustration and exasperation blew themselves to sparking anger.

"Not so," Gaston said, calm as ever. "Though I will freely admit that I see reasonable personal benefit, there's also the captain to consider: if he buys you, he stands to gain quite a bit. And you—if you work hard and cooperate, there's a very good chance you'll live longer than you might have otherwise, and that's even in addition to those other benefits I've mentioned. The silver lining wraps all the way around this situation." He smiled and set down his teacup. "But I digress. We've sat and chatted for quite long enough—and though tea was quite pleasant, I fear I must prepare for our guest. I'll be back shortly. Marianne will clean up the tray."

CHAPTER TWENTY-SIX
Crawford

Crawford stood on deck aboard *The Morigana*, his face downturned as Captain Nimune explained Gale's death to the crew. The men were silent, and Crawford saw that many of them also bowed their heads—though their reasons were nothing like his.

He shifted his feet, and his insides knotted and writhed and twisted into countless uncomfortable shapes. The twins stood on either side of him, and Devyn gave Crawford a companionable pat on the shoulder.

Crawford almost choked.

The wind blew cold across *The Morigana's* decks, hissing and whistling and whispering silent jeers as it wove through the rigging. The ocean was choppy, and the sky, though clear, was grey and empty. Even the gulls were gone. Crawford wished there was more noise in the world—he wished to be anywhere other than where he was—and most of all, he wished the captain would shut her mouth and let Crawford forget what he had done.

"—he was a good man," she said, looking around to each crew member in turn, lingering on Crawford a few moments longer than he liked. "Strong, brave, and committed to his work. Though Gale dines with ol' Mother Ainsley tonight, he won't be forgotten by us that still sail. Let us honor his memory by makin' it home safe to Alinor, and Brothers willin', let's keep it a fair few years 'fore we see Gale again. You know he wouldn't have it any other way, aye?"

"Aye!" the crew answered, and Crawford joined the cry half a beat behind. His voice felt oddly hoarse and his eyes were weirdly hot as the crew dispersed to get back to their various duties.

Daryl took him by the shoulders and looked into his eyes, forcing Crawford to meet his gaze. "You alright, lad? I know you two were solid mates—you need to take a day? I don't want you up workin' the winds if you ain't at your best."

Crawford cleared his throat and shook his head, forcing a weak smile. "Nah... Don't you worry 'bout me, mate, I'm fine an' fit to pull my weight. I'm just..." His voice cracked. The gold coins felt heavy in his pocket. "I got a lot on my mind. I reckon a good day's hard work'll clear my head."

Devyn clapped his hand on Crawford's shoulder again, and Daryl nodded. "Aye, I'll come too—keep you straight 'n steady. You know Gale's down there in Ainsley's Keep lookin' up at us that's left, havin' a grand ol' time an' wishin' us well. He wants to see us get home safe, even if he ain't comin' with."

"Aye," Crawford said, croaking out a chuckle, "I'll bet you're exactly right."

CHAPTER TWENTY-SEVEN
Gale

An hour and a half passed before Gaston returned to Gale's cell. Gale was left alone, and it was like a fog lifted—his mind was finally clear, and he found anger glittering in his heart like shards of ice.

Still, though, his hands were chained, and nothing he could do would free them. He sighed and closed his eyes, muttering a prayer—but was interrupted by a polite knock on the door.

Gaston entered a moment after, followed by a stranger. Gale sat up straight.

The new man was tall and broad, with a hard face burned by the sun and the wind. He wore a long, oiled sea-coat and a three-cornered hat, and his mouth was twisted into a constant scowl by an unfortunate scar on his chin. The man placed his hands on his hips and gazed down at Gale with dark, dispassionate eyes. A Captain's Mark shone pale on the man's tanned neck.

Gale met the man's eyes and stared back, refusing to be cowed. The man raised his eyebrow and snorted.

"This it? For the numbers you called, Gaston, I damn near expected to find some sorta god chained up in this tower. Seein' as this here's naught but a man, I reckon I oughta get a fair discount. Two, maybe three for the price o' this one."

Gaston laughed, sweeping his hair back from his face with an easy gesture. Gale took a deep breath, hardly caring about the angry draft his magic carried through the room.

"If you find yourself dissatisfied, friend, I'm sure we can renegotiate. However, my dear Vern, I suggest you wait to pass judgment until you've seen what I see. I promise you won't be disappointed. I suspect he's old blood—perhaps some little illegitimate sprout needed to be pruned from one of the more respectable family trees, or some such nonsense. Either way, he has power you're not likely to see again. If you're no longer interested, I'm sure I'll have no trouble finding another buyer."

Gale's frustration flared, sending another small gust blowing out the door without his conscious prompting. He could feel every little swirling eddy as the breeze caressed every corner of the room, and he let that consume him.

Captain Vern frowned slightly. "I dunno, Gaston. Sure, the boy's got some shoulders on 'im, but I don't reckon he's worth all that. I'm readin' his thoughts now an' there ain't much in his head but air."

So the Captain was a mindreader... The draft in the room picked up strength.

"I expect that's because he's a windworker," Gaston answered smoothly. "From what I've gathered, it seems that he's been working long enough to think in terms of air. I'm sure what you're seeing, my dear Captain, is mere proof of his experience 'before the mast,' as I believe your people say. I've seen for myself that the boy is unexpectedly clever, though I appreciate that one would not guess that from a glance."

"More likely he's a half-wit who got lucky enough to fool ye, Gaston. I ain't givin' you a copper 'til I see 'im in action."

"Of course not. Never fear, dear captain, I know just the place we can test our friend Gale. Don't worry, I'm sure you'll see his worth."

* * *

The sunlight was blinding after so long inside the tower. Gale's eyes watered and his limbs ached. He nearly tumbled down the first flight of stairs from Gaston's house to the seaside, and for most of the walk, it felt as though Vern's firm hand on his shoulder was the only thing keeping him upright. The shackles on his ankles did not help.

Gulls flocked in the sky above, swirling together in a gigantic, loosely spiraling cloud. The wind was cool and sweet. Gale closed his eyes and savored the light caress of the sun and the breeze—though his reverie ended when Vern shoved him forward.

Gale swallowed his anger. Birds spun in the clear blue sky—tiny crabs shuffled through the shell-banded sand—glittering patterns shifted on the patchwork ocean waves—the hot sun beat at the back of his neck—it was better to focus on that.

Off against the horizon, past the tiny fishing

boats, Gale saw a speck of a ship that he imagined might have been *The Morigana*. He inhaled sharply, and a sudden gust blew across the beach, picking up loose grains of sand and driving them together into a twisting sheet of airborne grit.

"None of that, now," Vern said, shoving Gale forward so that he stumbled again. "Your ol' ship has sailed. Best accept that now."

Gale took another deep, slow breath. "Aye aye, sir."

A tiny boat crewed by a pair of rough-looking hands drifted up to meet the trio on the shore. One— a stout, craggy man with short brown hair and a jutting jaw—was obviously a windworker, and the other—a lanky, broad-shouldered man with dark hair and a bored expression—was obviously in charge.

When the boat reached the sand, the lanky one hopped out and saluted. He did not glance at either Gale or Gaston.

Vern cleared his throat authoritatively, his hand tightening on Gale's shoulder.

"Gaston, I'd like ye to meet my first mate, Josiah Weatherman."

"It's a pleasure to make your acquaintance, my friend," Gaston said, smiling and bowing like a well-oiled machine.

Josiah's lips tightened. "We've met."

Vern smirked and raised his eyebrow. Gale kept his face impassive.

Gaston brushed a bit of sand from his shirtsleeve. "Have we?"

"Aye," Josiah confirmed, "you... 'introduced' me to my last captain."

"Josiah... Josiah... Oh! You're that lovely boy I

picked up at the Fishtail Tavern… Five years ago, wasn't it? It's good to see you're doing so well now, my friend!"

Josiah clenched his jaw. "You're no friend of mine."

Gaston tilted his head at an angle and tapped his finger to his chin thoughtfully. "Oh, yes—now I remember. You always were a rude one, Josiah. Not at all like my friend Gale. Regardless, I do hope you'll be kind as we put him to the test. The boat is ready, I trust?"

"Aye," Vern interjected, exchanging a nod with the windworker in the boat. "She's set an' ready. Josiah, I expect you to take the lad out and see all goes to plan."

Josiah nodded, and the next thing Gale knew, he'd been shoved into the little boat and the other windworker was pushing them both out into open waters.

After a few moments, the other windworker let his power fade. "Your turn," the man growled, glancing at Gale.

Gale summoned a breeze. The boat lurched forward. Gale took a deep breath, quieted his ire, and softened the wind.

He glanced at his new companions. The windworker stared vacantly at the swirling gulls. Josiah kept his flat gaze glued to the distant horizon.

After several minutes, the man spoke. "Give us a starboard turn, now."

Gale's fingers twitched, but he brought the boat into a tight, neat turn. Off to the port side, the Rose Line beckoned, whispering promises and apologies on the world's wind. *The Morigana*—Guinevere—

everything he knew and loved lay in that direction. Crawford sailed that way without him.

"Belay that drifting, now," Josiah said, his voice as flat as his gaze. "We're not aiming for the Line, today. You want to take her in a circle, here. Nice and easy."

"Aye, sir," Gale mumbled, softening the breeze and letting the taut sail slacken. The mast creaked mournfully as the other windworker angled the canvas to better catch the wind.

Slowly, point by point, the little boat turned her prow around.

Gale's eyes passed over the Rose Line again. The tiny speck of the distant ship was gone, and Gale's self-control snapped.

Magic washed over him. The boat lurched forward, skipping over the water as though about to take flight. Gale let loose a manic laugh that was echoed in the flapping canvas and strained singing of the taut lines.

Josiah shouted something—gestured wildly towards the shore—but Gale ignored him, pushing harder towards the horizon. The wind—the waves—the ship—motion was all that mattered.

Then Josiah hit him upside the head with a belaying pin and knocked Gale clean into the water.

Salt flooded his mouth—bubbles flooded his sight, swimming between shining spots of golden light. Gale's breath escaped and fled towards the surface as his shackles dragged him down—then strong arms grabbed him and hauled him back over the side of the boat.

Josiah slammed him up against the mast. "Take us back. Now."

Gale glanced around. The tiny boat had blown past the domain border and drifted well onto the Rose Line. The other windworker seemed nearly panicked trying to stop it.

Gale bared his teeth. "Give me one good reason why I should—'cause I see two reasons right there on shore why I shouldn't."

Josiah's lip curled. "They're back there. I'm right here. The thing about slavery—they wanna keep you alive. Right here, right now, I'm not so attached."

Gale scowled. "Some might say it's better to die free than to live as a slave."

Josiah leaned in until his face was mere inches away from Gale's—his dead eyes burning. "Would you?"

Gale clenched his jaw. Guinevere's face flashed through his mind. "No," he eventually conceded. The words were bitter on his tongue. "I would not."

"Good man," Josiah said, drawing back and letting Gale fall to the deck. "Now take us back."

Gale hung his head and summoned a landward breeze.

The boat inched forward slowly, barely making a ripple on the water. Josiah made no comment.

The breeze fell dead as soon as they hit the shore.

Josiah seized Gale's arm and pulled him from the boat, saluting Vern with his other hand. Gale did nothing to resist.

Vern crossed his arms over his chest. "Your verdict, Josiah?"

Josiah shoved Gale forward. Gale stumbled.

"He's strong and skilled, and he takes orders well. Give him half a chance and he'll take it, but he ain't in no hurry to die. I'd say power like his… he'll set us fair ahead if we can keep him in line. But there's an equal chance he'll prove more trouble than he's worth. It's up to you if you're lookin' to gamble, Cap'n."

Vern nodded. "Right. I've seen enough. Gaston—let's talk price."

CHAPTER TWENTY-EIGHT
Guinevere

Guinevere walked beside her father in the shipyard, helping him inspect the sleeping ships with their half-finished paint and their half-grown repairs. The place was empty but for the gently glowing, whispering ships—even the most passionately dedicated employees had yet to arrive.

Technically, curfew was still in effect at this hour, but hardly anybody cared. In the seaside district, such a law was little more than a joke. Guinevere yawned and rubbed at her eyes. She'd never been a morning person, but Markus liked to start his day well before dawn.

Guinevere yawned again. Her father leafed through a sheaf of papers he'd snagged from his desk, ticking another tiny box on the strip of squiggles he called a list.

"Remind me, father—what are we doing here at this ungodly hour?"

"Gettin' an early start, Guin. All hours are godly gifts an' I'm not one to see them wasted."

"Yes, well—why am I spending these particular hours here, when I could be spending them asleep? I'd understand if you needed my help somehow, but so far all I've done is shadow you."

Markus pulled his mouth into a tight smile. "Sorry, lass—I want you here when the Cleansers show up, and if I know a thing about Evelynn, she's the type that tends to be early. It's better you're here to start. But the idle time'll end soon, I promise you that. It'll be all work once the Cleansers and the Spellcrafters both join us."

Guinevere frowned. "There are Spellcrafters coming?"

"Aye, I wasn't keen on the idea either. But Evelynn reckons there's no harm gettin' a genius in to help this project find its feet, an' since she's footin' the bill I can't rightly argue. It's Caesar, at least—an' that one ain't as bad as some. A right cold fish, sure, but I've worked with him before and he knows his craft proper."

Guinevere sighed and nodded. "I suppose it could be worse. Anyway, if you don't need me for anything right this particular moment, I'm going to go get some coffee. Want any?"

Markus shook his head. "No thanks."

"Right. Well, I'll meet you by the gate when the bells ring."

With that, she wandered off—back in the direction of the tiny shack beside the warehouse that her father called his office. It was a sturdy little thing, with smooth stone walls and an orderly tile roof, but the sea air had worn away the polish—making the building look several years older than it was. Her father was always talking about remodeling it, but he'd yet to find the time.

Guinevere let herself in and triggered the spell to set the kettle boiling. As she waited for the water to heat, she sat herself down in her father's chair, propped her feet on his desk, and imagined for a moment how it would feel to run the company. She idly leafed through a pile of paperwork—mostly commission specifications and memos for employees, with the last few sheets being reminders Markus had written to himself.

She frowned and set the stack of papers down. As soon as she was in charge, she'd install a proper filing system. And maybe hire a secretary. And then once she'd overhauled the worst of her father's habits, Guinevere would get the business really rolling. Her father had built it from nothing, and she'd take it to the next level—more focus on innovation in addition to the usual work. They wouldn't just be builders, they'd be inventors—using the assets of the upper class to fill the needs of the rest. Sailors especially.

Guinevere nodded to herself and got up to finish fixing her coffee. She'd bring Gale into the business, too, once he was back and they were married. He knew the reality of life at sea better than anyone, and together they could make it better—usher in a new age, of sorts. Of course he'd have to finally learn to read, but that was no huge obstacle. Guinevere had always hoped to teach him, someday.

She took a sip of her coffee and set her feet back on the desk, dreaming of the world they'd create. After a few pleasant moments, her trance was broken by the city bells. Curfew was over. Guinevere stood and stretched and left to join her father, taking her coffee with her.

He was at the entrance when she arrived, greeting the Cleansers as the workers trickled in. Guinevere couldn't help but wonder if their perfect timing was coincidental, or if Shiro's mother had kept them waiting around the corner for the bells to begin their racket. She seemed the type who liked things exact.

Guinevere greeted them both with a smile and a polite hello. Evelynn returned it with a nod, and Shiro replied with a mostly-coherent "how do you do?" He seemed even less of a morning person than Guinevere.

"I'm quite well," Guinevere answered as her father flagged over some of the more important craftsmen to introduce to Evelynn. "Would you like some coffee, Shiro? You look like you could use some."

Shiro gave a rueful grin and rubbed his eye. "Do I really? I apologize—I do try to be professional, but alas: I am only human. Coffee would be wonderful, thank you."

"You're in luck. I just made some, so it's still fresh. Come this way." Guinevere waved Shiro on, assuring both their parents that they'd be back in a moment.

They went to the office and got Shiro his drink, and after the man had a moment to wake up properly, he thanked Guinevere and offered her a smile. "You know, I had a feeling before—I thought this partnership would be a good one, and now I'm certain: you have excellent taste in coffee, Guinevere."

Guinevere chuckled. "One of my father's old

shipmates has a hand in the trade, so we get a good deal. I'm afraid I can't take credit."

Shiro laughed. "Well, you're welcome to it anyway. On the subject, though—about your father… Is it true he was a painter before he became a shipwright? It doesn't really matter, but I came across the rumor while researching your business, and I can't help my curiosity."

"He painted houses on Midway Point, yes. And the way he tells it, he just happened to be walking past as a ship was loading up to leave, and when he saw they needed an extra hand, he set down his bucket, grabbed a crate, and never looked back."

"Just like that?"

Guinevere shrugged and smiled. "According to him. Either way, he fell in love with the sailor's life, and he realized he wanted to dedicate himself to building ships. And after a while, he met my mother and fell in love again—so however exactly it happened, we're all here now."

"So we are," Shiro agreed. "And I have no doubt that his expertise, your expertise—our expertise… It's just what we need to bring Alinor into the future."

"And beyond, perhaps. I see this as the first step. Who knows? If we can make this happen today—just think of what we can achieve tomorrow."

"Agreed. Now… I suppose we should be getting back, shouldn't we?"

"Yes, I suppose we should."

And so Shiro and Guin—both newly caffeinated—left the office to rejoin their parents.

They caught up just as Markus and Evelynn were finishing their tour.

Evelynn looked her son up and down. "Awake

now, are we?"

Shiro stood straighter. "Yes, Mother."

"Good."

Markus smiled. "You two have perfect timing. The Spellcrafters are here, and we're just looking to greet them." He nodded to one of the workers who'd been trailing the pair. "Leila—would you do the honors?"

The woman skipped forward to open the gate, beyond which a somberly-dressed duo stood like a couple of sleek and patient crows. They both pale, narrow faces, sharp green eyes, and smooth black hair. The one on the left was taller and older and exuded an air of authoritative grace, while the one on the right couldn't have been much older than sixteen or seventeen, and he carried himself in such a careful imitation of the other that Guinevere had to hold back a laugh. Clearly, the pair were father and son.

The father stepped forward first, and Guinevere's smile chilled when she saw the bluebell he had pinned to his jacket. Though subtle, she recognized the symbol of mourning, and she remembered a story she'd heard some weeks ago about a young boy drowned in an accident. She had no problem keeping her expression sober as everyone exchanged formalities.

Ceasar Spellcrafter gave a stiff bow. "Markus. Evelynn. It's a pleasure to work with you both. Please meet my son, Kai. He'll be assisting me, today."

Markus nodded, shaking both their hands warmly. "Pleasure workin' with you both."

He carried on to introduce everyone around, and when it was Guinevere's turn to shake hands, she accompanied her greeting with a sympathetic smile and a "Please allow me to offer my condolences about your son."

Caesar's lips tightened, and he nodded. "Thank you. This tragedy has been hard on my family, but all we can do is keep living. So let us begin." He turned to Markus. "I was told our work today would require analysis of an existing piece of technology. Where might we find this?"

"Built aboard every sailin' vessel approved for Line travel and most that ain't, that's where," Markus said. "Come this way an' I'll show ya."

He led them through the shipyard to a large, decadent vessel currently undergoing light repair. The workers—enchanters, mostly—were busy refreshing the protective spells and restoring the paint, but they moved aside as the group passed down into the depths of the ship to crowd around the natural wooden cistern in her heart.

"Here's the device," Markus said, "though I'm not sure the word right applies to part of a living vessel. We grow the bones of the ship, see—and as it all takes shape, we get our team to magic it to Ainsley's Keep an' back. By the end, we get a solid ship that takes up seawater and sends it up to this cistern fresh and ready for drinkin'. So I imagine what we need to do is break down the process, aye? Isolate what happens so's we can replicate it minus the ship."

Caesar nodded, while behind him Kai took notes. "That would be ideal."

Evelynn nodded as well, dipping her fingers into the cistern and pursing her lips.

"This is... interesting. The water is certainly potable, but I can feel traces—impurities we don't usually see. Shiro, come here. I want your impression."

Shiro leaned over and trailed his fingers in the water as well. "I quite agree, Mother. There are some odd elements here, however I imagine that they don't impact much beyond the flavor."

"I do hear sailors say that every ship tastes different," Guinevere said, half to herself. "They tell me you know you've found home when you meet a ship where the fruit and the water both taste right."

"Very nice, but hardly relevant," Caesar replied, frowning at the cistern. "Today's work does not depend on hearsay from sailors. Instead, I propose we begin discussing the means and methods by which we make our magic. My son will record."

Guinevere's expression tightened, but she nodded, and the conversation progressed to follow that path, meandering this way and that as the group compared notes and took measurements. All the while, poor Kai scribbled in his little notebook as though the world were ending. One minute Evelynn and Shiro would be explaining the standards by which water could be considered pure, the next, Guinevere and Markus would find themselves giving a joint dissertation on the intricacies of singing a ship to life, and then just as they thought they were getting somewhere, Caesar would drop some chilly comment about some obscure law of enchanting, and the whole process would begin anew.

Frustrating though the conversation was, Guinevere found she was enjoying herself. Despite the backtracking and argumentation, making headway here carried the same sort of detail-oriented satisfaction as a day spent weaving. This just happened to be louder.

After several hours, the group finally broke for lunch. Markus, Evelynn, and Caesar went one way, and their children went another. Personally, Guinevere would rather have kept the group together, but she found it hard to stay irritated when she saw how much more relaxed Shiro and Kai both seemed to become.

CHAPTER TWENTY-NINE
Crawford

It had been months since Crawford had slept. No matter how hard he worked himself, when the time came to close his eyes at the end of his shift, Crawford found himself unable to rest. He closed his eyes and settled into his bunk to sleep, but his dreams were too vividly painful—and when he was inevitably called to wake and work again, reality felt far too much like a dream.

So when the alarm bells sounded and the screaming began in the middle of Crawford's attempt to nap, Crawford was half-certain that it was only his mind playing tricks.

Until someone shook him awake, shouting something about a magic octopus.

Crawford stumbled from his bunk and staggered upright, rubbing desperately at his tired eyes. His tongue was made of boiled leather—his head was full of hot lead—he nearly fell over as he bent to pull on his shoes—but somehow he collected himself enough to scramble up the ladder to the deck. The sun was blinding—stabbing at his brain through his eyes. Crawford felt slightly nauseous and rather cold. He realized he'd forgotten to put on his shirt, but it was too late to worry about that.

The crew was in a state of panic, beating at the air as red and orange and deep purple *things* drifted down from the clouds in a gentle rain. Shapes plopped into the water and bounced lightly against the deck, and when Crawford looked up, they seemed to fill the sky—floating every which way on a myriad of contradicting breezes. People ran left and right, yelling orders and curses as they smacked the colored blobs out of the air and into the ocean, where they floated on the surface like so many tiny drops of oil before dipping down and disappearing into the murky depths.

Crawford prodded one stationary blob with the toe of his boot. It convulsed, stubby tentacles writhing as the thing squirmed to get airborne and away.

Nimune's voice rang above the chaos. "Get to work, Breezebender! Blow them away before they send us off course!"

Crawford snapped to attention, finally registering that both the twins were busy weaving an intricate pattern of air. Daryl struggled to keep the falling octopodes clear of the sky around the ship, while Devyn fought to keep *The Morigana* steady on the Rose Line. Crawford shook himself, smacked the side of his face in a bid for clarity, and scrambled to join them.

He sucked in a breath and called a breeze, willing the wind to catch the tiny creatures and whisk them away.

A shadow flickered in the corner of Crawford's eye. It looked like a person, but when Crawford turned his head, no one was there. He gritted his teeth and raised his hand, pulling the wind back and forth to sweep away the octopodes falling through the gap in Devyn's defenses.

He was only seeing things.

Something cold and rubbery smacked into Crawford's back and stuck, squirming uncomfortably against his bare skin. Crawford screamed and jumped—completely losing his hold on the wind. He flailed, trying to twist around to get at the thing, but it shuddered and scuttled away from his fingertips—sending cold shivers racing up and down Crawford's spine with every twitch.

"Crawford, get it together!" Devyn shouted, kicking aside an unusually large octopus that made it to the deck.

"Get it off me, first!" Crawford shouted back, practically writhing as the thing on his back crawled up to tickle the base of his neck.

Daryl growled, raising both his hands to sweep more of the octopodes that were still falling like so many snowflakes. "Get it off yourself—we ain't just sittin' on our hands over here!"

Crawford yelled something unintelligible as the tiny purple octopus crawled over his shoulder and extended a tentacle to wrap around his neck. It wasn't strangling him—the thing seemed more curious than anything—but Crawford could not bear the sensation of its suckers at his throat. He flailed, pulling at the tentacle—but the creature's grip only tightened. He batted at it—then sent a strong, panicked gust of wind straight at the thing's body.

The octopus finally got the message and detached, floating back into the sky and then down towards the ocean.

Crawford shuddered. Someone called his name in the chaos behind him. Crawford turned to look, but no one so much as glanced his way.

He shook himself, forcing his mind back to his job. He rallied his magic and swept a wind up and around, clumsily pushing aside a handful of octopodes that had drifted up to deck-level from the sea.

Crawford heard his name again—it sounded like Gale. No one was there. He suppressed a shiver, flicking a breeze at a particularly yellow octopus that was drifting towards the mast and playing havoc with the wind in the sails.

The octopus spun away, extending its tentacles as it was swept back out into the sky.

The three windworkers carried on like this for some time. Devyn pushed the ship, Daryl cleared the sky, and Crawford felt strangely incompetent as he worked around the edges and filled in the gaps. When the last airborne octopus finally plopped into the sea, Crawford was ready to go back to sleep.

"Was that... normal?" he managed to ask, his shoulders drooping into an exhausted slouch. His head pounded. The space behind his eyes felt hot and sour.

Devyn shrugged. "I haven't heard of an octo-fall happenin' on the Line for some years, but aye. They go up an' lay their eggs in the unshifting sky where it's safe, an' then the fresh-hatched young scatter on the winds. We musta been proper unlucky to get caught like that... I ain't fond o' octopus."

Crawford rubbed at his eyes and nodded, swaying slightly as his balanced wavered. "I don't mind one of 'em on a plate, but I don't like 'em fallin' on my head. I coulda lived my whole life without ever seein' that happen an' died perfectly happy."

"Aye... Now, mate—you might wanna swing by ol' Patcher 'fore you do much else. I dunno what that thing did to you, but you ain't lookin' so good."

Crawford narrowed his eyes, suddenly paranoid. "What do you mean by that?"

Devyn nodded towards Crawford's shoulder. "Look at your skin, mate."

Crawford glanced down. His bare shoulder was covered in round, purple blotches where the octopus had gripped him. He became suddenly aware of the strange, similar sting on his back.

Crawford swore. "What the... You don't reckon it's poison, do you?"

It was Daryl who answered. "Prob'ly not—I never heard of anyone bein' poisoned by a sky-sucker afore, but you ought to go down and get checked anyhow. You don't look too good."

Crawford opened his mouth, but then decided against protesting. He allowed himself to be led down to Patcher's door.

* * *

"What brings you down to ol' Eddy Patcher, lad?" the skinny, pale-eyed man leaned forward, edging in far too close to squint at Crawford's face.

Crawford leaned back, stabilizing himself against the door frame. He'd yet to retrieve his shirt, so the odd purple welts were still dark and obvious on his skin.

"Uh… There were… I got… An octopus fell from the sky and hit me."

Patcher gave a knowing nod. "Ah, right, that'd explain it. I thought—well, never mind what I thought. You want me to patch you, aye?"

Crawford nodded slowly. "Um… Yes? That's… why I'm here."

"Right, right. 'Course you are. Come on over here, lad, an' ol' Eddy Patcher'll patch your right proper—don't you worry 'bout a thing." He waved Crawford inside and gestured for him to sit on a cot in the center of the tiny cabin.

Crawford sat, his gaze wandering around the dimly-lit space, lingering on the shadows in the corners. Already, they bothered him—forming into almost-people in the corner of his eye the moment he turned his head away. Crawford blinked hard and shook his head.

He was seeing things. He was seeing things because he was tired. That was all.

Patcher walked up and made a show of examining the marks on Crawford's neck and back, clicking his tongue. "Them's some nasty welts you got there, lad—some nasty welts indeed. That octopus o' yours musta been mighty fond. I once heard of a man who got his face sucked clean off by one o' those things. I heard he lost his whole face, and there wasn't a thing left but smooth skin on his head. Now, I thought that was fair silly, since there's gotta be holes for the eyes and the mouth—you can't just lose a mouth, though I suppose you could maybe lose a pair of lips—but I guess it ain't as good a tale if a man gets his face ripped off an' there's still all the face-holes where they ought to be. It ain't as dramatic that way, I reckon."

Crawford opened his mouth, then shut it again when he realized he had absolutely no reply.

Patcher continued obliviously. "Aye—issa a better story, though I ain't ever seen the like. I did see a man once—some beast o' the outlands stole the man's left leg. Just the leg, mind you. Clean stole it when the bastard slept an' left the man with his ankle stuck straight to his hip. Man eventually got himself a prosthetic. Vowed to hunt the monster down and beat the thing to death with it, too. I heard he's out there now, scourin' the world for what he'd lost. Ain't that a tale?"

Crawford cast the man a sideways glance. "Aye, that's... somethin', alright."

"Aye, certainly somethin'. Now hold still a sec—" As he spoke, Patcher set his hand on Crawford's shoulder. A blue glow lit Crawford's wounds at his touch—each dark circle shining for a moment before winking out of existence. Crawford exhaled in relief. The magic was cool and soothing. It took the ache from his bones away along with the marks on his skin.

Patcher grinned and slapped Crawford's back when the last mark vanished. "Feel better?"

"Aye. Thanks for that." Crawford went to stand, but Patcher stopped him with a shrewd glance.

"Before ye go, lad... is that all that ails you? Because I been watchin' ye, lad—an' you're a tad jumpy. Ol' Eddy Patcher ain't no fool—he knows when somethin's up."

Crawford opened his mouth with an excuse, but he hesitated, grimacing. "I... ain't too sure what you're talkin' about, mate."

"Come on, lad—somethin's eatin' ye. I can tell. 'S the magic, y'see. I'm healin' you up, an' I can tell there's somethin' else, though it's outta my reach to chase away."

Crawford's jaw clenched, and he swallowed hard. "There's nothin'. I just... I ain't been sleepin' right, since Gale... What with... I'm overtired. That's all. Nothin' more."

Patcher gave a knowing nod. "Aye—Guilt'll do that to ye. Ol' Eddy knows."

Crawford's heart froze in his chest and shattered—he lurched forward slightly to gasp a breathless "—What?"

Patcher nodded again. "As a healer, I watched a good few mates o' mine die. Good men, all of 'em, and there wasn't a thing I could do—magic or not. Way I hear it told, Gale went and got himself killed steppin' in for ye, aye? That's a burden to live with, right enough—knowing your mate went an' gave it all up to give you a chance."

Crawford felt his eye twitch. He fought nausea. "Aye..."

Patcher smiled. "Way I figure, it's a burden—but that's all the more reason to go an' live your life as grand as ye can. Like he'd want, aye? No sense wastin' a gift like that."

"Aye..." Crawford croaked. He couldn't catch enough air to breathe.

Patcher just kept talking. "Trust me—Ol' Patcher knows from experience. Sometimes good people meet messy ends and there's not a thing you coulda done to stop 'em. When Violet-Eyed Order sculpted out the future, he wrote us all a plan an' a role to suit his grand design. When Orange-Eyed Chaos went an' broke everything, he granted us the freedom to make our own mistakes an' make the best o' this shattered world on our own. So when you're havin' a hard time sleepin', lad—I want you to remember: Gale made his own fate. He chose his path, an' now you gotta live on to choose yours."

Crawford nodded. He couldn't speak. His throat was dry. His own tongue tasted vile.

Patcher smiled, and clapped Crawford on the back again. "Right. Well, you go back now an' get some rest, lad. An' stop by if ever you need a chat. Ol' Eddy's always here for a nice chat, an' we need our windworkers sharp an' fit, now, with the year turnin' down to the dark months. But you go an' rest yourself up as best you can in the meantime. Sleep's a proper magic in itself."

CHAPTER THIRTY
Gale

Gale never found out how much Gaston had sold him for. He never found out how much he was worth. Gale never found out how much money Captain Vern had spent to claim his power, but Gale found out quickly that life aboard Vern's ship—*The Mother Morcades*—was close akin to life in hell.

Though the ship was a beauty from the outside—dark and sleek and large, with neatly-clipped strand and proud red sails—Gale had never known such hate as he found inside her hold. The crew was bitter and broken—hardened criminals working beside exhausted slaves, each man knowing that he had nowhere to go and nothing to hope for until Mother Ainsley claimed his soul. Supplies were scarce, beatings were regular, and the callous brutality the captain encouraged in his crew seemed to have seeped into the wood of the vessel—lending a bitter tint to the drinking water and withering the shipfruit on the vine.

Gale worked beside three other windworkers

aboard *The Mother Morcades*—the man from before; another man who had, at some point, lost his tongue; and another recent purchase with a story much like Gale's. Gale talked to the other new capture for a few days, until the second week at sea when the man fell overboard during the night. The deckhands said it was an accident. Gale did not believe them.

As if the company wasn't bad enough, the work was grueling. Since Gale's power outclassed the other windworkers', the captain had him pushing the ship as fast as he could as often as he could; Gale's shifts lasted until it was clear he could go no longer without overloading his magic, and then one of the others would take over until he had regained his strength—at which point Gale was sent back to the crow's nest to work again.

It wasn't long until the days and nights all blended together into a dismal haze of exhaustion and labor. The work made his bones ache. The sun burned his skin. The salt crusted into his hair, and the longer he spent focusing on the driving winds, the harder Gale found it to think in terms of the human world. Words slipped from his grasp even as his body grew stronger and his reserve of magic greater. Captain Vern, mindreader that he was, often commented—smirking as he remarked on the emptiness of Gale's head.

Gale never replied.

One day, as Gale stood in the crow's nest and summoned his wind, Josiah climbed up the ladder to stand as lookout beside him.

"Storm's coming in landward along the Line. It ought to meet us soon. Cap'n expects that you help unwind it 'fore you go off shift."

A long moment passed as Gale processed his words. "Aye aye, sir."

Josiah said nothing, he simply stood to the side, his eyes on the horizon.

Gale cleared his throat. "You…"

"Me?" Josiah's voice was cool, emotionless. His dead eyes never wavered.

"Yeah. You… you're first mate. Why?"

"Why?" Josiah glanced at Gale.

"Why," Gale repeated.

Josiah's eyes returned to the ocean. "I don't know what you mean."

"You do. You… Me… Didn't choose this. Why are… Why did…"

"Why haven't I gotten away yet?"

Gale nodded.

Another long moment passed as Josiah considered his answer. The man sighed. "By the time you work yourself high enough to have a shot at freedom, the life you had is gone. People don't wait. They say they do, but they don't. You're gone one year, your girl's got married. Your mother's dead. Your mates've scattered. Your life's been shot an' all a man has left waitin' for him is death in the arms of Mother Ainsley. May as well do the work to pass the time. Sooner you get used to that, easier it gets."

Gale let the wind slacken a bit so he could look the other man in the face. "No."

"What?"

"I said no."

Josiah raised an eyebrow, chuckling under his breath. "Are you… you're admittin' to plannin' escape? You're sayin' that to me?"

Gale turned his face back to the ocean and began

to sing low under his breath—a song he'd heard only
once before and hadn't understood until recently.

>*"Oh, I thought I heard the bosun say,*
>*Leave her, Johnny, Leave her.*
>*We've sailed the Line for many a day,*
>*An' it's time for you to leave her.*

>*"Leave her Johnny, Leave her—*
>*Oh leave her, Johnny, leave her,*
>*For the voyage is long and the ship won't go*
>*And it's time for you to leave her.*

>*"Oh, Captain, now yer gonna lose yer crew,*
>*Leave her, Johnny, Leave her.*
>*We've had enough of the ship, the grub, an' you,*
>*An it's time for you to leave her.*

>*"Leave her Johnny, Leave her—*
>*Oh leave her, Johnny, leave her,*
>*For the voyage is long and the ship won't go*
>*And it's time for you to leave her.*

>*"Leave her, Johnny, ye can leave her like a man,*
>*Leave her, Johnny, Leave her.*
>*Oh, leave her, Johnny, oh, leave her while ye can,*
>*for it's time for you to leave her.*

>*"Leave her Johnny, Leave her—*
>*Oh leave her, Johnny, leave her,*
>*For the voyage is long and the ship won't go*
>*And it's time for you to leave her.*

>*"Now I thought I heard the bosun say,*

Leave her, Johnny, Leave her.
One more good heave an' then belay.
An it's time for you to leave her.

"Leave her Johnny, Leave her—
Oh leave her, Johnny, leave her,
For the voyage is long and the ship won't go
And it's time for you to leave her.

"Oh I pray that we shall ne'er more see,
Leave her, Johnny, Leave her,
A hungry ship the likes of she,
And it's time for us to leave her."

Josiah hesitated before speaking. "That song's about mutiny. Bad luck to sing it on these waters, boy. Walls and waves have ears alike."

Gale let his silence speak for him.

Josiah crossed his arms over his chest, pensive. "You shouldn't have sung it—I ought to report this."

"You won't," Gale replied.

"You don't know that."

"I do."

Josiah hesitated again, squinting slightly as the breeze picked up around him. "How?"

Gale took a deep breath, relaxing his magic and reigning in his desperate hope. "You let me finish the song. You been thinkin' the same thing for years, I'd wager. Looking for an excuse. You knew what I was singin' as soon as I started singin' it, but you let me finish—an' you didn't try an' murder me outright. We wouldn't still be talkin' if you were fully opposed. An' if I'm readin' you wrong... Well, Brothers damn me—but I'll blow you overboard without a second thought about it."

Gale was surprised to find he meant it.

Josiah raised one eyebrow. "So that's how it is, eh? Threats?"

Gale shrugged, pushing a hand back through his hair. "That's how things work around here, an' I aim to make sure you understand. I reckon you were a good man once, Josiah. I reckon you were a good man, an' I want to give you the chance to be that man again. Help me take the ship. Help me right this wrong we're both suffering, an' you can get back to havin' a life worth livin'. I don't doubt the ship'll see a good captain in ya when we're through."

Josiah nodded slowly, staring out at the sea without so much as a flicker of emotion betraying his cold face.

Gale followed his gaze. A dense fog sat on the horizon ahead, even as dark clouds gathered on the Line behind *The Mother Morcades*. The world's wind picked up, stirring the shining waves higher as the watery domains shifted and replaced each other, adding more confusion to the haze. Gale thought he saw a patch of land appear—some rare, rogue domain that didn't care to remain with the others of its kind—but it was hard to be sure at this distance. Not that it mattered.

Josiah let a soft sigh escape. "You're a fool. You're a blamed thoughtless fool, an' damn you for it. I been livin' these years just fine without hope, but now you've gone an' given it to me, an' I won't be able to get the notion out of my head. Entertainin' the idea o' mutiny's fair certain to get me hanged, blast ye. I'd be proper furious if I had a thing left to lose."

Fierce delight whipped through Gale's mind,

stirring up an accidental crossbreeze that Gale quickly suppressed. "So you're in?"

"I'd have to be a bigger fool'n you to say no."

Gale allowed himself a mirthless grin. "Good. So. We take out the captain, an' afterwards it'll be your job to keep the crew in hand."

Josiah nodded. "What's your plan?"

"I'm gonna kill him." The words were a thrill, even as they chilled his spine. "I'm going to use the storm to blow him overboard tonight an' he ain't gonna see it coming."

Josiah frowned. "What about his lifeline?"

"That's your job. You find a sec in the havoc to get the thing untied or cut or somethin', an' I'll blow him right over the side into the deep."

"That's it? That's your master plan?"

Gale shrugged.

Josiah's expression twitched. "You don't have a clue what you're doing, do you?"

"Not a clue," Gale answered, rolling his shoulders as he let the world's wind take over for a moment. "I ain't in the habit of mutineering—I figure all I can do is wing it an' pray for Mother Ainsley's smile. Do you got a better plan?"

The other man pinched the bridge of his nose and sighed. "No... Smilin' or not—I get the funny feelin' we'll both be meetin' Ol' Ainsley sooner than I'd like."

Gale bared his teeth in a mirthless grin. "There are worse fates."

* * *

The storm rolled in as dusk fell, darkening twilight into pitch. Blue-white lightning forked through the air. Waves towered and tilted and crashed with sound to match the thunder. Rain fell so thick that Gale half-imagined he'd already sunk.

He and the other two windworkers were lashed to the crow's nest—the screaming wind tore at their clothes and buffeted *The Mother Morcades* so she careened and threatened to capsize. There was too much, and the wind was too strong—even the best of teams would have had trouble wrestling this storm into submission. Gale and his crewmates were nowhere near the best of teams.

The one man was sick and trembling, exhausted even before the storm had arrived. The other man had little skill and did not know how to read the air. Gale was strong, and he was skilled—but he could not keep his attention on the task at hand.

His blood rushed in his ears, echoing the howl of the wind in the rigging as he stared down at the dark figure of Captain Vern on the deck below. The ship leaned dangerously close to the water. Gale wrenched the writhing wind to push it back into place.

Vern stood steady on the pitching deck, gripping the railing with one hand as he barked orders to his scrambling crew. His coat flapped wildly, his lifeline hung slack, and the Captain's Mark on his neck seemed to glow in the darkness. Gale grit his teeth and scrubbed the rain from his eyes. Josiah clutched the other railing and relayed the captain's orders, inching closer toward the secured lifelines every time the ship steadied enough to take a step.

Gale grimaced and whispered a prayer.

Lightning tore across the sky. Gale flinched and

whirled around. He was too late to catch the bolt, but he saw a faint blue glimmer on the horizon. Thunder crashed. The other trembling windworker swore softly and collapsed into his lifeline. The wind he'd held came loose, slamming into Gale and nearly drowning him with horizontal rain. Gale cursed, wrenching the gust away as *The Mother Morcades* began to tilt.

The mast creaked and groaned protest. Lines snapped, and the sails flapped wildly. Gale growled and heaved the winds up and away—earning a moment of calm for the sailors below, who took advantage of the lull to repair the lines with a flash of green light. Lightning burst the sky again. The other remaining windworker was trembling, now—his expression locked into a silent rictus.

Gale's knees began to shake, but he summoned his voice. "Hold fast," he said, glancing down at Josiah. "There's hope for us, yet."

The wind snatched his voice away. The other man did not hear.

Gale strained, shoving the ship out from under a mountainous wave. He panted for breath, pushed his hair back from his face with a hand, and risked another glance down at the deck.

Josiah was close, now. Three feet away from his goal. The ship lurched. Josiah slipped and slid across the deck. Gale's blood froze. A wave washed over the side of the ship and swept Josiah into the sea.

Gale yelled wordlessly, heaving with all his strength to pull the ship upright again. Josiah was nowhere to be seen—but his lifeline was taut. Gale cursed in relief. The man was still there.

All of a sudden, the wind slowed almost to a halt.

The clouds parted. The rain petered out to a gentle stop. A domain had shifted, and the storm was fading.

Gale sank to his knees and thanked the gods. Through the slats in the railing, he could see to the deck below. The rest of the crew was just as exhausted. The captain—still alive and well—moved to pull Josiah back on board the ship.

Gale's heart dropped like a stone. The last of the breeze fell dead around him.

Josiah flopped to the deck, gasping and still clutching at his lifeline. The captain offered him a hand up. Josiah took it, and the captain froze.

He shoved Josiah down and drew his sword. He shouted, but Gale could not make out the words. Josiah shook his head. The captain shouted something else. Josiah shook his head again and held up a hand in an unmistakable plea.

The captain's sword leapt—a flash of steel. Josiah's head hit the deck, and his lifeless body slumped at the captain's feet in a spray of blood.

Gale sank further down and found that his whole body was shaking. His strength was gone. He wanted to be sick.

Two deckhands heaved Josiah's body over the side, tossing his head into the waves like an afterthought. Captain Vern barked an order and pointed up at the crow's nest—at Gale.

* * *

Gale was forced to his knees at Captain Vern's feet. The captain's sword was still drawn, still dripping with Josiah's blood. Gale couldn't help but stare at it, his throat dry and his eyes wide and wild.

Josiah was dead.

Vern said something. Gale blinked up at the man, uncomprehending. Around him, the crew stood, wet and exhausted, watching silently. Only the wind stirred, whispering soft comfort into his ear.

Josiah was dead.

Vern scowled and repeated himself. Gale strained to understand. He could almost make out the words on the breeze, but the captain's speech was foreign to him.

The captain spoke again. His sword came to rest at Gale's throat. Gale swallowed hard and focused harder.

Josiah was dead.

"...what?" Gale croaked, slowly pulling himself back to the present and into the realm of man. Guinevere's face flashed through his mind—she'd be expecting him home, soon. The wind picked up slightly.

Josiah was dead.

Vern twitched his sword, letting the point drag lightly down Gale's neck. "You heard me, boy. Answer the question, 'fore I decide a quick death's too good for ye."

"What... what was the question?"

There were a few snickers from the crew. Vern growled, and the flat of his blade bashed against Gale's head, knocking him down. The sharpened edge bit into Gale's cheek. Stars swam before his eyes, but the pain called him the rest of the way back to reality.

Josiah was dead.

Vern snapped his fingers, and a pair of deckhands grabbed Gale by the shoulders and hauled him back upright. Nobody noticed when the wind began to blow across the Line.

Gale let his head loll. One of the men who held him up seized his hair and pulled his head back so the captain could see his face.

Josiah was dead.

Vern leered, his face far too close. His voice was dangerous and soft. "You made me kill him, lad. You made me kill my mate Josiah—his blood's on my blade, but it's on your hands. How?"

Gale sucked in a deep breath, coaxing the breeze around and willing it to blow a little stronger. "All I did was talk to him, Cap'n. Reminded him how hope feels. He—he was gonna be a good man again. Until you killed him."

Vern narrowed his eyes and scoffed. "Aye, that ain't crazy talk in the least. What's in your head, boy? How far's this mutiny go?" He glared into Gale's eyes, probing his mind with magic.

Josiah was dead—and Gale's only hope had died with him. The wind rose up, raw and hot in response to his anger. Gale didn't bother to stop it.

"I'm done," he murmured, his voice coming as though from a long way away. "I'm sorry, Guin. I swore I'd come home, but I can't push on further."

Vern's brow creased. "Who are you talking to?"

Gale closed his eyes and let the wind blow stronger. "You rest easy—I'll take the bastard to the depths with me. I hope the Brothers grant you the happiness I couldn't bring."

Vern sighed and took a step back. "The lad's gone an' snapped. Figures a mind as empty as his'd be easy to lose. You—Braithe—" he pointed to the man on Gale's left "—you're first mate, now. Toss this idiot in the brig, then see the other windworkers get up an' movin'. Come dawn tomorrow, we're keelhaulin' this blasted Brother-scorned mutineer—an' if that don't kill him, I'll skin him alive and feed him his own guts."

Gale gave the man a strange smile. "It's too late for that."

The captain ignored him, continuing to shout orders. The men started to drag Gale away.

Gale laughed and raised his voice. "It's too late for that! It's too late for you! Haven't you noticed, Captain? Don't you see—we've blown off course! We're off the Line! There's no hope for any of us, 'cause we've drifted an' I ain't puttin' us back!"

The crew froze. The captain's face went white. As one, every man on deck went to peer over the side, and every one of them found that his words were true. *The Mother Morcades* had left the Rose Line and floated onto the trackless Thousand Seas.

Gale gave them all a smile.

Captain Vern stormed back across the deck and grabbed Gale by the collar, shaking him violently as he shouted blasphemy and ordered Gale to return the ship to the Line.

Gale spat in the captain's face. "Tempest take you. Tempest come and take us all—I ain't dyin' alone."

The air blurred—the colors all ran together, swirling and pooling and reforming to reveal a new patchwork of sea as the domain shifted. The Rose Line was gone, and a decrepit storm-tossed ship with tattered sails and strand tangled into an unearthly veil loomed in its place.

Captain Vern threw Gale to the deck, swearing louder. "What have you done? Idiot—what have you done? You said her name—you called her right to us!"

One of *the Tempest*'s leaves writhed through the air and wrapped around his throat. In an instant, the captain was gone—suspended from the strand with snapped neck and still-kicking legs. Men screamed and scrambled—but one-by-one they were plucked into the air after their captain.

Gale's grin widened even as tears leaked down his face and stung his bleeding cheek. He was ready when the glowing leaf fluttered down against the wind and wrapped itself around his chest.

CHAPTER THIRTY-ONE
Crawford

When *The Morigana* landed at Midway Point, Crawford did not disembark. Instead, he lay in the fo'c'sle, trying and failing to ease into sleep. The sighing breezes and creaking wood haunted his mind like the groans of the condemned. No matter how hard he tried, Crawford could not find rest.

When *The Morigana* returned to sea on the final leg of her journey, Crawford found that no matter how hard he worked himself, the story was always the same—he would lay in his hammock, but the rocking sea merely turned his stomach and invited his mind to play tricks.

He knew it wasn't real—he knew the grotesque faces that swam before his eyes were false, because real faces disappeared when he closed his eyes. He knew the voices he heard as he drifted on the edge of sleep were impossible, because no sailor aboard *The Morgana* could sing in those unearthly tones. He knew it wasn't real, because no one else ever heard the beastly screams that woke him every time he nearly slept. He knew it wasn't real, because there was no real way Gale's voice could have come to replace the tone of Crawford's own thoughts.

But that didn't stop him looking over his shoulder when he stood at his post alone, and it didn't stop the thrill of terror that leapt in his head every time a shadow flickered at the edge of his sight.

So when the violet-blue lights flared to life atop the mast, Crawford froze dead in his tracks and stared in unblinking, uncomprehending horror. They did not vanish. Crawford looked at the lights straight-on, but they did little more than waver.

"They're not real," Crawford assured himself, whispering the phrase like a mantra. But when Devyn came to relieve him at his post, the other man nodded towards the unearthly glow.

"It's a lucky night when the soul candles glow, eh lad?"

Crawford shuddered, almost sobbing. "You can see them too?"

Devyn gave him an odd look. "Aye, mate—it ain't just you. Ye feelin' alright?"

Crawford nodded and gestured to the violet flames that still burned against the dark wood of the ship. "Aye, they—they just... I been starin' at the sea so long... what are they?"

"You never seen the soul candles afore, lad? Well, don't you fret about it—they're a good omen. Souls lost to Mother Ainsley's Keep peepin' back through the cracks in the world to keep an eye on us still livin'. Don't know if it's true—but that's what they say, an' I find it a right comfort."

Crawford gave a shaky nod, though his whole body trembled with sudden weakness. He opened his mouth to reply, but all that came out was a nearly inaudible whimper.

Devyn didn't hear, and when the man spoke again, his words seemed to come from a long ways away—as though Crawford were hearing him from the bottom of a deep pit. "So you take heart, Crawford. Gale might be gone, but I'd reckon he's still got his eyes on your back. These candles are here to prove it."

Crawford's throat seized, his stomach heaved, and he fainted dead away.

CHAPTER THIRTY-TWO
Guinevere

The year was long in passing, but Guinevere weathered it as firmly and stolidly as any stone. However, when the stretching seasons finally cycled around to begin again and each new sunrise broke the horizon without bringing *The Morigana* home, Guinevere could no longer ignore the ache in her anxious heart. It pulled her to the shore to greet the dawn, and though she was able to recapture herself and act as normal during the day, it carried her back to watch the sea as those long days faded away to the bruised purples and dead blacks of night.

Then a fog rolled in—a thick fog, tainted with some strange wild magic that kept it in place despite the weatherworkers' best efforts—and for days, it lingered. Guinevere could no longer watch the horizon, but every dawn and dusk still took her down to stare at the empty sea.

At last, one morning, after she'd already spent far too long chasing imaginary shapes through the shifting gray-white haze, Guinevere's tired eyes found a set of familiar sails.

Guinevere blinked and rubbed her eyes. The ship remained. Her heart trilled.

She leapt to her feet, scattering pebbles every which way as she dashed to greet the ship at the docks. Guinevere arrived just in time to watch the ship pull in and come to a gentle halt.

The world seemed eerily silent even as the men bustled about under the captain's shouted orders. There was a hush in the air—a dampening stillness. The fog was heavy. The air, cold.

Guinevere shivered and wrapped her arms tightly around herself, straining for a sight of Gale.

The bustling quieted. The gangplank lowered. One by one, the sailors walked the length and were home.

Gale was not the first off the ship, nor was he the second. When the third and fourth and fifth man walked by, Guinevere frowned. A chill ran through her, settling down to linger in her bones.

And then Crawford stepped off the ship, alone. The man's head was bowed. His gray cap was low over his eyes, and Guinevere could not see his face. His shoulders were hunched as though under some great weight.

Guinevere's heart froze to lead, and the whole world threatened to dissolve into mist. When Crawford came hesitantly before her, she could see straight through him to the void beyond.

He did not meet her gaze, and she did not greet him. He set down his bag, and fumbled with the fastenings a moment, before drawing out a small bundle. Three gold coins, wrapped in a length of green cloth.

"For you," Crawford whispered hoarsely, "from him."

He apologized and croaked condolences, but Guinevere barely heard him. She stood silent, gripping the cloth and the coins with numb fingers. Though she held reality within her hands—felt the smooth fabric and the slick coins and the chilled sea breeze—none of it seemed real. None of it was real. Guinevere was a soul trapped in a body of stone and a world of mist.

Water ran down her cheeks, though her face remained immobile. "I see," she said, her voice all too soft and calm. "Thank you."

Crawford nodded, and Guinevere turned and walked away. Her step was steady, though the world careened wildly around her.

She made it all the way back to her room before the sobs caught up.

CHAPTER THIRTY-THREE
Gale

Gale giggled quietly to himself as he dangled aloft in *The Tempest's* strand. All around him, corpses kicked amidst clacking bones—morbid windchimes to punctuate the forlorn sighing of the lonely breeze.

He swung vaguely. That small part of his mind that clung to rationality wondered why he still lived, while all his former crewmates choked and gasped around him. The rest of his mind—that fractured, fragmented part of his spirit that had given up on logic in the face of irrational cruelty—was too busy reveling to care.

He was free. It was a dark freedom shadowed by death and soaked in blood, but it was his. He'd won it.

The Tempest dropped him. Gale hit the deck in a heap of limbs and wild-eyed curses, and there he lay for a long moment. His breath hitched, and he coughed, and then he sobbed, and then he could not stop sobbing. Gasp after ragged gasp invaded his lungs, tearing in through his throat and then racing out again without leaving any air behind.

It was a long time before the sobs stopped wracking his body and left him panting, forsaken and nauseous like some beached fish upon the deck. It was a long time before Gale found his senses and regained sensibility, but eventually he pushed himself up to his hands and his knees and looked around the ghastly ship.

She was in a sad state of disrepair—everywhere Gale turned, he saw cracked, flaking paint and splintering wood, held together, it seemed, by little more than a haphazard tangle of overgrown vines.

She didn't look seaworthy. She shouldn't have been seaworthy. Yet somehow she sailed.

Gale took a deep breath and risked a glance up. He saw tattered sails and snared strand littered with corpses in every state of decay, the last dangling vestige of so many souls lost to the sea without even the breath of memory to revive them.

Gale looked away, a new wave of nausea sweeping through him. He'd have vomited, had his stomach not been empty.

He swallowed hard, holding back another desperate giggle as he clutched his head. Air—he needed air. Gale sucked in breath after breath as though he were drowning, until at last his trembling limbs stilled and he felt he could stand without falling to pieces.

The Tempest creaked and groaned, whistling eerily as he found his feet and stumbled those first few steps away from where he had fallen. Dark liquid pattered down against the deck. Gale did not look up.

He staggered forward, aimlessly falling from step to step until he found himself at the door to the captain's cabin. There was nothing to do but go inside.

It had been a sensible, homely chamber once, with the sturdy furniture and impressive—if rather outdated—instruments one might expect to find in any well-to-do merchant vessel. However, time had not been kind. The respectable furniture was warped and broken beyond use, and the instruments were now little more than bashed-up bits of corroded metal and faded paint. Vines grew up the wall and over everything, pinning the past in place, and the faintly glowing leaves dangled everywhere in a tattered sort of veil. They fluttered, reaching towards Gale like so many pale fingers, and he recoiled—forgetting that it was the wind of his own magic that made them stir.

Another deep, resonant creak rang out from somewhere in *The Tempest*'s hull. Gale frowned. She was laughing at him.

He turned and almost walked back out onto the deck, but the corpses stopped him. They were out there and he was in here, but he could feel their eyes on his skin and it froze his blood. This cabin—though horrible in its own way—was the dry, forsaken kind of dead. The ghosts were old and placid. But out there... Gale's mind was too hot and scattered. His hands were still tacky with blood, and the crew wouldn't like that. They wouldn't care that the blood was his own.

Having decided, Gale let his eyes roll back and his legs fold gently beneath him. He was unconscious before his face hit the floor.

* * *

Gale woke gradually. He dreamed he was with

Guinevere, until he remembered that he was lost to her and her image vanished, leaving Gale alone in darkness. Then his body returned to him. The pleasant numbness leaked away from his bones, leaving him with a dull, empty ache in the pit of his stomach. He was sore and stiff, and all his joints felt twisted at the wrong angle. When Gale opened his eyes and vision returned to him from the blurry haze, he saw where he was and remembered.

Gale found that he was cold.

He pushed himself up slowly. His arms trembled. The ship groaned. His face stung. Gale reached up a hand to touch his cut cheek and found that his skin was caked with old blood he'd forgotten to wipe away.

He groaned and forced himself to his feet. Water—there would be fresh water in the basin. There was always water in the basin.

He stumbled out the cabin door and found the lower decks without ever taking his eyes from his feet.

Belowdecks, things were much the same as they were in the captain's cabin; battered by the tides of time and overgrown with tangled vines. Holes had been knocked in the hull in several spots, only to be crudely repaired by the ship's own growth—and every so often Gale would come across a knot of vines that might have once been a sailor's trunk or a pair of long-forsaken boots. If he didn't know he was on a ship, Gale might have thought that *The Tempest* was a jungle.

Eventually, he found his way down the basin room. The little cabin was usually the neatest, cleanest place on a ship, but the basin room of *The Tempest* was more overgrown than any cabin Gale had yet seen.

Thick vines wove over every surface, lacing the entryway shut so that Gale had to climb through on his hands and knees. The strand-leaves lit the tangled growth with a soft, white-green light that made Gale's eyes feel fuzzy. The cabin seemed more akin to a spider's web than any part of a ship.

He crawled towards the basin. It was half his height, as wide as a table, and deep enough that a man could submerge his arm to the shoulder—but the vines had claimed it, snaking their way over the surface so that Gale could hardly wet his fingers in the pure water below.

He heard the last fragile bit of hope shatter in his chest, but he ignored the sound and examined the basin anyway. Vines covered nearly every inch, but many of them were thin, and all of them were haphazardly interwoven. A tug here, a push there— after perhaps an hour of careful, patient work, Gale made a hole the size of his fist. After another hour, the hole was wide enough that he could drink and clean his face.

Finally, his head felt almost clear. He blinked, and breathed, and stretched. He ached all over. He was hungry and unshaven, and the cut on his face would probably not heal well—but he was alive. He was breathing. He was lost and alone and trapped on a ship of the damned—but it could be worse. He was alive. He was breathing. And Guinevere was out there somewhere.

Gale clambered back out of the basin room to the galley, and he helped himself to some shipfruit from the vine. *The Tempest* seemed a solid ship, despite the murdering, and she had plenty of water and food. All she lacked was a crew and a captain—but that could be worked around. Gale would find a way.

* * *

Gale spent as long as he could belowdecks, clearing away the growth and cutting back the untended mess of ages in the belly of *The Tempest*. He knew, in a distant sort of way, that days and nights were passing—but the movement of the sun in the world beyond seemed meaningless. Gale ate when he was hungry, slept when he was tired, and bent himself to fixing what he could without caring where *The Tempest* drifted. Going abovedecks—back into the sun—meant facing the corpses. Gale preferred to forget about them.

Then the day came that *The Tempest* gave a fearsome shudder, lurching to a halt that threw Gale against the wall. He swore under his breath, and the ship creaked an echo.

Gale picked himself up and hesitated—but *The Tempest* screamed, every timber groaning at once in a fearful cacophony. Gale leapt to his feet and was halfway up the ladder before his brain could catch up to think twice.

When it did, the memory of dangling corpses made him pause—but *The Tempest* creaked so urgently that Gale's fear took a backseat to hers. He pushed open the trapdoor and crawled out into the pale blue starlight.

The waves roared, and the world's wind rushed furiously past Gale's head—loud enough to drown *The Tempest's* scream. She shuddered and shook, but she did not move except to tip gently to the side.

The Tempest had hit land.

It was not an island or coastline or any bit of land that had any reason to be anywhere near water—it was a miles-long, irregularly-shaped chunk of grassland that, for some reason, had decided to unstick itself from the continental pattern and materialize in the middle of the patchwork ocean. Waves beat at the straight-cut boundaries where land met water, and the sea breeze whipped the rolling hills so that the grasses bent and rippled like water. Several tawny, eight-legged creatures galloped around, running from one boundary to the next, heedless of the ship that now sat stranded on the border.

Caught between land and water, *The Tempest* screamed. Gale felt the blood drain from his face. If either domain shifted while *The Tempest* was between them, she would be ripped in two. Gale scrambled to the side of the deck that was still over water and began to pull at the winds.

He felt weak. With no momentum and the world's wind against him, Gale may as well have been pushing at a wall. *The Tempest's* tattered sails billowed and fluttered, but she did not move except to creak.

Gale gritted his teeth and heaved, but his wind slid through the holes in her sails and did nothing. A straight gust was not enough, and Gale was exhausted. He tried again, pulling the wasted wind around before it lost speed. The ship groaned and tipped, skidding a few inches back towards the water. Sweat dripped into Gale's eyes, but he could not mind the sting.

Inch by arduous inch, the ship slid back to the sea—and then she shrieked, timbers groaning in terror. Gale risked a glance over his shoulder, and the world blurred. The prow of the ship wavered in a shimmering haze—the greens of the land and the browns of the deck dispersed into a pulsing mix to swirl with the blackish-blues of the water and sky. A scream tore up Gale's throat, and he threw himself into one final push. *The Tempest* lurched, scraping to freedom just as the hillside domain vanished—taking two feet of the bowsprit with it.

Gale staggered beneath a wave of nausea. The world spun and blurred again, sea melding with sky to become a haze of indistinct blue—and then it all went black.

CHAPTER THIRTY-FOUR
Guinevere

Guinevere folded her shirt and pants precisely, carefully stowing them in the canvas bag beside the others. Her world was small and in sharp focus, though she felt strangely drunk as she pulled the drawstring tight and stood. Outside, rain fell in a steady, misty drizzle—not unusual for the season.

She threw on her father's old sea coat, shouldered her bag, and crept out of her room—easing the door shut so the latch barely clicked. Every tiny noise sent her heart skittering through her chest and stole her breath away. She crept along the edges of the hallway to keep the floorboards from creaking on her way to the front door.

Her hand was on the handle when her father cleared his throat behind her.

Guinevere whirled around. Markus was in the shadow of the grandfather clock, invisible from the entryway. Though Guinevere's face burned, she met his eyes.

"What's this about, Guin?" he said. His tone said

he knew.

Guinevere's mouth was dry as she answered. "I'm leaving."

"Where to?" He wasn't accusing—just asking. That made it worse.

"To sea. To find him." As the words left her mouth, a part of Guinevere recognized how ridiculously desperate they sounded. The rest of her didn't care.

Her father nodded. "How?"

"I'm going to sail the Line. I'll find him."

"And if he's in the arms of Mother Ainsley?"

Guinevere's throat threatened to close. Tears brimmed behind her eyes. Her voice stayed steady. "Then I'll know for myself."

Markus sighed. "I can't forbid you, Guin. Not when I'd be doin' the same in your place. But... I want you to think about this. Gale's one man in a wide and deadly world. His mates have no reason to lie to you, an' even if they're mistook and the lad's just... mislaid... you could search your whole life and still never find a trace of him."

Guinevere sucked in a shuddering breath. "I have to look. He—he's out there. He promised."

Her father stepped forward and ushered her into a hug. "I know. I'm sorry, lass. These things... not even the best of men can keep a promise when the gods throw the world against him. You can do all in your power and still fall short." He trailed off, then sighed. "Guinevere... I hope you can forgive me. I was only trying to do right."

Guinevere sobbed in answer.

* * *

Life goes on, and all we can do is keep living. When Caesar first said those words, Guinevere had thought him cold—but now she felt she understood. Gale was gone, but the sun still rose and fell and the tides still turned. He was gone, but the winds still blew and the city bustled exactly as it always had. Her heart still beat, broken and empty though it now felt as she waited for the man who would never come home.

It was surprisingly easy to carry on, which was part of what made it so hard.

But each morning, when Guinevere rose to help at the shipyard and tend to her shop, she pinned a bluebell to her jacket and told herself to smile.

He would have wanted her to be happy.

It wasn't her fault.

This was how he'd wanted to go.

Charlotte and Ell both cried with her when they heard the news. And Shiro—his normally cool demeanor broke when he saw her sorrow and realized what had happened. He sat with her for hours and he listened as she told stories about Gale and all the things she would miss. He insisted on listening. He said it would help. And though each story broke her heart anew, he was right. Afterward, he gave her a journal—a little book in which she could write all the good memories and so recall them when things got hardest. That's what he had done when he lost his father, he explained. And he assured her she was welcome to ask should she ever need any kind of help.

Guinevere thanked him.

The Spellcrafters came forward in sympathy too,

rigidly formal though they were. Caesar and his wife invited the Syrens and the Cleansers to a celebratory dinner once the purification device's design was finalized, and they made a point to make sure Guinevere knew she was not alone. Though the whole ordeal was beyond awkward, Guinevere appreciated the sentiment.

So life went on, and Guinevere folded her grief into her bridal train and hid it deep at the bottom of her closet.

CHAPTER THIRTY-FIVE
Gale

Gale awoke on the deck of *The Tempest* again, feeling as though his entire body had been pulled inside out, set on fire, then doused in the sea and left to dry under the blistering sun for hours.

The blistering sun part was even true. Even through closed eyes, it was too bright, and his skin felt hot enough to put fire to shame. Gale thought he had known pain before—thought his life at sea, his time on the Line, his hardship under Captain Vern had hurt him as deeply as a man could hurt without dying—but no. No, Gale knew now that there was always further to sink.

He twitched his arm. Agony shot through his body, tearing along his spine. Gale convulsed, unable to even scream as searing heat and sharpened ice raced each other through his veins and left his bones hollow. When it was over, he lay still, afraid to breathe as he listened to the ringing in his ears.

A tiny whimper clawed up Gale's throat. He was no stranger to magical overload, but he had never felt it like this.

Hours passed. Gale rested until he felt strong enough to risk another twitch, then he rode out the agony until he could bear to try again. He wished he could give up and die, but even that required strength Gale did not possess.

Evening fell. Gale cracked open his eyes. As daylight died, *The Tempest's* strand began to glow, and he watched it flutter until he fell at last into a fitful doze.

He woke with the dawn and felt better. Not much better—every move was still agony—but now the pain was slightly less. He was, over the course of the morning, able to roll over and drag himself a few feet towards the galley.

The wind shifted when he was halfway across. He couldn't sense the flow the way he normally could, but he saw grey clouds rolled in above him, and he felt the deck move as the waves picked up. A light rain kissed Gale's face.

By nightfall, he was inside the door. By dawn, Gale could move well enough to pull himself up a wall and sit. By noon, he had gathered enough shipfruit to make a kind of meal.

Peeling the fruit was a struggle, but once he got them open, they were the best thing Gale had ever tasted.

He slept again, after eating, and he did not know how long it was before he woke again. But after his rest, he found he could force himself to stand, so long as he kept a hand against the wall.

That discovery helped him towards the cistern, where he plunged his face into the water to drink. Then he ate again, and slept, and after two more days of struggling, he felt fit enough to risk going up to the deck again.

The moon was high in the sky when he emerged on unsteady feet—it grinned at him from between the stars. A gust of wind blew, tossing Gale's ragged, salt-crusted hair into his eyes. He reached to blow it away with magic, but that power was still beyond his grasp as he staggered up towards the ship's prow.

The Tempest's bowsprit was short, now, severed more neatly than any human hand could hope to cut.

Gale whistled under his breath. "Looks like you and me got lucky, gal," he mumbled, his voice hoarse from disuse.

The Tempest creaked in reply. In agreement, Gale imagined.

He missed the sound of human voice, so he spoke again. "Praise Ainsley... I feel like hell."

The Tempest groaned sympathy.

Gale managed a smile. "I can only imagine you feel the same, after all these years driftin'. We're a right wrecked pair, ain't we?"

Another groan. A stray leaf from the strand fluttered down to brush Gale's arm. He shuddered, the horror of hanging rising back into his mind at the touch. Captain Vern was still up there.

"But not as wrecked as some." He paused and took a deep breath, mumbling, "One of these days I'll cut that lot down. When I'm strong enough."

Though he spoke softly, *The Tempest* creaked a loud reply. The strand whipped around in another gust of wind, and the old bones rattled.

Gale frowned. "Don't take that tone with me. It's all good for you, but those bastards are dead an' even the worst of 'em deserve to be cast down. Mother

Ainsley can't right judge 'em if they're all stuck up here. It ain't right to leave 'em hangin'."

The strand whipped harder—but Gale realized he did not care. He crossed his arms. "Yeah, go ahead. Hang me too. See where that gets ya. If you wanna rot alone on the Thousand Seas 'til the day you splice yourself proper, do as you damn well please."

The wind died down, and the strand stopped thrashing. *The Tempest* groaned apologetically.

Gale nodded. "So there we have it. I'm cuttin' 'em down."

The ship gave a hurried groan, and to Gale's surprise, the strand swirled contrary to the wind and the dangling bodies fell from the leaves like so many overripe fruit. After a brief rain of bits and bones, the strand was clear—fluttering back in line with the world's wind as though nothing had happened. One of the tendrils fluttered past and brushed Gale's face. He recoiled—then gathered himself enough to chuckle.

"Who'd have thought? She can be reasoned with…"

The Tempest creaked. Gale could not help but laugh.

* * *

The days that followed were better. Gale's strength trickled back, and with the corpses no longer overhead, he could almost bring himself to relax. The feverish panic faded from his brain. He no longer felt crews of ghosts glaring over his shoulder, cursing him for living where so many had died. At last, Gale began to feel like himself.

He fell into an easy routine in those empty days on those empty seas. He would wake before dawn, and he would fish—casting nets at first, then casting tiny cyclones as his magic slowly returned. The nets were undoubtedly more effective, but Gale knew no better game than to pluck fish from the water with a neat twist of wind for *The Tempest* to catch from the sky. It helped him regain his strength.

After he'd caught his dinner, Gale would return belowdecks and spend the hottest part of the day restoring *The Tempest*, talking to her all the while. He told her stories as he worked, about the trouble he'd found and the wonders he'd seen, and she seemed to enjoy it—the vine-wrapped cabins would untangle themselves as he talked, and three weeks of work would get done in an afternoon. But Gale never dared mention Guinevere. Not with Johnny's ghost still staring at his back.

Then, as the day grew old and the setting sun threw rainbow shades across the shattered sky, Gale would return abovedecks and propel *The Tempest* through as many domains as he could manage in hopes that the gods would smile and place him back in sight of the Rose Line's familiar pink glow.

On those evenings, he had plenty of time to watch the world, and Gale saw many strange things—lights like candles dancing beneath the waves, great pale faces like islands staring up from the depths in stoic silence, fish that leapt from the waves and shifted into birds; and stranger things, like the enormous writhing shadows that twisted unknowably in the deeps, or the silent domains where the water glowed with an eerie phosphorescence and Gale had to work twice as hard to make the winds blow. Yet he never wavered—he chased the horizon with single-minded hunger, as though to outrun Mother Ainsley herself.

One morning, when Gale was going through the captain's cabin, he found a small box at the bottom of an overgrown chest. The hinges were rusted and the latch was stuck, but it opened well enough when Gale smashed it against the captain's desk. Among the splinters, Gale found the remains of a gentleman's shaving kit. The ivory-handled razor was dull, and the delicately patterned mirror was deeply discolored and coated in a thick layer of grime. Gale rubbed the mirror against the rag that was once his shirt, wiping away the dust of empty years—and he nearly dropped the thing when he saw the man inside.

Sun-bleached yellow hair hung in a tangled mane around a hollow face burned dark by days of labor. An ugly scar crossed one cheek and vanished into a scraggly, unkempt beard. And through the mess of hair stared a pair of intense, colorless eyes—pale and haunted and hungry. The frightful glare kept Gale pinned in place for a long moment—until he recognized the face as his.

He rubbed the mirror on his shirt and looked again. The haggard castaway stared back, meeting his gaze with the same sharp hunger. Gale rubbed his eyes. He had been gone too long.

He took a deep breath, set down the mirror, and lifted the razor. Though dull, it was not in bad condition. He cleaned and sharpened it carefully, letting the familiar action become his world. It felt as though years had passed since he'd last done this. He'd almost forgotten how. Gale fetched some water from the cistern, sat himself down at the captain's desk, and set to remembering the rest.

Slowly, he carved away his beard, using the same patient care as when he worked to untangle *The Tempest*, and gradually the face in the mirror morphed back into his own. But as Gale angled the mirror to shave beneath his chin, he caught sight of something new—a curved, pale scar twisted to match the glyph on *The Tempest's* hull.

She'd Marked him. He was captain, now.

Gale set down the razor and gingerly touched the symbol. It was neither raised nor puckered—it was smooth as the rest of his skin, and it spanned from the corner of his jaw, just below his ear, to almost the center of his throat, and it curved down to almost touch his collarbone. He frowned slightly, tracing it with his thumb. As much as he'd once dreamed of captaining a vessel, he'd hoped to have had some say in the matter. Even if he made it home, the Mark would never fade.

And it was only on his face because she'd been looking for Johnny.

Gale stroked the Mark and frowned.

CHAPTER THIRTY-SIX
Guinevere

Grief is a weight that settles in the heart and stays there, but Guinevere carried it gracefully. It weighed down her smile and her step and her voice so that she did not feel like laughing or walking or singing, but life went on and she lived as best she could. If nothing else, the weight of grief made it easy to sit and weave for hours on end. The clack and rattle of the loom kept her thoughts at bay. She had little enough to do, now that she was no longer needed on the production team, and she did not have the heart to return to the shipyard.

Instead, she numbed her mind with routine, rising each day without thought and going through the motions until it was time for bed.

One day, Shiro came to visit her at her shop. He arrived quietly, politely—almost sheepishly. He cleared his throat softly to call her attention away from her loom.

Guinevere glanced up and summoned a smile. "Hello, Shiro. I didn't expect to see you, today."

Shiro smoothed back his hair and showed his teeth in a nervous grin. "I hope it's no trouble. I simply wanted to... Well, I figured I would stop by to chat."

Guinevere paused her weaving. "Is something the matter, Shiro?"

He wrung his hands. "No, not at all. Well, mostly not. The matter is—well, it's not small, but—"

"Shiro, you're babbling."

"I'm sorry, Guinevere. I really am. It's just that... Well, do you remember when we met? Almost a year ago, now."

"Of course I do. Has it really been so long?"

"Unfortunately, yes."

"Why is it unfortunate?"

"Do you remember what I told you, back then, about my mother's ultimatum?"

Realization dawned, settling in Guinevere's heart atop the cold stone of grief.

"Oh. You want me to marry you." Guinevere was surprised by the lack of emotion in her voice.

Shiro wrung his hands tighter, his expression pained. "Please don't misunderstand, I'm not—it's not—" He sighed. "I don't want you to think ill of me, Guinevere, but I had to ask. My mother believes we would make a good match—both personally and professionally—and I have to admit in this past year I've come to think of you as a very dear friend. Dear enough that I could spend my life with you, if you would have me—though I understand if you refuse. If that's the case, I swear to you now that I'll never mention it again—but... Please, consider me."

"Okay."

"And I hope that I'm clear—I don't imagine I

261

could ever replace Gale, nor do I ever expect you to… love me… like… Did you just say 'Okay?'"

Guinevere shrugged, turning back to her weaving. "I did. Your mother is right. We're a well-matched pair, and I do consider you a good friend. It still feels as though my heart died with—with him, but… if ever I learn to love again, I suppose I wouldn't mind if I came to love you. So yes. I'll consider."

Shiro nodded and smiled, though his face remained tinged with regret. "Thank you, Guinevere. I'm… sorry to have asked this of you. If it were up to me… Well, never mind that. I appreciate your consideration. And please know that, should you decide to refuse, I shall accept your decision unequivocally and it shall not damage our friendship."

Guinevere nodded. "I'll discuss the matter with my family tonight."

* * *

"What?" Ell's half-shrieked question was the first thing to break the silence after Guinevere's announcement at the dinner table. "You're going to do *what?*"

Guinevere brought her fork to her mouth before answering. "I'm only considering, Ell. Nothing's settled, yet."

Ell was on the edge of her seat, food forgotten. "What about Gale?"

"What about Gale?" Guinevere lowered her eyes. "I can't keep living in yesterday's dream. Eventually I have to wake up and move on and face tomorrow. He'd have wanted me to be happy."

Markus cleared his throat. He set down his fork and waited until Guinevere met his eyes. "Are you sure this'll make you happy, lass?"

Guinevere shrugged. "Shiro is a nice man. He cares about me. Beyond that, his family is of at least equal wealth and of higher standing—so I can say without doubt there is no chance he intends to merely leech off our assets." She said the words without a trace of irony. "It's an advantageous union in every respect, Father."

"Aye, Guin. But will it make you happy?"

Guinevere paused before answering. "From where I stand now, I can't imagine anything else that might."

Ell pouted. Markus rubbed his face and sighed. "If this is what you want, Guin, then you have my blessing. Just make sure you're doing this for you. Marriage is a drastic thing to do on a whim."

CHAPTER THIRTY-SEVEN
Crawford

Crawford was not sober when he heard the news. He'd hardly been sober in the half-year since he returned to shore.

He slept better drunk.

Gale's voice haunted him from every breeze. Not even the drink could drown it. Several times Crawford considered throwing himself off a dock, but no amount of rum could give him the courage to face Gale's ghost directly.

But news of Guinevere's wedding was the last straw. Crawford stumbled out of the bar in which he'd been wallowing and set himself towards the little shop in the alley off Palm Street. The bell rang when he entered. Missus Smith looked up from her book.

"Hoy, Crawford. I ain't seen you in ages. You look rough."

Crawford staggered forward and gestured with his bottle. He'd forgotten he'd been holding it.

"Gale ain't dead," he blurted.

Missus Smith frowned. "What're you sayin',

boy?"

"He ain't. I know you pr'y heard he was—but he ain'tn't."

Smith's voice was cold. "Crawford, go home. You're drunk."

"Aye, I—I—I am, but he... He ain't." A sob bubbled up despite Crawford's best efforts, and tears fell freely down his face. The floor pitched beneath his feet and it was all he could do to stumble forward and grip the countertop.

Missus Smith leaned away, disgusted as Crawford croaked, "Gale ain't dead. Or maybe he is—I dunno—but he... he—he weren't. He weren't dead 'til after he was, unnerstan?"

The woman's lip curled, and she raised an eyebrow. "Aye, Crawford, that's how it tends to work."

"No!" Crawford yelled, louder than he meant. His bottle slammed against the counter as he waved his arm, the contents sloshing out and spilling everywhere. "No—you don'—you ain't gettin' it—Gale—he—I..."

A rough, hiccuping sob tore his sentence to shreds. "'S my fault. 'S all my fault. Gale ain't never comin' home causa me—an'—an'—I'm th'only one who knows it!"

"We all know, Crawford." Her face was stone.

"Nononono—issa—issa lie. Isalla lie."

Missus Smith stood up. She was by no means a tall lady, but her anger made her giant. Crawford stumbled back.

"Get outta my shop, Crawford, 'fore I call the Dogs on ya. This ain't no way for a man to behave."

"You don'—you don' unnderstand—"

"I understand everything I oughta, Mister Crawford Breezebender. I understand my boy Gale is lost 'cause o' you an' I had to hear 'bout it from the friend of a friend of a man in your crew 'cause the one sailor aboard who knew I'm the closest thing the boy's got to a mother didn't have the spine to come tell me himself!"

She was yelling, now. Crawford whimpered.

"And now," she continued, "I understand that the same blamed coward has the gall to *finally* show up, drunk beyond reason, babblin' 'bout lies an' provin' beyond all doubt that he don't deserve the life Gale saved!"

"I know," Crawford said. "I know."

Missus Smith clenched her fists and growled through her teeth. "Get outta my shop before I call the Dogs to come scrape your remains off the floor."

Crawford turned and didn't stop running until he tripped face-first into the gutter.

CHAPTER THIRTY-EIGHT
Gale

Gale did not know the sound of hope until he heard the gulls cry over the open sea.

He awoke from an uneasy doze at the helm and saw four of them sailing together just below the clouds. They were normal birds, too—the scrappy, rough-throated, narrow-winged forktails of the Line—not the broad, colorful birds that made their homes on the shifting seas.

Gale turned to see where they'd flown from, hardly trusting his eyes. There, glittering pink among the blues and greens and greys of the broken waters, was the Rose Line—not twenty minutes aft of *The Tempest*.

A ragged yell escaped Gale's throat. He slung the wind around, pulling the wheel in a turn so sharp *The Tempest* nearly careened. She groaned in protest, but Gale pushed the wind harder through her ragged sails. The world was shining again for the first time in far too long.

"C'mon, darlin'!" he crowed. "It's here! Ol'

Mother Ainsley—both the Brothers—they're smilin' on us, now! We don't gotta be lost no longer!"

The Tempest creaked—reluctantly shifting around until her prow faced the pink—then she stopped. Gale's wind whistled uselessly through her sails.

"Please!" His voice cracked in a sob. He tugged at the wheel harder, as though that were the problem. "Move! Damn you—you can't do this!"

The Tempest did not budge. She bobbed in the waves like a log.

Gale screamed in frustration and dove overboard—but *The Tempest* caught him in her strand before he felt so much as a drop of spray. She dumped him back onto the deck like so much flotsam.

"You can't keep me here!" Gale yelled, "You don't own me! I have to get back! I promised! I promised I'd make it back!"

He scrambled to his feet and ran for the side again, but *The Tempest* tangled him in an instant and did not let go. Gale thrashed and screamed and cursed, but she only bound him tighter.

His voice broke when the domain wavered. He stopped struggling when the world blurred and blended and shifted away, taking his last hope with it.

Gale hit the deck hard and did not move for a long moment.

The Tempest's strand fluttered over his face, suddenly gentle.

Gale bolted up and yanked it away, his patience gone.

"No. I'm not playing this game anymore. I tried to be nice. I tried to understand. I tried to keep sympathy for you who've been lost so long an' lost so much—but here I am givin' you all I got an' now I see you ain't lost a thing you didn't throw away. You never saved my life—you stole it from those who stole it from me—and damn us all, I want it back!"

The Tempest gave a plaintive creak.

"Oh, aye—always so innocent, you are. So wounded. You're so sad an' lonely, an' that's the reason you kill and steal an' hurt. But you know what? You know what? It's all your own damn fault."

The Tempest shivered with a terrible sound.

"No! I'll say it again! It's all your own damn fault! You killed your Johnny when you refused to go ashore—you killed your crew when they got sick of wandering—and you damn well took my life, too!"

The shaking was violent, now. *The Tempest* shrieked, strand whipping like a maelstrom. Gale yelled over the din.

"You better hang me, too, you thrice-cursed sun-forsaken devil-begot boat! You better carve this mark off my face and resign yourself to an eternity alone with your sins—'cause I—I—" Realization struck Gale with the force of lightning. The strand still thrashed and whipped—but it was driven by *his* wind. Gale's blood roared in his ears, but the ship was silent.

Gale sucked in a breath and slowly released his magic. *The Tempest* creaked a quiet question.

"I don't understand," he managed through clenched teeth.

The Tempest groaned softly, the strand fluttering towards him once again. It brushed his face, lingering over the Captain's Mark on his neck.

"No. I'm not Johnny. He's been dead a long time."

The Tempest shuddered and went still.

"Every sailor knows the story," Gale continued, not hiding the bitterness in his voice. "Johnny was in love with a woman. You didn't understand that the love a sailor has for ship and sea ain't the same as the love of flesh and blood, so you stood becalmed 'til the crew got good and desperate and they mutinied in hopes it would change something. You killed him. You killed them. And that weren't enough for ya, so you been sailin' since, killin' every Jack and Jane you ran upon who didn't suit your fancy. Up 'til now when you killed me. I got a girl back home, you know. Waitin' for me. But I'll never see her again. I had a chance—it was worse odds'n one in a million, but I had it—and you scuppered it. A man don't get that lucky twice. So thanks. I hope you're happy. Because maybe you had a chance of makin' it work—findin' a one like Johnny—but if your hope was me, you scuppered that, too. I'm done. I ain't goin' with this flow a moment more."

The Tempest was quiet. Gale sighed and smoothed back his hair. The storm in his heart had blown out.

He sat down on the deck with his back to the mast and his arms crossed atop his knees, and he wondered how it might feel to drown. Probably unpleasant, but he reckoned it was better than life as an owned thing, without point or purpose or hope.

He sighed and shook himself. That was no way to think.

The world's wind picked up from a new direction and tousled Gale's hair. He set his jaw and turned his face toward *The Tempest's* crow's nest where he imagined her eyes might be.

"Make your peace with a lonesome eternity,

Tempest. Come dawn tomorrow, I'm leaving. Try'n stop me if you want, but I'm makin' port again even if I gotta burn you to ash and sail away on driftwood to do it.

The Tempest creaked in weak alarm.

"I don't know the reason ships need sailors, but sailors need ships to sail. *I* need to sail. An' if all you wanna do is drift, my odds are better without you."

The Tempest creaked again, a long and low complaint. Gale didn't need words to understand her fear.

He climbed to his feet and went belowdecks to search for supplies and anything seaworthy enough to float, and he spent the next several hours trying and failing to lash broken barrels into any sort of serviceable raft. Gale fell asleep draped over one of the more solid barrels and awoke some time later to a low whistle from *The Tempest.*

Gale raised his head, rubbed his face, and hauled himself towards the upper decks. The moon was a bright wedge and the water glittered black.

"Whassit?" Gale mumbled groggily, half-expecting the strand to whip down and hang him right then and there.

But *The Tempest* did not hang him—her strand merely fluttered towards a particularly dark and glittery patch of sea.

Gale squinted at it. "Somethin' else out to kill us, is it?"

The Tempest did not answer. Gale sighed and swung himself into the rigging for a better look. A dark blob sat on the horizon, gleaming with a strange, unwavering yellow light—like the glow that sometimes coalesced deep beneath the water.

"What's that?" Gale asked, not daring to guess.

The Tempest gave a very final creak.

"You don't mean…?"

She creaked again.

Alinor. She had brought him home.

Gale whooped, elation soaring up and lifting the wind with it, rustling the strand and the lines and carrying out far over the water. Gale laughed, and laughed, and laughed until he was giddy with joy.

"Take us in—faster, now! You've done it darlin'—we're home!"

The Tempest whistled in the wind, her lines humming.

"Didn't you miss this?" Gale cried, bustling about as much as one man could—nearly driving himself into a frenzy as he scrambled to make ready. "Back to where the sailors sing and the seabirds cry and the long-lost-loves stand waitin'! I'm gettin' married, darlin'—I'm gettin' married!"

The Tempest whistled again, and Gale hummed an old tune.

> *"Rolling down to Alinor, my lads,*
> *Rolling down to Alinor!*
> *We're homeward bound*
> *From the Rose Line around*
> *Rolling down to Alinor!"*

* * *

It was a challenge, bringing *The Tempest* to port without a crew, but with her help, he managed. For better or worse, her anchor was rusted away—so when they pulled into the harbor, Gale said, "*Tempest,*

I know you've been proper lonely, out there on the water all these years. And I know in all this time, you've been scared an' bleedin—an' that's why you done all these terrible things. That's no excuse—but I say I'm willing to take the sentence as near-served. If you're willing to promise me you won't kill another soul or keep from port again, I'll wear your Mark with pride. We'll hire a good crew—get you treated proper with a fresh coat o' paint... I reckon we could go places. A ship like you that can wander the world like none but the Knights... it'd be a cryin' shame to fall through the cracks again.

"What I'm tryin' to say..." Gale paused, collecting his thoughts, then continued. "I ain't Johnny. Won't ever be. But I'll serve as your captain if you're willing to serve me back. Give an' take—that's how it's s'posed to go, aye? So stay, if you want. Anchor or no, I know it don't matter to you. I won't try'n tie you down. If you'd rather leave, you can sail off an' I won't say a word about it—but if you decide to stay, I'll see you're looked after. Thank you for bringing me home."

The Tempest creaked softly, her timbers settling. Her glowing strand drifted faintly in the natural breeze, and she was still. Gale smiled, grabbed a line, and swung himself down onto the dock. His feet struck land with a solid thump, and Gale's first stumbling steps brought tears to his eyes. He'd almost forgotten how good it felt to walk on stable ground.

Gale laughed, his face sore from smiling, and his magic swept a gentle breeze across the shore to sing through all the nooks and crannies of his long-awaited home.

The Tempest groaned plaintively behind him. Gale

turned and gave her a heartfelt smile. "Don't worry, darlin'. I'll be back. So long as you're here waitin', I'll return—sure as I'm a child of the sea."

With that, Gale walked away, down from the docks to the solid stone streets of the city. The unwavering yellow lamps were a nice change after so long beneath the dim glow of the ship-strand, though the rising nighttime fog made everything feel like a dream. Gale trailed his fingers along the weatherbeaten buildings as he walked, just to feel something solid.

They stayed as they were under his touch. When he turned to glance around, everything was still as it had been. In fact, nothing had changed in all the time he'd been gone—it was exactly as he'd left it, which made the world seem all the more unreal. Surely Alinor could not remain the same when Gale was so different. He was a stranger, now. Alinor was no longer his home.

Gale smiled to himself. He'd fix that, soon.

A sailor stumbled out of a bar a ways ahead of Gale, sauntering around with the easy, unsteady confidence of a Linesman celebrating his safe return. Gale grinned and stepped aside to let the man pass, happy beyond reason to see another soul.

"Evenin', mate," Gale said.

"Evenin," the man replied, passing Gale. Then he stopped and rubbed his eyes, squinting ahead into the mist where *The Tempest* sat glowing. "'Hoy, mate—do you see that?"

Gale turned as well, not hiding his mirth. "See what?"

"That ship. It wasn't there, before."

"Just docked, it did," Gale replied.

The man hesitated, then gave a nervous laugh. "Aye, right. Funny thing—that vessel had me spooked. In this light she don't half look like *The Tempest*. Ain't that a laugh? Here I was for a minute thinking some old curse had come to port."

Gale laughed along. "Aye, mate—that's a lark. But I wouldn't worry—I'm fair certain she's given up that curse stuff."

The man paused, humor draining from his face. "What?"

"You got a good eye to recognize her right off, sailor. But I reckon that the omen business is through. 'Least so long as she keeps that new captain of hers."

The sailor gaped like a fish. "You ain't sayin' that's her?"

"I am, mate."

"Ainsley save us," the man whispered, staggering backwards. Gale steadied him.

"Easy now, friend—she's just a ship like any other. Temperamental, maybe—quick to pick a fight—but a right lady all through."

The man made a strangled noise—a wordless question. Gale clasped the sailor's shoulder in reply.

The man looked at him, face pale. "Who are you?"

Gale laughed again. "Just another one of Ainsley's boys returned, mate. Now tell me, is the Sunrise Blue Tavern still up an' open, nowadays?"

The man nodded slowly.

Gale clapped his shoulder again and flipped the sailor a coin from the pocket of the sea coat he'd taken from *The Tempest*. Thankfully the captain had left behind his share of cash. "Thankee, mate. Here's for your trouble."

The man stared down at the coin as though he expected it to eat him. Gale snickered and decided to let him be, setting out towards his old favorite haunt.

Before anything else, Gale needed a good meal and several questions answered.

CHAPTER THIRTY-NINE
Crawford

Crawford was at the bar when the man walked in, though he did not turn around to see. He was too sober—far too sober to care who came and went, though he was by no means on his first drink.

"'Hoy, Cap'n," the bartender said, "I ain't seen your face afore—if you just pulled in to town, you might find the Risin' Star Tavern more t' your taste. We don't get too many upper folk in here—no offense meant—an' we prefer to know the ones we got."

"What's this, you don't know me, Roger Barkskin? I only been comin' here near nine years of my life. Here I thought I'd be welcome after missin' this last one."

A hush fell and Crawford froze. He thought he'd shaken his ghosts—drowned them in booze—but here they were again, back to haunt him. He downed his drink and risked a glance over his shoulder. He was almost numb to the chill along his spine.

The man in the center of the room was different

than in most of his nightmares. He wore a great sea coat, had a mane of yellow hair tied loosely behind his head, and bore an unfamiliar ship's Mark on his neck—but his face was the same. His face was always the same.

This one had not seen him, yet.

The barman spoke again, slowly. "Who are you?"

It was odd—normally other people did not respond to Crawford's visions. He must be deep in a dream, now.

Gale stepped forward and spread his arms, smiling. That was odd, too. Crawford's visions didn't usually smile.

"It's Gale, mate. Don't tell me you forgot me already."

After a split-second hesitation, the barman hopped the counter to embrace Gale, along with every other regular who was still awake and sober enough to care.

Gale always had been popular. Crawford did not move, though his tears began to run. He couldn't stop them if he tried, these days. The other men said he'd gone mad.

Crawford never denied it.

Behind him, somebody—probably the barman—said, "Gale! I don't believe it! We all heard you were dead!"

Gale laughed. It hurt Crawford to hear.

"Not dead, just delayed. I'm only the other kind of late. I'll admit—I got proper lost, but I'm good an' found, now."

"An' a captain too, by the looks of it," another man added. "What ship?"

"*The Tempest*," Gale said.

Crawford choked, and by the sound of it, he wasn't the only one.

"*The Tempest?*" somebody exclaimed. "Boy, I'd call you a liar if you weren't back from beyond here before me! How'd that happen?"

"I'll tell you all about it later. First I need a meal cooked proper, a bed that don't move, an' someone to tell me what I've missed. Blast it all if it ain't good to see friendly faces again."

"Speakin' of," the barman said, "there's someone you oughtta talk with, Gale." He lowered his voice, but Crawford could still hear every word. "You an' Crawford—you were mates, aye? He ain't been right since he came back without you. Seein' you breathin' might do him good."

Crawford sank, flinching at the chill in Gale's voice.

"Where?"

"Right there in the corner. Been a sorry sight, lately. Poor kid."

Crawford's skin crawled and a dull horror gnawed at his gut as Gale came to stand behind him. A hand grabbed Crawford's shoulder and roughly spun him around. He came face to face with Gale's mirthless grin.

"'Hoy, shipmate. How ya been?"

Crawford began to sob.

Gale looked to the bartender. "We're goin' on a walk, him and me," he said—and the next thing Crawford knew, he'd been dragged out back into a darkened alley and the ghost had him pinned against the cold stone wall. It was just as well. Crawford's legs weren't holding his weight.

Gale's ghost grinned, a mad light in its eyes as it

279

leaned in close. "I been lookin' forward to seein' you, shipmate. Spent the long months dreamin' 'bout what I'd do when I finally got back face to face. Now tell me, Crawford—give me one good reason I shouldn't sell you to a slaver for a handful of gold."

Crawford choked out a whimper. "Gale—I'm so sorry. I don't have a reason. I'm so sorry. I tol' you I din't mean it—I tol' you. But now you're dead and there's no takin' that back even if I did give Guin the money. I know that. I knew he was no good but I let him fool me an' now you're gone an' issal ruined an' issal my fault. Please—please jus' lemme die in peace, Gale. I can't live with you hauntin' me no more."

Gale's ghost gritted its teeth. Crawford whimpered. Then the ghost punched him very hard in the jaw.

Crawford hit the ground and sprawled. Golden stars swam around his face and the world spun, but his head felt strangely clear. No ghost or vision had ever done that before.

Crawford blinked. Gale offered him a hand up.

"I ain't dead, Crawford, so quit your blamed cryin' an' jus' tell me what happened."

"What?"

"I said quit your cryin'! Stand up! I was gonna kill ya, but right now I can't even bear to look your way. Stop bein' so pathetic an' just tell your half the story 'fore I give up an' turn you over to someone far less patient."

Crawford stared for a long moment, numb from within. He took the offered hand and managed to speak with barely a hiccup.

"I was... you were drunk. I was tired and jealous and annoyed. That bastard Gaston said all the right things—like he understood—then tricked me into sayin' yes to a vague bargain I didn't think was more than scuttlebutt. I was complainin'—that's all—but when I woke up, you were gone, an'... I had the money. Far as I looked, nobody'd heard of either you or him. What could I do? Go to the Dogs talkin' crap 'bout some noble type? Tell the captain I—I sold you off but had second thoughts? I... couldn't bear. Couldn't face. Couldn't. Tol'em you were dead, I did... I went an' said you saved me so they'd know it weren't your fault. But... it didn't... didn't... I knew. I still knew."

Crawford rubbed at his eyes, his voice cracking. "Stopped sleeping, after that. Kept... kept seein' you. Hearin' you. Everywhere. An' every day made it worse. An' then after I gave Guin the... after—blast it, Gale—Guinevere's gettin' married!"

CHAPTER FORTY
Gale

Gale's heart dropped. "Say that again?"

"Guinevere's gettin' married! I don't know a thing about it 'cept it's happenin' an' it's—dammit—I think it's today!"

Gale reeled, grabbing at the opposite wall for support. He couldn't be angry. He was too stunned to be angry. But the wind whipped around him, clattering through nearby shutters and signs. Crawford flinched. Gale swore through his teeth.

"I don't believe it. I don't believe it! Where? When? Who?"

Crawford shied back and returned to stammering. "I—I don't—these months have been—"

"Crawford, spit it out an' tell me! You thought it was hell before? I can give you hell! I don't half owe it to ya—but I swear, tell me what I need to know and someday I just might forgive ya!"

Crawford gulped and nodded, eyes wide. He was so pale—so broken. Threatening him made Gale feel dirty.

"I—I don't… I spent most o' these last months drunk or lost off my head, an' Guin—I ain't… I ain't been able to look her in the face—I ain't been able to hear her name without thinkin' back to… well, to you. I don't know much. Groom is some noble. As for where… best I've got is 'some ritzy church, probably today.' So I don't know, Gale. I don't know, but… Come to think of it, I know who might."

* * *

Hardly half an hour later, the two men stood outside the door to Missus Smith's shop. The sun was up now, and curfew was lifted—but it was still early enough that Gale compulsively knocked on the door before entering. Missus Smith would be up, of course—she'd always been an early riser—but courtesy was courtesy.

Crawford slunk off to wait outside as the little bell announced Gale's entrance.

"Missus Smith! I need your help!"

Misses Smith had a mug of coffee halfway to her mouth, but it slipped from numb fingers and shattered on the floor.

"Gale? Chaos claim me, lad—you're s'posed to be dead!" The woman stood and took a faltering step forward.

Gale smiled and swept her into a hug. "Nah, ma'am—I'm s'posed to be married, but I hear my bride's run off with another man. What do you know about it?"

Missus Smith cuffed Gale upside the head. "Here I've been mourning you these past four and a half months—that's half a year, Gale—an' that's all you've got to say to me? I'm practically your mother! How's a 'how d'ya do' too much to expect?" There were tears in her eyes as she scolded him, and at the end, she embraced him again even more tightly. "I missed you, lad."

Gale nodded and planted a kiss on her forehead. "Aye, ma'am. I missed you, too."

Before he could get further, Missus Smith withdrew and took Gale's chin in her hand, turning his head so she could examine his Captain's Mark.

"*The Tempest,* eh? Gale, you have some explaining to do."

"Aye aye, ma'am—I'll tell ya later. We'll have all the time in the world. But now, please—what do you know about Guinevere? You gotta know—you know everyone."

Missus Smith sighed. "Aye, Gale, but… You'd best forget her. Your girl—she's moved on, boy. You been gone a long time, an' as much as I hate to say, she's in her right."

"Just tell me, ma'am—please. Who, where, and when. That's all I need."

"An' what'll you do if I say, Gale? Show up at the wedding, fight the groom and sweep her off her feet?"

"If I have to."

"No. She chose this, Gale. Maybe you'd best let her be."

"I can't—not without seein' her. I gotta try. So who, where, and when?"

"Promise me one thing, first."

Gale crossed his arms. "Name it."

"If you get caught bein' an idiot, I've a right to come tan your hide in jail."

Gale chuckled. "Aye aye, ma'am. I'd figured that always stood."

Missus Smith sighed again. "Shiro Cleanser, his name is. A big name in the upper circles. Real old money, with class to go with it. Not someone you want to be crossin'."

"That's my mistake to make, ma'am," Gale replied.

"Aye, lad—but I don't fancy losin' you again quite yet. There are other girls."

"I've sailed to the end of the world and back for Guin's love, Missus Smith. I have to see her. I have to know for myself."

Smith relented. "Kingsown Church, boy. Invitation only. Ceremony starts at noon an' it's quite a walk. Not to mention the bride's gonna be squirreled away gettin' ready, so your odds are slim. I dunno what you expect to be able to do, Gale."

"Whatever I can," Gale replied.

"And that's why I worry."

* * *

Crawford was gone when Gale came back outside to meet him. His body was there, but the man's eyes were glazed. He stared at the blank wall, his expression set in a mask of vague horror.

Gale frowned and tapped Crawford's shoulder, snapping his fingers in front of the man's face. "'Oy—Crawford. Crawford! You with me? Hey!"

Crawford started, flinching back from Gale with a small yelp.

"Crawford, what's got into ye?" Gale said.

Crawford gasped for breath and seemed to come

to. "Gale?"

"Aye."

"You—you're back?"

"Aye, mate. We've been through this."

Crawford ran a hand down his face. "I thought it was all another dream..."

"Nah, mate—'s time to rise an' shine. We gotta get into Kingsown Church 'fore noon, y' got that?"

Crawford nodded. "Aye aye, Cap'n. How?"

"No idea," Gale said, sweeping Crawford into his wake as he strode out of the alley, "but I reckon we'll make somethin' up when we get there."

* * *

It took them over an hour to find the church. Though Crawford and Gale were both native Alinorians, they'd spent their lives by the shore and rarely ventured inland. Trips to the merchant quarter were rare, and trips to the palace district, where the church was, were rarer. It was like a whole other world, there—the buildings were taller and cleaner, with more windows and less rust, and Gale could hardly hear the sea.

The people seemed strange, too. More polished and posh, with clipped accents and shiny clothes. Gale could feel them staring as he and Crawford sized up the formidable church gate.

It was all spikes and spires and stone—probably enchanted, too—to keep out uninvited guests.

"That's the place?' Crawford asked.

"Aye, so it'd seem."

"Real romantic, ain't it? How we gonna get in? I reckon those stone walls run all the way 'round, an' that doorman don't look the type to let us slide through without a paper."

Gale agreed. The doorman was a grizzly bear shifter wearing an elegantly tailored suit complete with an absurdly tiny hat.

"We might be able to snag an invite off someone," Gale hazarded. "Y'know, jus' send up a breeze to snatch it away."

"Aye, that'd work fine—'cept invites're usually addressed with names and suchlike, an' I reckon it'd take more'n a spit-shine to pass you off as a lord, Gale."

"Blast it, you're right. My odds're better just askin' nicely."

"I hope that's not your best plan, Gale, because there's bad plans, an' then there's bad plans."

Gale shrugged. "I'm still thinkin'."

"Well, think fast. We've only got another hour or two 'fore thing's over and done."

"Don't remind me. Is—uh—is there a back way?"

Crawford shrugged. "May as well check."

Gale nodded. "I'll take starboard, you circle port."

The two went around the building and met again in the back.

"Anything?" Gale asked.

Crawford shook his head. "Only door I saw was locked tight an' started heatin' up the moment I got to playin' with it."

"Blast. There was nothin' on my side."

"So what—" Crawford trailed off, distracted by something only he could see, but he shook himself and came back. "What now?"

Gale shrugged, ignoring the frantic flutter in his chest. "I... I don't know. If we can't get through or around... maybe over?"

"Over?"

"Aye, you see those thief types on the roofs a lot—right? Maybe that way's worth a shot."

"S'pose so," Crawford said doubtfully, "up until you've fallen down."

Gale laughed. "I'll worry 'bout that when I get there. C'mon—let's find a way."

They walked around the church again, but all four walls were sheer and spiked. However, there was one spot where a neighboring building overshadowed the high wall *just* enough that a daring man might be able to make the jump.

Crawford said Gale was crazy—after all, there were spikes—but Gale insisted, and Crawford eventually relented. So they walked around that building and found that it was sheer, too, but Gale saw a spot where a careful man might step from a neighboring rooftop and reach a windowsill and climb up from there, so they walked around that building, and so on, and further—and by the time they found an alley connecting to an accessible roof, another hour had passed.

"Hey, Crawford, gimme a leg up," Gale said. "I can reach if I just get a little boost."

Crawford knelt and laced his fingers to make a step, clearing his throat nervously. "Uh—Gale? It might be my eyes playin' tricks again, but it looks like we got company."

Gale was already halfway up the wall when he turned his head and saw the pair of police officers—a stocky woman with reddish hair and a scar on her cheek, and a wiry young man with spots on his face. Both of them were laughing.

"Hate to interrupt, boys," the woman said, "but what's all this?"

Gale and Crawford exchanged a quick glance, and Gale used Crawford's shoulder to climb the rest of the way up as Crawford stood and raised both hands.

"I'll tell you the truth, ma'am—it's for true love. My mate just got back from bein' lost at sea an' he's gotta get into the Kingsown 'cause his love's marrying another man in less than an hour. You get it, right?"

It was the Dogs' turn to exchange a glance. The woman scoffed. "You expect us to believe that? You on the roof—get down! I know you sailor folk are always climbing around out there, but that's not how we do things here on land."

Gale ignored her. He was too busy wobbling with the motion of a rolling ship no longer beneath his feet.

The Dogs both ran forward. "Whoa—steady!" the man called. "Are you drunk? Get down from there!"

Gale flailed his arms and caught his balance well enough to sweep a bow. "Drunk? Officers, I'm just' finding my land legs. I ain't touched more'n water in… Ainsley praise—I'm a whole year sober!"

"Sure, kid. Now come on down before you hurt yourself."

"What time is it?" Gale called.

"Half past!" Crawford answered.

"Sorry, officers—catch me later!"

Gale began to run, scrambling up the steeply sloping roof. Behind him, he heard Crawford say, "I know it sounds proper crazy, ma'am—but he really is jus' tryin'a get back to—"

But the officer interrupted. "Donner, go after our climber. He's gonna kill himself up there. And fun as that could be to watch, we should probably get him down."

"Or at least find a better view," the man agreed, sounding breathless. Gale guessed he was climbing, too—but Gale didn't bother to check. A tile shifted under Gale's foot and he wobbled, pitching backwards into the empty sky. The Dog behind him shouted a warning—but Gale was ready. A strong gust of wind pushed at his back and righted him.

Gale scrambled up to the point of the roof and leapt, grabbing for the next ledge. He missed his grip and fell—catching a narrow bit of decorative siding instead. He dangled one-handed for an instant—then swung himself up to shuffle along inch-by-inch toward the nearest windowsill. It was twice as wide as his ledge—and nearly a foot above his head.

Behind him, the Dog yelled, "Would you just stop? Seriously! You'll break both your legs—if not your neck! Hang on for half a damn second and we'll find someone to catch you!"

Gale took a deep breath, kicked off the wall, and reached. He caught the sill and caught his breath—giving his heart a moment to remember how to beat.

Someone clapped on the street down below. Gale risked a glance over his shoulder and saw the woman standing beside a nervous Crawford. They appeared to be chatting, and the woman seemed to be enjoying the show.

"You better pick up the pace, Donner!" she called. "He's getting away! Give him a run for it, Sea

Monkey!"

Gale assumed she meant him. Then his hands began to slip and his mind came rushing back to task. He grabbed the windowsill with both hands and heaved himself up, carefully edging his feet onto the ledge with the wind supporting his back. The woman behind the window looked up from her embroidery and screamed. Gale nearly fell. Behind him, the cop swore and ordered him down again.

Gale took a deep breath, caught his balance, and jumped—grabbing the top edge of the windowsill with his fingertips and scrambling up to the roof before good sense could catch up with him. He paused for an instant, then sprinted—leaping the gap to the next rooftop.

This wasn't that bad—not compared to scaling a ship in a storm.

The Dog cursed and leapt after him. The man's luck was better—he landed straight on the roof his first try.

"Please—will you think about this? You're being ridiculous!"

Gale turned his head and grinned. "Aye, mate—but I don't know any other way to be!"

The next wall was an easy climb, with plenty of swirled ornamentation that was almost as good as a ladder—until Gale touched the wrong swirl. It must have been some hidden glyph left by an enchanter to deter thieves, because suddenly Gale's face was full of fire. He swung a panicked gust at it. The fireball swerved and shot into the sky an instant before Gale's face was consumed.

More applause rang from below. The cop called him crazy, but Gale didn't turn. He darted up the wall, stretched to the windowsill of the next building, sidled from ledge to ledge, and scrambled up to the final rooftop.

He paused for a breath and glanced behind him. The Dog was stuck working his way up the enchanted wall, prodding each section before advancing. On the street below, the other Dog stood with Crawford and an audience of casual, curious passerby.

Gale waved to them. Several of them waved back—including the Dog, who turned into a hawk and flew up to join him on the rooftop.

The other cop, still stranded on the enchanted wall, yelled something profane.

The woman smirked and shouted back, "You're on duty, Donner! You're supposed to set a good example!" She grinned at Gale and jerked a thumb at her partner. "New kid. Gotta put him through his paces."

Gale nodded, pretending to understand, and the woman continued.

"Anyway, we had our fun—but now that's over. Come with me nice and easy, and we'll let you off with a warning. You put on a good show."

Gale shook his head. "I can't do that, ma'am."

The woman raised her eyebrows. "Can't you? See—if you don't, I don't get to do things the easy way, and that's really, really annoying. It'll be better for everyone if you come quietly."

"Please, ma'am. I can't stop now. I gotta get into that church—I gotta see Guinevere."

The woman crossed her arms. "Guinevere?"

"The love of my life, ma'am. Like we said—she's marrying another man in—" The city bells began to chime, welcoming midday. "—blast it, it's happenin' now! Please, I gotta get down there!" Gale ran to the edge of the roof, but the woman stepped in front and pushed him back.

"I can't let you do that."

The cop's partner hauled himself up the final edge to join them. He was charred and breathless and very much displeased as he panted, "Good, you—you got him."

Gale tried to push past, but the woman was stronger than she looked. Her partner came and grabbed Gale's arms from behind, and together, the Dogs herded him back towards the center of the roof.

"No!" Gale cried, struggling. "You can't—I fought the world to be here! I fought the world—you can't stop me here! Get out of my way! *Get out of my way!*"

The woman seemed taken aback. "Gee, mister. I thought you had to be desperate to run that obstacle course, but wow—you are *desperate*. What's your plan, anyway?"

"I just wanna see her—that's all. I have to see her."

The woman gave a long, slow sigh, looked to her partner, and then looked at the sky. "You know what, Donner? Mister Sailor Man over here doesn't actually seem drunk. And climbing on buildings—though frowned upon—isn't technically illegal. Let him go. I wanna see what happens next."

"What?" the other cop said.

Gale echoed with, "Really?

"Yeah," the woman continued, "I don't know how you plan to get down there in time, but your antics are bound to be more interesting than patrol. Go for it, kid. We can always hit you with 'breaking, entering, and resisting arrest' if it turns out we gotta."

Gale almost melted. "Thank you, ma'am. Thank you—I'll—I'll—" Unable to properly speak, Gale gave the officer a kiss on the cheek and vaulted off the building.

He sailed over the church wall and had just enough time to wish he'd paused to think before he hit the tree. Branches snapped and cracked and broke as Gale crashed through. Leaves went everywhere. Gale smacked the ground hard and was left thoroughly stunned.

Gale heard the policewoman's voice drift down from high above. She laughed and said, "What do you know? I think he lived!"

Gale rolled over and shook his head, clearing the twigs from his hair and the stars from his eyes. He staggered up, and sharp pain shot through his left ankle—overwhelming the dull ache that throbbed through the rest of his body.

A pleasant garden hummed around him. Bees as large as Gale's fist bumbled through flowers in neatly ordered beds, and tall trees rustled, lending quiet shade to the sculpted pebble path. The neatly arranged swirls of stone were probably enchantments of some kind, but Gale could only guess at their purpose.

The path led through the outer garden to the center of the church, which was hemmed in by tall, white-flowered hedges. Beyond the hedge, soft music played.

Gale limped forward and stopped beneath the green archway where the hedge broke. There, past the silent trees and waiting flowers, past the watching guests and beneath the statues of the Brother Gods, stood Guinevere—dressed in sunset purple, arm in arm with a man in orange who could only be her groom.

Gale stopped, and found he could not breathe. She was beautiful, she was smiling, and Gale could not bear to take that from her. He could not bring himself to leave, but he could not bear to take the new life she'd made and demand she choose—so Gale stood and watched in silence, the wind carrying his grief to whisper through the leaves.

CHAPTER FORTY-ONE
Guinevere

Guinevere smiled as she stood before the Brother Gods, wedding wreath in hand, feeling very much trapped in a dream. Everything was lovely, but none of it was real. The weather was perfect, but wrong. The golden sun was a bit too hot, and not a breeze stirred the vibrant rows of flowers. Everything was decked in soft purples and warm oranges, but Guinevere felt as though she were looking at it all through a layer of thick glass.

Her family sat with Shiro's on blankets in the grass, among the flowers. Her father was there, and Ell and Charlotte and everyone—but their encouraging faces seemed miles away. Elsewhere. Distant. Even Shiro, who stood a foot and a half to her left with a wreath of his own, seemed unreachable. The priest in front of her was farther than the moon.

Only the bluebell pinned to her dress was real. Guinevere smiled. He'd have wanted her to be happy.

A gentle breeze whispered through the church.

For a moment, Guinevere imagined she smelled the sea. She turned to scan the garden again—and saw him, standing battered and bruised beneath the archway. His hair was a tangle, his clothes were rags—he seemed little more than a specter of some castaway captain—but he was undeniably Gale.

The world fell away beneath Guinevere's feet. Gale said nothing—did nothing. He could have been a statue, visible only to her.

Guinevere opened her mouth, but she could not find her voice. Gale took a half step forward. The priest said something, but his words were only noise. An expectant silence followed. Shiro looked to Guinevere and asked if she was alright.

She nodded and managed to whisper, "Do you see him?"

Shiro glanced over and frowned. "Who's that?"

Guinevere choked back a noise—a laugh or a sob, she couldn't tell. "Brothers above, you see him, too!" She ran forward, and Gale's face lit up with the brightest smile. He met her midway and swept her up in a hug.

A long moment passed before Guinevere found the strength to pull away and look Gale in the eye. She took in his features and placed a hand at the side of his face. There was a scar on his cheek—old, now, but unfamiliar. She traced it with her thumb.

"Where have you been?"

"Looking for you." He pulled her into a kiss.

Eventually, Guinevere remembered her audience. Shiro cleared his throat—but before he could speak, Evelynn Cleanser got to her feet.

"I demand to know the meaning of this."

Gale pulled away, but he didn't let go of

Guinevere's hand. He gave an awkward little chuckle. "Right... I'm interruptin' somethin', aren't I?"

Guinevere looked around, squeezing Gale's hand lightly. "I... suppose you are." There were so many shocked and staring faces. Ell looked as though she were about to explode.

Gale nodded to Shiro and Evelynn, then looked back to Guinevere. "Should I leave?"

"No," Guinevere answered, "please stay."

Evelynn raised her voice again. "Who is this man? Shiro! What's going on?"

Shiro sighed, straightening his sunrise-colored suit. "Mother, I can only assume this is Gale. He is Guinevere's true love, if you believe in that sort of thing."

"But she is your fiancée! You are at the altar! About to exchange—"

"Mother," Shiro interrupted, "look at them."

"I see, Shiro." She sounded angry. "How did he even get in here?"

Gale raised a hand. "Apologies, ma'am. I knew I wasn't invited, what with me just rollin' in this morning, so I climbed a roof and jumped."

Guinevere turned to Gale. "You did what now?"

Gale had the grace to look sheepish. "It was the only way I could think to get in."

Evelynn pinched the bridge of her nose. "This is ridiculous."

Markus chuckled from his seat. "Ain't it just? Now, obviously this situation's gotten a fair bit tangled. I say we call a rain check and sort it all out."

"We can't 'call a raincheck' on a wedding!" Evelynn snapped. "This is the Kingsown Church! Do you know how long it takes to schedule—"

"Well, here now—" Markus interrupted, "we can hardly continue with—"

The two began to argue, and the church came alive with chatter as everyone sought to give comment. Gale passed Guinevere a helpless glance and murmured, "I'm sorry, Guin. This played out neater in my head."

Guinevere laughed and leaned over to kiss his cheek. "Mine, too. You should have been back half a year ago, Gale. What kept you?"

"I made mistakes, Guin," he said slowly, "Got carried away—which got me carried onto the wrong ship and then carried off again into open waters. But I made you a promise, an' it takes more'n worldshift to keep me. Now Guin, I gotta ask—" He brushed a strand of hair from her face and met her eyes, his gaze intense. "Am I still the man you want to marry?"

Guinevere looked, considering the question. A lot can change in a year, but beneath the new scars and the Captain's Mark and the new pain Guinevere saw etched in the lines of Gale's weatherbeaten face, she found the same soft kindness—the same gentle sincerity that she'd come to love so long ago.

"Yes," she answered, nodding. "I believe you're still him."

Gale smiled, and they almost kissed again—but Shiro yelled before they could. The whole church fell quiet to look at him. Even the bees stopped buzzing.

When he had everyone's full attention, Shiro smoothed back his hair, straightened his clothes, and said, "Let's be rational, please. There's no reason to argue. Look at them—those two are in love. Mother, I know how much you wanted to see me wed today—but how can you expect me to separate them now that Gale is alive and with us again? I love Guinevere enough that I cannot bear to stand between her and happiness."

"But Shiro—it was going to be perfect—"

"And it still can be. For them. I see no reason to waste a perfectly good cake." Shiro looked around at the guests, almost fierce as he dared them to argue. "Any objections?"

Markus turned towards the priest. "Can we do that?"

The priest threw up his hands in a helpless shrug. "I don't see why not. I've never conducted a wedding that switched partners midway through—but in the words of Orange Eyed Chaos: 'There's a first time for everything.'"

Markus turned to Gale and Guinevere. "Is this what you want?" He addressed them both, but of course his eyes lingered on her.

Guinevere glanced to Gale, who replied with a shrug. They both nodded.

"I won't object," Gale said, chuckling.

Guinevere smiled. "Shiro's right, it would be a shame to waste the cake."

Shiro's mother crossed her arms. She looked Gale up and down, glowering.

"This is a farce. Shiro, he doesn't have a wreath—"

"He can use mine, of course."

"—much less any family to present it. He's not even wearing the proper color."

Shiro turned to Gale. "Have you anyone we can fetch, Gale?"

Gale shrugged. "There's ol' Missus Smith in the shop off Palm Street—she's the closest I got to a mother. An' there ought to be a man outside—an ol' shipmate who... well, I dunno if I want him passin' my wreath, but I s'pose you may as well let him in anyway."

Shiro nodded and clicked his fingers at one of his cousins. "Jared, please go fetch them both. Take a cab, it'll be faster. Also, Gale—might I say, it's a pleasure to meet you. Guinevere's told me a great deal."

Gale grinned and ran his fingers through his hair in a motion so familiar Guinevere wanted to cry. "'S a right pleasure meetin' you, too, Shiro. I s'pose I oughtta thank you for takin' this all so well."

Shiro waved the thanks away. "Don't mention it. Now, my dear mother is right about getting you into the right color. Unfortunately, I doubt my jacket would fit." He called to the assembled families again. "Does anyone have anything orange they'd be willing to lend?"

There was a general shaking of heads, until Ell piped up.

"I have an idea!" She stepped up and whispered in the priest's ear. He smiled and nodded, directing Ell away into another part of the garden.

Gale staggered suddenly, and everyone collectively remembered the height he had just leapt from. Shiro called a healer forward to help.

Then Gale's guests arrived and Ell emerged with an orange flower crown she'd made herself. She set it on his head, and Shiro ushered everyone back to their places. He positioned Guinevere and her father in front of the statue of Order, led Gale and Missus Smith to stand before the statue of Chaos, then he sat down on the blanket in the grass beside his own mother, looking pleased with himself.

The priest cleared his throat and called the gathering to attention again. Guinevere and Gale reluctantly released each other's hands.

Softly, the priest began to sing in the old tongue—a welcome, and a wish that the gods look on in favor. When he finished, he nodded to Markus and Missus Smith, who passed the wreaths they held to Gale and Guinevere. The priest explained the symbolism—each flower in the wreath was a wish and a prayer; a gift of hope from all who love the souls about to wed. At his signal, Guinevere and Gale exchanged their wreaths, and the priest explained how the families were now joined to support each other in shared love behind the couple. Then he had Gale and Guinevere present their wreaths to the gods together. Gale placed Guinevere's wreath before Chaos, and she placed his before Order.

Then they stood and clasped hands again. Guinevere fought back happy tears, and the priest smiled.

"This world is made of forces in opposite. Day and night. Fire and water. Order and Chaos. Though these forces stand contrasting, they exist in perfect balance—a harmony, and neither can exist without the other. Look no further than this garden church: within these walls, we have a union. Every flower, no matter how randomly planted, holds within it the spirals of Order's design, and no matter how carefully tended, seeds will fall and sprout and grow as Chaos wills.

"Apart, order grows stagnant and chaos cannot stay, but together, in the balance, there is life and beauty. Here, in the eyes of the gods and all who love you, I pray that you find this balance between yourselves. Let your strength always stand to aid your partner when they falter, and know that when you fall in weakness, your partner will be there to lift you again. Two parts together make a new whole and reach new heights. Brothers bless you both. Take this seed and let your garden grow."

The priest pressed a large seed into the couple's hands. Guinevere smiled at Gale, and he smiled back. Together, they walked forward and knelt to bury the seed in the soft earth. When it was done, they shared a kiss. Everyone clapped.

Gale chuckled. "What d'you know, Guin—we're married now. There was a time I thought this day would never come."

Guinevere laughed, wiping away a happy tear and kissing Gale again. "And to think, this morning I thought you were dead."

CHAPTER FORTY-TWO
Crawford

—Two Years Later—

A heavy mist hung over Alinor as the city bells announced the morning. Though the mist was short of a proper rain, Crawford was soaked within minutes. He pulled his cap over his eyes and hunched his shoulders against the chill. Though the skies were dark and the world was grey, he'd promised Gale he would be at the docks.

A small crowd waited by *The Tempest*—sailors said goodbye to anxious families, while curious spectators lingered, waiting to see the infamous ship's first departure under her new captain. Crawford loitered on the edge of things, hands in his pockets. He never felt comfortable on the docks anymore.

He cast his gaze toward *The Tempest*. She was beautiful now, sleek and whole—no longer dressed in the tatters of decay. Her sails where white and broad, her new paint was bright and cheerful, and though her long strand still had an unnerving habit of drifting contrary to the wind, she no longer looked like an omen of death. Crawford almost thought he heard her singing—creaking and whistling with the shantyman's tune.

He grinned. In the two years since their wedding, Gale and Guin had worked a miracle.

A voice called Crawford's name, but he ignored it. Most of what he heard these days was real, but sometimes his mind still played tricks. When he heard his name again, however, he turned his head to see.

Gale was there, grinning broadly and looking every inch a captain. He even had a fancy hat, now.

"Crawford," Gale said, "I was starting to wonder if I'd see you."

Crawford chuckled. "I almost didn't show. I woke this mornin' half convinced you'd left yesterday an' I'd gone and missed it."

"So you're coming, then?"

Crawford tried to smile. "Sorry, mate. Not this time. I ain't cut out for life on the Line."

"You sure, Crawford? This crew could use a windworker like you and you know it. Nothing that happened before was your fault."

Crawford chuckled. "This crew's got you. I reckon they'll be happy to make do."

"It won't be the same," Gale protested.

"It will, though. That's the problem. I still wake up, sometimes, thinkin' you're dead and these past years were a dream. As soon as I'm out of sight of the shore, that's only gonna get worse."

Gale sighed, his lips tightening in a halfhearted smile. "An' we can't be havin' that. You look after yourself, Crawford—you hear?"

"Aye aye, Cap'n." Crawford gave a mock salute.

"Don't you fret—them aboard *The Osprey* have my back well enough. I might not be a Linesman, but I'm still a damn good sailor. If either of us need looking after, mate, it's you. I still can't believe you're headed back onto the Line."

Gale chuckled. "I got promises to keep, mate. An' at this point it's in my blood. I couldn't stay away if I tried."

"Aye, just… take care of yourself, mate."

"I will."

Guinevere appeared from the crowd and planted a kiss on Gale's cheek. "Don't worry too much, Crawford. I'll be watching out for him, too. If he gets himself into trouble, *The Tempest* and I will sail to Mother Ainsley's Keep to drag him back. Speaking of, Gale—time and tide don't wait. We ought to get rolling soon."

"Aye aye, love," Gale said. "Well, Crawford—keep safe. Stay well. We'll see you when the year's up."

Crawford nodded. "Good luck out there—the both of you. And Guinevere—you're off to sell your inventions, aye? You make sure to do your own bargaining. Gale's a fine sailor, but he don't got the head for numbers."

Guinevere smiled. "We're working on that. But I wouldn't have him any other way."

Somebody else yelled to the couple, calling them away. Crawford smiled and bid them both a fond farewell before they were swept away by the crowd.

Crawford recognized most of the faces. Shiro was there with Charlotte, and El and Markus and Missus Smith—even the Spellcrafters came down to watch the departure. There were a lot of hands to shake and farewells to make, but eventually Gale and Guinevere made it onto *The Tempest* with the crew.

Crawford couldn't help but grin. The old joy stirred in his heart at the thought of a voyage, though he was not sailing with them. He swept the cap from his head and waved, cheering with the rest as Gale summoned a breeze and *The Tempest*'s sails ballooned wide and white.

She slid away from the dock, her strand streaming before her. Guinevere struck up a shanty, and the whistling wind matched her tune.

THE END

ABOUT THE AUTHOR

Mara Mahan lives in Virginia with her family, her dog, and her steadfast swashbuckling crew. She spends most of her time writing, and the rest of her time juggling, reading, playing video games, and occasionally even sleeping.

Follow her on Twitter and Tumblr **@MaraMahan**, and check out her website for news about upcoming books and other random ramblings.

www.MaraMahan.wordpress.com

Share your opinion! Show your support! Don't forget to leave a review on Amazon.com and Goodreads!

Now read on for an excerpt from Wardbreaker!

WARDBREAKER

CHAPTER ONE

Only the bravest of the brave, the strongest of the strong, and the wisest of the wise could join the Knights of Alinor. Legend held that only heroes could pass through the Stronghold's iron gates.

Kyrin brushed his hair out of his eyes and regarded the enchanted lock that sealed the famous gate, ignoring the rat that clung to his shoulder.

When I rob this place, I'll go down in history.

The ward protecting the lock was a thing of beauty, a tapestry of language woven by a master enchanter from lifeless iron and his own inner magic. However, like a tapestry, while the guardian spell had taken great effort, great skill, and great talent to weave, a man only needed to pull the right thread to unravel everything. Kyrin almost had it—he could almost see the common theme. Everything fit together and was related within the spell, and if he could find the flaw, he could take the whole ward apart.

Kyrin drew his prized lock picks from the pocket

1

near his heart. He had hoarded his money for three years to pay for them, skipping meals and going without sleep until he could afford to hire a specialist smith willing to work from his design. Now he never let them out of his sight. The picks were the perfect tools for undoing mundane locks and wards alike, and not a similar set existed anywhere in all of Alinor. At least, that is what the man's face had suggested when he had seen Kyrin's diagrams.

Kyrin had wanted his picks to be perfect, as few things in his life were. All nine of the picks had been imbued with one of the nine elements of magic, and through elegant glyphs carved on a puzzle-like band at the handles, the base powers could be refined and directed. In the right hands, the bands, the glyphs, the magic itself could be twisted and reformed to dismantle even the most devilish of wards without so much as a touch of outside magic. One only needed knowledge, cunning, and a steady hand.

The smith had been excellent. Kyrin probably should have refrained from stealing so much from him afterward, but the temptation of winning back his hard-earned fortune with his new picks had been too much to resist. But no regrets—that day had been Kyrin's first big step towards glory. Remorse was pointless.

Soon, even the Faceless will revere me.

"What's the plan, Shadow?" Rat chuckled, scratching at his torn ear with a dirty paw as he dug his tiny claws into Kyrin's shirt. "Stumbling already? Gonna trip over the first hurdle? Drop the dream and go home, kid. Even the Faceless hasn't cracked this egg, and if the Guild leader can't get in, how could a cripple like you?"

"Shut your stupid mouth, Rat, before I make you eat those words. I'm not like the rest of you streetscum."

"Obviously. The rest of us are human. You... You're just a *shadow* under our feet. Pathetic." Rat's voice rang with spiteful joy as he savored the flavor of each insult.

Kyrin had to sigh. "Yeah? Well how about you switch back to your human form, will ya? It's demeaning, having to talk to vermin like it's a person."

"Funny thing," Rat's voice grew deeper and more manlike as he leapt from Kyrin's shoulder and obligingly shifted his shape, his filthy matted fur lengthening to oily dark hair, his pointed snout and wormlike tail shrinking away as his body bulged and stretched its way back into the likeness of a crouching human, "that's what I said when the Faceless paired me off with you, *partner*. Same word I used too, demeaning."

Kyrin's eyes narrowed and his scowl deepened. "Like you have the guts to talk in front of the Faceless. Last I heard, the one and only time you entered the Inmost Court, you weren't able to do anything but snivel face-down on the floor."

Rat's pale eyes narrowed. "Yeah? An' what do you know about that, Shadow? Last I heard, you weren't allowed to show your pathetic face anywhere near the Inmost Court, *cripple.*"

Again, that word... Kyrin closed his eyes and willed himself to relax, to keep his voice cold and professional and free from anger. "Rat, I promise you," he said, unconsciously slipping back into the more cultured accent of his childhood, "when this is

3

over and the Faceless finally ends our partnership, I'll—"

"You'll what?" Rat interrupted, cutting Kyrin off mid-threat. "Beat me? Kick me? Make me regret? I'd like to see you try, *dreck*. I'm a shifter, and you're… You're a nothing. A worthless, hopeless, spineless little *cripple* without even a drop of magic in your blood. You're gonna die in there, even if the Knights *are* out!"

"Shut up!" Kyrin cried. Across the street, a set of shutters flew open and a figure leaned out to peer around the deserted street. Kyrin's heart leapt to his throat and he threw himself to the ground. After an annoyingly long moment, the figure pulled the shutters closed again, and Kyrin allowed himself to breathe.

"Rat, *please*," he hissed through clenched teeth, "cut this incessant babble before the Dogs show up. You might be able to shift and scram, but all I've got are my own two feet. Lose me, and the Guild'll fine you an arm and a leg—and you know how the Faceless is about figures of speech."

The partnerships were the Faceless' little joke. Some teams were strategic dreams, legends in the Guild, with powers and personalities carefully selected to complement each other and manage perfect crimes. Others, like Shadow and Rat, were more akin to a waking nightmare—perfectly incompatible and perfectly stupid, holding together only through fear of the Faceless and through a mutual reluctance to face the fines the Guild charged for losing a partner.

Soon, though, Kyrin knew his fortunes would change. No one would dare laugh or call him "cripple" after he robbed the Knights. A hero among thieves was still a hero. Glory was glory no matter where you stood.

Kyrin leaned in for a better look at the ward, repressing a manic grin.

It was a tall gate, made of dark iron—cold, forbidding, and practically unclimbable on account of both the sharpened steel spikes mounted on top, and the powerful ward spells woven into the hard metal. The ringing hum of the hidden magic was nearly audible on this silent moonlit night, and if it weren't impossible, Kyrin would have been willing to swear he felt the deep resonance echo within his bones.

Unless that was just his suppressed anxiety. This gate was the first big hurdle to the ultimate prize.

Wealth. Power. Respect... After this job, it'll all be mine. I just have to get inside...

"You gonna admire the thing all night, Shadow? Or are you actually gonna try and crack it?" Rat's slouching silhouette crossed its arms, and the man's booted foot tapped invisibly in the darkness.

Kyrin made a strangled noise somewhere between a sigh and a growl. "Shut. Up. I'm working on it. I know what I'm doing—don't pretend you do."

Rat responded, throwing back some venomous reply, but Kyrin barely registered his words. The heavy iron lock that barred the Stronghold's massive gate had his full attention. Kyrin dared not give it less.

Years ago, in the garden of a wealthy merchant, Kyrin had encountered a ward woven on the ground by shadows cast from magelight. When night fell and the streetlights lit themselves, the garden itself became a trap invisible to all but the experienced eye. Kyrin had missed the signs until it was nearly too late, and

5

he had been forced to burn several pages from his notebook to break the darkness and escape with his life. The scars on his legs still ached some nights, and that twisted darkness often writhed back through his dreams to trap him in chains of bladed black.

Compared to that trap, this lock looked tame. But looks, Kyrin knew, were deceiving.

Rumor held that this particular lock had been forged back in the age when the pictorial script was still common among Alinor's literate population, so it utilized nearly every form of magical defense. Many of Kyrin's childhood textbooks had described the Stronghold's gate as a tangled rat's nest of violate enchantment and misleading wordplay—they had called it the unpickable lock.

"Yet every lock has its pick, and every ward has its flaw..." Kyrin muttered to himself as he bent his neck for a better angle. Though his teachers had repeated that mantra with a different intent, Kyrin lived his life by the simplistic dogma. Nothing was fail-safe, and a way would always open to the creative and determined individual. Kyrin just had to be clever enough to find it.

"I guard the heroes who guard our land..." Kyrin translated, tracing a gloved finger over the ancient words as he mumbled, "Alinor's Knights are safe in my hand..."

"You're making that up." Rat peered over Kyrin's shoulder at the lock. "There's nothing there but squiggles."

"Shut up, Rat. You can't even read plain Common. Don't talk."

"Nope!" Rat chuckled, smirking. "Ordinary folk like me don't need your fancy letters. I got my magic and no cause to *compensate*."

"Shut up. Now where was..? Oh—right. Hand. Let's see... Blah blah blah, something about pure brave heart, land where only heroes tread, poetic nonsense about worthiness..." Kyrin twisted around to read the side of the lock, giving in to his urge to flaunt his skill at Rat.

He finished his reading with a broad flourish. "Basically, the ward is telling us it's a ward, and declaring its intent to never, ever let anyone through who doesn't have the Knight's Key—on pain of a horrific and possibly embarrassing death."

"I coulda told you that, genius. So much for your fancy learning. How's that supposed to get us in?"

"Ah, but you see, Rat," Kyrin explained, letting the genius comment slide, "the important thing isn't *what* the ward says, it's *how* the ward says it."

"What? Get to the point, Shadow."

"The point is, *partner,* that the message the ward spells is less important than the glyphs used to spell it. Everything in the old script is highly contextual, so a symbol that means one thing in one place can mean something else entirely somewhere different. Like— for example, this swirl here means "hero" But I've also seen it to mean 'shield' before."

"...Eh?" Rat's eyes began to glaze. Kyrin smothered a grin.

"Likewise," Kyrin continued, kneeling down beside the lock and fishing in his pockets for his tools, "a lot of glyphs can name the same word, but all have different connotations. I can think of at least five different ways to write "hero" off the top of my head, and each has a completely different feeling behind it. The trick is to not only know what a word means, but to also know what it might mean elsewhere, and what it means beneath its first meaning. If you have the sense to read the words that were written the way they weren't meant to be read, the ward'll tell you what it is, what it does, what'll happen if you trip it, and it'll practically give you step-by-step instructions on how to take it apart. So like here—"

"Shut up! Shut up! I get it!" Rat cried, throwing his hands in the air, "You've read a book! Now will you just shut up and take the blasted thing apart? I don't have all night, Shadow! Got better things to do than listen to you talk my last good ear off, you know. Get moving!"

"Yeah yeah yeah," Kyrin had expected Rat to snap after the second sentence, never anticipating the crook would allow him to lecture as long as he had. "Forgive my tryin'a shove some wisdom into that thick skull of yours. Now stand back, will ya? I don't need you breathing down my neck for this. You don't even wanna know what happens if you make me screw up."

For once, Rat obliged without comment. Everyone knew what happened when a ward went off on a thief, and Kyrin knew that, if he failed, Rat would want to be far enough away to watch the show in safety.

But no matter. Now was the time for Kyrin to lose himself in the realm of carven glyphs and mirrored meanings.

Though the gate's spell started off looking like a standard flare-ward—the kind that adorned most middle-class merchant shops in the city—the enchantment soon began picking up undertones of ice and earth, touches added specifically to make unraveling the ward more difficult.

The mix was odd—classically, one would counter fire with water, but here, water was an integral part, negating the negation and tying the whole mess in a paradoxical loop. Kyrin did not know what to think—nothing made sense, and many elements seemed to spring from nowhere for no reason. Whenever Kyrin began to suspect he had found a flaw in one aspect, another sneaked up and kicked him in the pants.

One wrong move, and he would wind up tangled in a web of ancient words to be eaten alive by the old magic at the center. Doubt crept into Kyrin's heart and started gnawing at his core. It would be so easy to step wrong, so easy to fumble and lose life, limb, and pride in one fell blow.

The longer Kyrin examined the thing, the more complex the spell seemed to become. New dimensions threw themselves into the mix at every turn—elements of light and darkness floated into view, with barely noticeable references to ancient history and classic poetry drifting up to join them from the unknowably layered depths of context and meaning. Marks Kyrin had taken as meaningless decoration turned into obscure glyphs—words and words within words. He had never seen the like.

Kyrin closed his eyes to think.

If he had come alone, he could back out without incident, but Kyrin would never live it down if he ran away now, with Rat watching. Kyrin wanted to hand his partner another cause to mock him exactly as much as he desired a fireball in his face—much for the same reasons. He gnawed his lip and resigned himself to trusting his gut. Kyrin's instinct, his ingenuity, and his willpower would have to be enough to carry him through.

Wait half a minute… willpower… strength of will… Courage! That's it! That's the key! Through courage and will, humanity had gained mastery over the elements, over darkness, over light, over magic itself. The old poetry, the history, it all pointed back to human will. Even that old saying: "only a Hero may enter…" What was a hero but a courageous man? Gods—it was all so *easy!*

Kyrin selected the lock pick imbued with the essence of human agency, the ninth element, and twisted the bands around until the glyphs formed a crude reflection of courage and determination. The easy part—the brain work—was over. Now came the tricky bit. If he had guessed wrong, if he had missed something, if his hand slipped, Kyrin would find out—and it would be…unpleasant. Possibly even excruciating. Wards were never gentle, but Kyrin hardly cared.

The thrill was intoxicating. If he had to die, this was how Kyrin wanted to go; pulled to pieces by a spell as he himself pulled it apart.

Here, now, on the edge between success and failure, Kyrin was alive.

Using the tip of his lock pick, he tapped one of the tiny glyphs carved into the surface of the lock, waking it up. The ward started to ring quietly as it came alive under his hand, yawning and stretching like an animal roused from hibernation. Kyrin tapped one word, then another, then another, each stroke confusing the meaning of the magic and confounding the spell long enough give Kyrin a chance to pick the mundane portion of the lock. Since keys automatically took care of everything all at once, Kyrin had to move quickly to keep the ward from noticing his intrusion. Hesitation was his greatest enemy—if the ward caught him now, he would die.

As soon as the non-magical part of the lock was picked, Rat sauntered back to Kyrin's side. "That all, Shadow? I coulda done that. So much for your one talent."

Kyrin ignored him. Though he had picked the mundane lock, he still had to appease the ward and send the spell back to sleep. One careless slip would still kill him. He pulled his pick from glyph to glyph, gently countering and rearranging the imaginary lines of meaning that lay between the symbols.

Finally, after what seemed an age, Kyrin straightened up and stretched. "Shut up, Rat. Now, you can keep your mouth closed and follow me, or you can go on ahead—I don't care. The other wards won't get me if they're busy with you."

"Not on your life, Shadow," Rat said as he once again shrunk down into his second form, "I ain't going first, and I'm not about to get left behind." Before Kyrin could do more than flail, Rat climbed his trouser leg, scrambled up his shirt, and found a perch on Kyrin's shoulder. "I'm with you, *partner*, and that means we stick together."

Kyrin wrinkled his nose in distaste, but he knew better than to try brushing the vermin off. Though Rat's rodent form was small, his human form was tall, strong, and mean, and Kyrin had no desire to become better acquainted with the man's fist.

Privately resolving to hire a dozen cats when he was wealthy and had a house of his own, Kyrin grimaced and shut his mouth.

Ambition drove his steps. Hatred filled his mind. Kyrin passed the Stronghold's gate and entered
the land only heroes tread.